Mark Twain

Mark Twain's Sketches, New and Old

Mark Twain

Mark Twain's Sketches, New and Old

ISBN/EAN: 9783337011284

Printed in Europe, USA, Canada, Australia, Japan

Cover: Foto ©Andreas Hilbeck / pixelio.de

More available books at **www.hansebooks.com**

BY

MARK TWAIN.

NOW FIRST PUBLISHED IN COMPLETE FORM.

TORONTO :

BELFORDS, CLARKE & CO.

MDCCCLXXIX.

PREFACE.

I have scattered through this volume a mass of matter which has never been in print before (such as "Learned Fables for Good Old Boys and Girls," the "Jumping Frog restored to the English tongue after martyrdom in the French," the "Membranous Croup" sketch, and many others which I need not specify): not doing this in order to make an advertisement of it, but because these things seemed instructive.

MARK TWAIN.

HARTFORD.

CONTENTS.

CONTENTS.

SKETCHES BY MARK TWAIN.

THE RECENT GREAT FRENCH DUEL.

MUCH as the modern French duel is ridiculed by certain smart people, it is in reality one of the most dangerous institutions of our day. Since it is always fought in the open air, the combatants are nearly sure to catch cold. M. Paul de Cassagnac, the most inveterate of the French duellists, has suffered so often in this way that he is at last a confirmed invalid; and the best physician in Paris has expressed the opinion that if he goes on duelling for fifteen or twenty years more,—unless he forms the habit of fighting in a comfortable room where damps and draughts cannot intrude—he will eventually endanger his life. This ought to moderate the talk of those people who are so stubborn in maintaining that the French duel is the most health-giving of recreations because of the open air exercise it affords. And it ought also to moderate that foolish talk about French duellists and socialist-hated monarchs being the only people who are immortal.

But it is time to get at my subject. As soon as I heard
of the late fiery outbreak between M. Gambetta and M.
Fourtou in the French Assembly, I knew that trouble
must follow. I knew it because a long personal friendship with M. Gambetta had revealed to me the desperate
and implacable nature of the man. Vast as are his physi-
cal proportions, I knew that the thirst for revenge would
penetrate to the remotest frontiers of his person.

I did not wait for him to call on me, but went at once
to him. As I expected, I found the brave fellow steeped
in a profound French calm. I say French calm, because
French calmness and English calmness have points of
difference. He was moving swiftly back and forth among
the debris of his furniture, now and then staving chance
fragments of it across the room with his foot; grinding a
constant grist of curses through his set teeth ; and halting
every little while to deposit another handful of his hair
on the pile which he had been building of it on the table.

He threw his arms around my neck, bent me over his
stomach to his breast, kissed me on both cheeks, hugged
me four or five times, and placed me in his own arm-chair.
As soon as I had got well again, we began business at once.

I said I supposed he would wish me to act as his second,
and he said, "Of course;" I said I must be allowed to act
under a French name, so that I might be shielded from
ŏblŏquy̆ in my country, in case of fatal results. He
winced here, probably at the suggestion that duelling was
not regarded with respect in America. However, he
agreed to my requirement. This accounts for the fact

that in all the newspaper reports M. Gambetta's second was apparently a Frenchman.

First, we drew up my principal's will. I insisted upon this, and stuck to my point. I said I had never heard of a man in his right mind going out to fight a duel without first making his will. He said he had never heard of a man in his right mind doing anything of the kind. When we had finished the will, he wished to proceed to a choice of his "last words." He wanted to know how the following words, as a dying exclamation, struck me:—

"I die for my God, for my country, for freedom of speech, for progress, and the universal brotherhood of man!"

I objected that this would require too lingering a death; it was a good speech for a consumptive, but not suited to the exigencies of the field of honour. We wrangled over a good many ante-mortem outbursts, but I finally got him to cut his obituary down to this, which he copied into his memorandum book, purposing to get it by heart:—

"I DIE THAT FRANCE MAY LIVE."

I said that this remark seemed to lack relevancy; but he said relevancy was a matter of no consequence in last words,—what you wanted was thrill.

The next thing in order was the choice of weapons My principal said he was not feeling well, and would leave that and the other details of the proposed meeting to me. Therefore I wrote the following note and carried it to M. Fourtou's friend:—

Sir: M. Gambetta accepts M. Fourtou's challenge, and authorises me to propose Plessis-Piquet as the place of meeting; to-morrow morning at day-break as the time; and axes as the weapons. I am, sir, with great respect,

MARK TWAIN.

M. Fourtou's friend read this note and shuddered. Then he turned to me, and said, with a suggestion of severity in his tone :—

"Have you considered, sir, what would be the inevitable result of such a meeting as this ?"

"Well, for instance, what *would* it be ?"

" Bloodshed !"

"That's about the size of it," I said. "Now, if it is a fair question, what was your side proposing to shed ?"

I had him, there. He saw he had made a blunder, so he hastened to explain it away. He said he had spoken jestingly. Then he added that he and his principal would enjoy axes, and indeed prefer them, but such weapons were barred by the French code, and so I must change my proposal.

I walked the floor turning the thing over in my mind, and finally it occurred to me that Gatling guns at fifteen paces would be a likely way to get a verdict on the field of honour. So I framed this idea into a proposition.

But it was not accepted. The code was in the way again. I proposed rifles; then, double-barrelled shot-guns; then, Colt's navy revolvers. These being all rejected, I reflected a while, and sarcastically suggested brick-bats at three-quarters of a mile. I always hate to fool away a humorous thing on a person who has no perception of humour; and it filled me with bitterness when this man went soberly away to submit the last proposition to his principal.

He came back presently, and said his principal was charmed with the idea of brick-bats at three-quarters of a mile, but must decline on account of the danger to disinterested parties, passing between. Then I said,—

"Well, I am at the end of my string, now. Perhaps *you* would be good enough to suggest a weapon? Perhaps you have even had one in your mind all the time?"

His countenance brightened, and he said with alacrity,—

"Oh, without doubt, monsieur!"

So he fell to hunting in his pockets,—pocket after pocket, and he had plenty of them,—muttering all the while, "Now, what could I have done with them?"

At last he was successful. He fished out of his vest pocket a couple of little things which I carried to the light and discovered to be pistols. They were single-barrelled and silver-mounted, and very dainty and pretty. I was not able to speak for emotion. I silently hung one of them on my watch-chain, and returned the other. My companion in crime now unrolled a postage-stamp containing several cartridges, and gave me one of them. I asked if he meant to signify by this that our men were to be allowed but one shot apiece. He replied that the French code permitted no more. I then begged him to go on and suggest a distance, for my mind was growing weak and confused under the strain which had been put upon it. He named sixty-five yards. I nearly lost my patience. I said,—

SKETCHES BY MARK TWAIN.

"Sixty-five yards with these instruments? Pop-guns would be deadlier at fifty. Consider, my friend, you and I are banded together to destroy life, not to make it eternal."

But with all my persuasions, all my arguments, I was only able to get him to reduce the distance to thirty-five yards; and even this concession he made with reluctance, and said with a sigh,—

"I wash my hands of this slaughter; on your head be it."

There was nothing for me but to go home to my old lion-heart and tell my humiliating story. When I entered, M. Gambetta was laying his last lock of hair upon the altar. He sprang towards me, exclaiming,—

"You have made the fatal arrangements,—I see it in your eye!"

"I have."

His face paled a trifle, and he leaned upon the table for support. He breathed thick and heavily for a moment or two, so tumultuous were his feelings; then he hoarsely whispered,—

"The weapon, the weapon! Quick! what is the weapon?"

"This!" and I displayed that silver-mounted thing. He caught but one glimpse of it, then swooned ponderously to the floor.

When he came to, he said mournfully,

"The unnatural calm to which I have subjected myself has told upon my nerves. But away with weakness! I will confront my fate like a man and a Frenchman."

He rose to his feet and assumed an attitude which for sublimity has never been approached by man, and has

seldom been surpassed by statues. Then he said, in his
deep bass tones,—

"Behold, I am calm, I am ready; reveal to me the distance."

"Thirty-five yards."

I could not lift him up, of course; but I rolled him
over, and poured water down his back. He presently
came too, and said,—

"Thirty-five yards,—without a rest? But why ask?
Since murder was that man's intention, why should he
palter with small details? But mark you one thing: in
my fall the world shall see how the chivalry of France
meets death."

After a long silence he asked,—

"Was nothing said about that man's family standing up
with him as an offset to my bulk? But no matter; I
would not stoop to make such a suggestion; if he is not
noble enough to suggest it himself, he is welcome to this
advantage, which no honourable man would take."

He now sank into a sort of stupor of reflection, which
lasted some minutes; after which he broke silence with,—

"The hour,—what is the hour fixed for the collision?"

"Dawn, to-morrow."

He seemed to be greatly surprised, and immediately said,

"Insanity! I never heard of such a thing. Nobody is
abroad at such an hour."

"That is the reason I named it. Do you mean to say
you want an audience?"

"It is no time to bandy words. I am astonished that

M. Fourtou should ever have agreed to so strange an in-
novation. Go at once and require a later hour."

I ran down stairs, threw open the front door, and almost
plunged into the arms of M. Fourtou's second. He said,

"I have the honour to say that my principal strenuously
objects to the hour chosen, and begs that you will consent
to change it to half-past nine."

"Any courtesy, sir, which it is in our power to extend
is at the service of your excellent principal. We agree to
the proposed change of time."

"I beg you to accept the thanks of my client." Then
he turned to a person behind him, and said, "You hear,
M. Noir, the hour is altered to half-past nine." Whereupon M. Noir bowed, expressed his thanks, and went
away. My accomplice continued:—

"If agreeable to you, your chief surgeons and ours
shall proceed to the field in the same carriage, as is customary."

"It is entirely agreeable to me, and I am obliged to you
for mentioning the surgeons, for I am afraid I should not
have thought of them. How many shall I want? I
suppose two or three will be enough?"

"Two is the customary number for each party. I refer
to 'chief' surgeons; but considering the exalted positions
occupied by our clients, it will be well and decorous that
each of us appoint several consulting surgeons, from among
the highest in the profession. These will come in their
own private carriages. Have you engaged a hearse?"

"Bless my stupidity, I never thought of it! I will

attend to it right away. I must seem very ignorant to you; but you must try to overlook that, because I have never had any experience of such a swell duel as this before. I have had a good deal to do with duels on the Pacific coast, but I see now that they were crude affairs. A hearse,—sho! we used to leave the elected lying around loose, and let anybody cord them up and cart them off that wanted to. Have you anything further to suggest?"

"Nothing, except that the head undertakers shall ride together, as is usual. The subordinates and mutes will go on foot, as is also usual. I will see you at eight o'clock in the morning, and we will then arrange the order of the procession. I have the honour to bid you a good day."

I returned to my client, who said, "Very well; at what hour is the engagement to begin?"

"Half-past nine."

"Very good indeed, Have you sent the fact to the newspapers?"

"*Sir!* If after our long and intimate friendship you can for a moment deem me capable of so base a treachery—"

"Tut, tut! What words are these, my dear friend? Have I wounded you? Ah! forgive me; I am overloading you with labour. Therefore go on with the other details, and drop this one from your list. The bloody-minded Fourtou will be sure to attend to it. Or I myself —yes to make certain, I will drop a note to my journalistic friend, M. Noir"—

"Oh, come to think, you may save yourself the trouble; that other second has informed M. Noir."

"H'm! I might have known it. It is just like that Fourtou, who always wants to make a display."

At half past nine in the morning the procession approached the field of Plessis-Piquet in the following order; first came our carriage,—nobody in it but M. Gambetta and myself; then a carriage containing M. Fourtou and his second; then a carriage containing two poet-orators who did not believe in God, and these had MS. funeral orations projecting from their breast pockets; then a carriage containing the head surgeons and their cases of instruments; then eight private carriages containing consulting surgeons; then a hack containing the coroner; then the two hearses; then a carriage containing the head undertakers; then a train of assistants and mutes on foot; and after these came plodding through the fog a long procession of camp followers, police and citizens generally. It was a noble turnout, and would have made a fine display if we had had thinner weather.

There was no conversation. I spoke several times to my principal, but I judge he was not aware of it, for he always referred to his note-book and muttered absently, "I die that France may live."

Arrived on the field, my fellow-second and I paced off the thirty-five yards, and then drew lots for choice of position. This latter was but an ornamental ceremony, for all choices were alike in such weather. These preliminaries being ended, I went to my principal and asked him if he was ready. He spread himself out to his full width, and said in a stern voice, "Ready! Let the batteries be charged."

The loading was done in the presence of duly constituted witnesses. We considered it best to perform this delicate service with the assistance of a lantern, on account of the state of the weather. We now placed our men.

At this point the police noticed that the public had massed themselves together on the right and left of the field; they therefore begged a delay, while they should put these poor people in a place of safety. The request was granted.

The police having ordered the two multitudes to take positions behind the duellists, we were once more ready. The weather growing still more opaque, it was agreed between myself and the other second that before giving the fatal signal we should each deliver a loud whoop, to enable the combatants to ascertain each other's whereabouts.

I now returned to my principal, and was distressed to observe that he had lost a good deal of his spirit. I tried my best to hearten him. I said, "Indeed, sir, things are not so bad as they seem. Considering the character of the weapons, the limited number of shots allowed, the generous distance, the impenetrable solidity of the fog, and the added fact that one of the combatants is one-eyed and the other cross-eyed and near sighted, it seems to me that this conflict need not necessarily be fatal There are chances that both of you may survive. Therefore, cheer up; do not be down-hearted."

This speech had so good an effect that my principal immediately stretched forth his hand and said, " I am myself again ; give me the weapon."

I laid it, all lonely and forlorn, in the centre of the vast solitude of his palm. He gazed at it and shuddered. And still mournfully contemplating it, he murmured, in a broken voice,

"Alas, it is not death I dread, but mutilation."

I heartened him once more, and with such success that he presently said, "Let the tragedy begin. Stand at my back; do not desert me in this solemn hour, my friend."

I gave him my promise. I now assisted him to point his pistol toward the spot where I judged his adversary to be standing, and cautioned him to listen well and further guide himself by my fellow-second's whoop. Then I propped myself against M. Gambetta's back, and raised a rousing "Whoop-ee!" This was answered from out the far distance of the fog, and I immediately shouted,

"One,—two,—three,—*fire !*"

Two little sounds like *spit ! spit !* broke upon my ear, and in the same instant I was crushed to the earth under a mountain of flesh. Buried as I was, I was still able to catch a faint accent from above, to this effect,—

"I die for . . . for . . . perdition take it, what *is* it I die for ? . . . oh, yes,—FRANCE! I die that France may live!"

The surgeons swarmed around with their probes in their hands, and applied their microscopes to the whole area of M. Gambetta's person, with the happy result of finding nothing in the nature of a wound. Then a scene ensued which was in every way gratifying and inspiriting.

The two gladiators fell upon each other's necks, with floods of proud and happy tears; that other second embraced me; the surgeons, the orators, the undertakers, the police, everybody embraced, everybody congratulated, everybody cried, and the whole atmosphere was filled with praise and with joy unspeakable.

It seemed to me then that I would rather be the hero of a French duel than a crowned and sceptred monarch.

When the commotion had somewhat subsided, the body of surgeons held a consultation, and after a good deal of debate decided that with proper care and nursing there was reason to believe that I would survive my injuries. My internal hurts were deemed the most serious, since it was apparent that a broken rib had penetrated my left lung, and that many of my organs had been pressed out so far to one side or the other of where they belonged, that it was doubtful if they would ever learn to perform their functions in such remote and unaccustomed localities. They then set my left arm in two places, pulled my right hip into its socket again, and re-elevated my nose. I was an object of great interest and even admiration; and many sincere and warm-hearted persons had themselves introduced to me, and said they were proud to know the only man who had been hurt in a French duel for forty years.

I was placed in an ambulance at the very head of the procession; and thus with gratifying *eclat* I was marched into Paris, the most conspicuous figure in that great spectacle, and deposited at the hospital.

The cross of the Legion of Honour has been conferred upon me. However, few escape that distinction.

Such is the true version of the most memorable private conflict of the age. My recovery is still doubtful, but there are hopes. I am able to dictate, but there is no knowing when I shall be able to write.

I have no complaints to make against any one. I acted for myself, and I can stand the consequences. Without boasting, I think I may say I am not afraid to stand before a modern French duellist, but I will never consent to stand behind one again.

THE GREAT REVOLUTION IN PITCAIRN.

LET me refresh the reader's memory a little. Nearly a hundred years ago the crew of the British ship Bounty mutinied, set the captain and his officers adrift upon the open sea, took possession of the ship, and sailed southward. They procured wives for themselves among the natives of Tahiti, then proceeded to a lonely little rock in mid-Pacific, called Pitcairn's Island, wrecked the vessel, stripped her of everything that might be useful to a new colony, and established themselves on shore.

Pitcairn's is so far removed from the track of commerce that it was many years before another vessel touched there. It had always been considered an uninhabited island; so when a ship did at last drop its anchor there, in 1808, the captain was greatly surprised to find the place peopled. Although the mutineers had fought among themselves, and gradually killed each other off until only two or three of the orignal stock remained, these tragedies had not occurred before a number of children had been born; so in 1808 the island had a population of twenty-seven persons. John Adams, the chief mutineer, still survived, and was to live many years yet, as governor and patriarch of the flock. From being mutineer and homicide, he had turned Christian and teacher, and his nation of twenty-seven persons was now the purest and devoutest in Christendom. Adams had long ago hoisted the British flag and constituted his island an appanage of the British Crown.

To-day the population numbers ninety persons,—sixteen men, nineteen women, twenty-five boys, and thirty girls,—all descendants of the mutineers, all bearing the family names of those mutineers, and all speaking English, and English only. The island stands high up out of the sea, and has precipitous walls. It is about three quarters of a mile long, and in places is as much as half a mile wide. Such arable land as it affords is held by the several families, according to a division made many years ago. There is some live stock,—goats, pigs, chickens, and cats; but no dogs, and no large animals. There is one church building,—used also as a capitol,—a school house, and a public library. The title of the governor has been, for a generation or two, "Magistrate and Chief Ruler, in subordination to her Majesty the Queen of Great Britain." It was his province to *make* the laws, as well as execute them His office was elective; everybody over seventeen years old had a vote,—no matter about the sex.

The sole occupations of the people were farming and fishing; their sole recreation, religious services. There has never been a shop in the island, nor any money. The habits and dress of the people have alway been primitive, and their laws simple to puerility. They have lived in a deep

Sabbath tranquillity, far from the world and its ambitions and vexations, and neither knowing nor caring what was going on in the mighty empires that lie beyond their limitless ocean solitudes. Once in three or four years a ship touched there, moved them with aged news of bloody battles, devastating epidemics, fallen thrones, and ruined dynasties, then traded them some soap and flannel for some yams and bread-fruit, and sailed away, leaving them to retire into their peaceful dreams and pious dissipations once more.

On the 8th of last September, Admiral de Horsey, commander-in-chief of the British fleet in the Pacific, visited Pitcairn's Island; and speaks as follows in his official report to the Admiralty :—

"They have beans, carrots, turnips, cabbages, and a little maize; pineapples, fig-trees, custard apples, and oranges; lemons, and cocoa-nuts. Clothing is obtained alone from passing ships, in barter for refreshments. There are no springs on the island, but as it rains generally once a month they have plenty of water, although at times, in former years, they have suffered from drought. No alcoholic liquors, except for medicinal purposes, are used, and a drunkard is unknown.

"The necessary articles required by the islanders are best shown by those we furnished in barter for refreshments: namely, flannel, serge, drill, half-boots, combs, tobacco, and soap. They also stand much in need of maps and slates for their school, and tools of any kind are most acceptable. I caused them to be supplied from the

public stores with a union-jack for display on the arrival
of ships, and a pit saw, of which they were greatly in
need.   This, I trust, will meet the approval of their lord-
ships.   If the munificent people of England were only
aware of the wants of this most deserving little colony,
they would not long go unsupplied. . . .

"Divine service is held every Sunday at 10.30 a.m.
and at 3 p.m., in the house built and used by John Adams
for that purpose until he died in 1829.   It is conducted
strictly in accordance with the liturgy of the Church of
England, by Mr. Simon Young, their selected pastor, who
is much respected.   A Bible class is held every Wednes-
day, when all who conveniently can attend.   There is
also a general meeting for prayer on the first Friday in
every month.   Family prayers are said in every house
the first thing in the morning and the last thing in the
evening, and no food is partaken of without asking God's
blessing before and afterwards.   Of these islanders' religious attributes no one can speak without deep respect.
A people whose greatest pleasure and privilege is to commune in prayer with their God, and to join in hymns of
praise, and who are, moreover, cheerful, diligent, and
probably freer from vice than any other community, need
no priest among them."

Now I come to a sentence in the admiral's report which
he dropped carelessly from his pen, no doubt, and never
gave the matter a second thought.   He little imagined
what a freight of tragic prophecy it bore!   This is the
sentence:

"One stranger, an American, has settled on the island, —*a doubtful acquisition.*"

A doubtful acquisition indeed! Captain Ormsby, in the American ship Hornet, touched at Pitcairn's nearly four months after the admiral's visit, and from the facts which he gathered there we know all about that American. Let us put these facts together, in historical form. The American's name was Butterworth Stavely. As soon as he had become well acquainted with all the people,— and this took but a few days, of course,—he began to ingratiate himself with them by all the arts he could command. He became exceedingly popular, and much looked up to; for one of the first things he did was to forsake his worldly way of life, and throw all his energies into religion. He was always reading his Bible, or praying, or singing hymns, or asking blessings. In prayer, no one had such "liberty" as he, no one could pray so long or so well.

At last, when he considered the time to be ripe, he began secretly to sow the seeds of discontent among the people. It was his deliberate purpose, from the beginning, to subvert the government, but of course he kept that to himself for a time. He used different arts with different individuals. He awakened dissatisfaction in one quarter by calling attention to the shortness of the Sunday services; he argued that there should be three hour services on Sunday instead of only two. Many had secretly held this opinion before; they now privately banded themselves into a party to work for it. He showed certain of the women that they were not allowed sufficient

voice in the prayer-meetings; thus another party was
formed. No weapon was beneath his notice; he even
descended to the children, and awoke discontent in their
breasts because—as *he* discovered for them—they had not
enough Sunday-school. This created a third party.

Now, as the chief of these parties, he found himself the
strongest power in the community. So he proceeded to
his next move,—a no less important one than the impeachment of the chief magistrate, James Russell Nickoy;
a man of character and ability, and possessed of great
wealth, he being the owner of a house with a parlour to it,
three acres and a half of yam land, and the only boat in
Pitcairn's, a whale-boat; and, most unfortunately, a pretext for this impeachment offered itself at just the right
time. One of the earliest and most precious laws of the
island was the law against trespass. It was held in great
reverence, and was regarded as the palladium of the people's liberties. About thirty years ago an important case
came before the courts under this law, in this wise: a
chicken belonging to Elizabeth Young (aged, at that
time, fifty-eight, a daughter of John Mills, one of the
mutineers of the Bounty) trespassed upon the grounds of
Thursday October Christian (aged twenty-nine, a grandson of Fletcher Christian, one of the mutineers). Christian killed the chicken. According to the law, Christian
could keep the chicken; or, if he preferred, he could
restore its remains to the owner, and receive damages in
"produce" to an amount equivalent to the waste and injury wrought by the trespasser. The court records set

forth that "the said Christian aforesaid did deliver the aforesaid remains to the said Elizabeth Young, and did demand one bushel of yams in satisfaction of the damage done." But Elizabeth Young considered the demand exorbitant; the parties could not agree; therefore Christian brought suit in the courts. He lost his case in the justice's court; at least, he was awarded only a half peck of yams, which he considered insufficient, and in the nature of a defeat. He appealed. The case lingered several years in an ascending grade of courts, and always resulted in decrees sustaining the original verdict; and finally the thing got into the supreme court, and there it stuck for twenty years. But last summer, even the supreme court managed to arrive at a decision at last. Once more the original verdict was sustained. Christian then said he was satisfied; but Stavely was present, and whispered to him and to his lawyer, suggesting, "as a mere form," that the original law be exhibited, in order to make sure that it still existed. It seemed an odd idea, but an ingenious one. So the demand was made. A messenger was sent to the magistrate's house; he presently returned with the tidings that it had disappeared from among the state archives.

The court now pronounced its late decision void, since it had been made under a law which had no actual existence.

Great excitement ensued, immediately. The news swept abroad over the whole island that the palladium of the public liberties was lost,—may be treasonably destroyed. Within thirty minutes almost the entire nation were in

the court room,—that is to say, the church.   The impeachment of the chief magistrate followed, upon Stavely's
motion.   The accused met his misfortune with the dignity
which became his great office.   He did not plead, or even
argue : he offered the simple defence that he had not med-
dled with the missing law; that he had kept the state
archives in the same candle-box that had been used as
their depository from the beginning; and that he was innocent of the removal or destruction of the lost document.

But nothing could save him ; he was found guilty of
misprision of treason, and degraded from his office, and all
his property was confiscated.

The lamest part of the whole shameful matter was the
reason suggested by his enemies for his destruction of the
law, to wit, that he did it to favour Christian, because
Christian was his cousin !   Whereas Stavely was the only
individual in the entire nation who was *not* his cousin.
The reader must remember that all of these people are
the descendants of half a dozen men ; that the first children intermarried together and bore grandchildren to the
mutineers ; that these grandchildren intermarried ; after
them, great and great-great-grandchildren intermarried :
so that to-day everybody is blood-kin to everybody.
Moreover, the relationships are wonderfully, even astound-
ingly, mixed up and complicated.   A stranger, for instance,
says to an islander,—

" You speak of that young woman as your cousin ; a
while ago you called her your aunt."

" Well, she *is* my aunt, and my cousin too.   And also my

step-sister, my niece, my fourth cousin, my thirty-third cousin, my forty-second cousin, my great-aunt, my grand-mother, my widowed sister-in-law,—and next week she will be my wife."

So the charge of nepotism against the chief magistrate was weak. But no matter; weak or strong, it suited Stave-ly. Stavely was immediately elected to the vacant magis-tracy; and, oozing reform from every pore, he went vig-orously to work. In no long time religious services raged everywhere and unceasingly. By command, the second prayer of the Sunday morning service, which had custom-arily endured some thirty-five or forty minutes, and had pleaded for the world, first by continent and then by nation-al and tribal detail, was extended to an hour and a half, and made to include supplications in behalf of the possible peoples in the several planets. Everybody was pleased with this; everybody said, " Now, *this* is something *like*." By command, the usual three-hour sermons were doubled in length. The nation came in a body to testify their grati-tude to the new magistrate. The old law forbidding cook-ing on the Sabbath was extended to the prohibition of eat-ing, also. By command, Sunday school was privileged to spread over into the week. The joy of all classes was complete. In one short month the new magistrate was become the people's idol.

The time was ripe for this man's next move. He began, cautiously at first, to poison the public mind against Eng-land. He took the chief citizens aside, one by one, and conversed with them on this topic. Presently he grew bolder, and spoke out. He said the nation owed it to itself, to its honour, to its great traditions, to rise in its might and throw off "this galling English yoke."

But the simple islanders answered,—

"We had not noticed that it galled, How does it gall? England sends a ship once in three or four years to give us soap and clothing, and things which we sorely need and gratefully receive ; but she never troubles us ; she lets us go our own way."

"She lets you go your own way! So slaves have felt and spoken in all the ages! This speech shows how fallen you are, how base, how brutalized, you have become, under this grinding tyranny! What! has all manly pride forsaken you? is liberty nothing? Are you content to be a mere appendage to a foreign and hateful sovereignty, when you might rise up and take your rightful place in the august family of nations, great, free, enlightened, independent, the minion of no sceptred master but the arbiter of your own destiny, and a voice and a power in decreeing the destinies of your sister-sovereignties of the world?"

Speeches like this produced an effect by and by. Citizens began to feel the English yoke ; they did not know exactly how or whereabouts they felt it, but they were perfectly certain they did feel it. They got to grumbling a good deal, and chafing under their chains, and longing for relief and release. They presently fell to hating the English flag, that sign and symbol of their nation's degradation ; they ceased to glance up at it as they passed the capitol, but averted their eyes and grated their teeth ; and one morning, when it was found trampled into the mud at the foot of the staff, they left it there, and no man put his hand to it to hoist it again. A certain thing which was sure to happen sooner or later happened now. Some of the chief citizens went to the magistrate by night, and said,—

"We can endure this hated tyranny no longer. How can we cast it off?"

"By a *coup d'etat.*"

"How?"

"A *coup d'etat.* It is like this: Everything is got ready, and at the appointed moment I, as the official head of the nation, publicly and solemnly proclaim its independence, and absolve it from allegiance to any and all other powers whatsoever."

"That sounds simple and easy. We can do that right away. Then what will be the next thing to do?"

"Seize all the defences and public properties of all kinds, establish martial law, put the army and navy on a war footing, and proclaim the empire!"

This fine programme dazzled these innocents. They said,

"This is grand,—this is splendid; but will not England resist?"

"Let her. This rock is a Gibraltar."

"True. But about the empire? Do we *need* an empire, and an emperor?"

"What you *need* my friends, is unification. Look at Germany; look at Italy. They are unified. Unification is the thing. It makes living dear. That constitutes progress. We must have a standing army and a navy. Taxes follow, as a matter of course. All these things summed up make grandeur. With unification and grandeur, what more can you want? Very well,—only the empire can confer these boons."

So on the 8th day of December Pitcairn's Island was proclaimed a free and independent nation; and on the same day the solemn coronation of Butterworth I., emperor of Pitcairn's Island took place, amid great rejoicings and festivities. The entire nation, with the exception of fourteen persons, mainly little children, marched past the throne in single file, with banners and music, the procession being upwards of ninety feet long; and some said it was as much as three quarters of a minute passing a given point. Nothing like it had ever been seen in the history of the island before. Public enthusiasm was measureless.

Now straightway imperial reforms began. Orders of nobility were instituted. A minister of the navy was appointed, and the whale-boat put in commission. A minister of war was created, and ordered to proceed at once with the formation of a standing army. A first lord of the treasury was named and commanded to get up a taxation scheme, and also open negotiations for treaties, offensive, defensive, and commercial, with foreign powers. Some generals and admirals were appointed; also some chamberlains, some equerries in waiting, and some lords of the bed-chamber.

At this point all the material was used up. The Grand Duke of Galilee, minister of war, complained that all the sixteen grown men in the empire had been given great offices, and consequently would not consent to serve in the ranks; wherefore his standing army was at a stand-still. The Marquis of Ararat, minister of the navy, made a similar complaint. He said he was willing to steer the whale-boat himself, but he *must* have somebody to man her.

The emperor did the best he could in the circumstances; he took all the boys above the age of ten years away from their mothers, and pressed them into the army, thus constructing a corps of seventeen privates, officered by one lieutenant-general and two major-generals. This pleased the minister of war, but procured the enmity of all the mothers in the land; for they said their precious ones must now find bloody graves in the fields of war, and he would be answerable for it. Some of the more heart-broken and inappeasable among them lay constantly in wait for the emperor and threw yams at him, unmindful of the body-guard.

On account of the extreme scarcity of material, it was found necessary to require the Duke of Bethany, post-master-general, to pull stroke-oar in the navy, and thus sit in the rear of a noble of lower degree, namely, Viscount Canaan, lord-justice of the common pleas. This turned the Duke of Bethany into a tolerably open malcontent and a secret conspirator,—a thing which the emperor foresaw, but could not help.

Things went from bad to worse. The emperor raised Nancy Peters to the peerage on one day, and married her the next, notwithstanding, for reasons of state, the cabinet had strenuously advised him to marry Emmeline, eldest daughter of the Archbishop of Bethlehem. This caused trouble in a powerful quarter,—the church. The new empress secured the support and friendship of two-thirds of the thirty-six grown women in the nation by absorbing them into her court as maids of honour; but this made deadly enemies of the remaining twelve. The families of the maids of honour soon began to rebel, because there was now nobody at home to keep house. The twelve snubbed women refused to enter the imperial kitchen as servants; so the empress had to require the Countess of Jericho and other great court dames to fetch water, sweep the palace, and to perform other menial and equally distasteful services. This made bad blood in that department.

Every body fell to complaining that the taxes levied for the support of the army, the navy, and the rest of the imperial establishment were intolerably burdensome, and were reducing the nation to beggary. The emperor's reply—"Look at Germany; look at Italy. Are you better than they? and haven't you unification?"—did not satisfy them. They said, "People can't *eat* unification, and we are starving. Agriculture has ceased. Everybody is in the army, everybody is in the navy, everybody is in the public service, standing around in a uniform, with nothing whatever to do, nothing to eat and nobody to till the fields."—

"Look at Germany; look at Italy. It is the same there. Such is unification, and there's no other way to get it—

no other way to keep it after you've got it," said the poor emperor always.

But the grumbler only replied, " We can't *stand* the taxes—we can't *stand* them."

Now right on the top of this the cabinet reported a national debt amounting to upwards of forty-five dollars —half a dollar to every individual in the nation. And they proposed to fund something. They had heard that this was always done in such emergencies. They proposed duties on exports; also on imports. And they wanted to issue bonds; also paper money, redeemable in yams and cabbages in fifty years. They said the pay of the army and of the navy and of the whole governmental machine was far in arrears, and unless something was done, and done immediately, national bankruptcy must ensue, and possibly insurrection and revolution. The emperor at once resolved upon a high-handed measure, and one of a nature never before heard of in Pitcairn's Island. He went in state to the church on Sunday morning, with the army at his back, and commanded the minister of the treasury to take up a collection.

That was the feather that broke the camel's back. First one citizen, and then another, rose and refused to submit to this unheard-of outrage—and each refusal was followed by the immediate confiscation of the malcontent's property. This vigour soon stopped the refusals, and the collection proceeded amid a sullen and ominous silence. As the emperor withdrew with the troops, he said, " I will teach you who is master here." Several persons shouted, " Down with unification!" They were at once arrested and torn from the arms of their weeping friends by the soldiery.

But in the meantime, as any prophet might have foreseen, a Social Democrat had been developed. As the emperor stepped into the gilded imperial wheelbarrow at the church door, the social democrat stabbed at him fifteen or sixteen times with a harpoon, but fortunately with such a peculiarly social democratic unprecision of aim as to do no damage.

That very night the convulsion came. The nation rose as one man—though forty-nine of the revolutionists were of the other sex. The infantry threw down their pitchforks; the artillery cast aside their cocoa-nuts; the navy revolted; the emperor was seized, and bound hand and foot in his palace. He was very much depressed. He said—

"I freed you from a grinding tyranny; I lifted you up out of your degradation, and made you a nation among nations; I gave you a strong, compact, centralized government; and, more than all, I gave you the blessing of blessings—unification. I have done all this, and my reward is hatred, insult, and these bonds. Take me; do with me as ye will. I here resign my crown and all my dignities, and gladly do I release myself from their too heavy burden. For your sake I took them up; for your sake I lay them down. The imperial jewel is no more; now bruise and defile as ye will the useless setting."

By a unanimous voice the people condemned the ex-emperor and the social democrat to perpetual banishment from church services, or to perpetual labour as galley-slaves in the whale-boat—whichever they might prefer. The next day the nation assembled again, and re-hoisted the British flag, reinstated the British tyranny, reduced the nobility to the condition of commoners again, and then straightway turned their diligent attention to the weeding of the ruined and neglected yam patches, and the rehabilitation of the old useful industries and the old healing and solacing pieties.   The ex-emperor restored the lost trespass law, and explained that he had stolen it—not to injure any one, but to further his political projects. Therefore the nation gave the late chief magistrate his office again, and also his alienated property.

Upon reflection, the ex-emperor and the social democrat chose perpetual banishment from religious services, in preference to perpetual labour as galley-slaves "*with* perpetual religious services," as they phrased it; wherefore the people believed that the poor fellows' troubles had unseated their reason, and so they judged it best to confine them for the present.   Which they did.

Such is the history of Pitcairn's "doubtful acquisition."

\

THE STORY OF THE BAD LITTLE BOY.

———

ONCE there was a bad little boy whose name was Jim— though, if you will notice, you will find that bad little boys are nearly always called James in your Sunday school books.   It was strange, but still it was true that this one was called Jim.

He didn't have any sick mother either—a sick mother who was pious and had the consumption, and would be glad to lie down in the grave and be at rest but for the strong love she bore her boy, and the anxiety she felt that the world might be harsh and cold towards him when she was gone.   Most bad boys in the Sunday books are named James, and have sick mothers, who teach them to say "Now, I lay me down," etc., and sing them to sleep with sweet, plaintive voices, and then kiss them good night, and kneel down by the bedside and weep.   But it was different with this fellow.   He was named Jim, and there wasn't anything the matter with his mother—no consumption, nor anything of that kind.   She was rather stout than otherwise, and she was not pious; moreover, she was not anxious on Jim's account.   She said if he were to break his neck it wouldn't be much loss.   She always spanked Jim to sleep, and she never kissed him good night; on the contrary, she boxed his ears when she was ready to leave him.

Once this little bad boy stole the key of the pantry, and slipped in there and helped himself to some jam, and filled up the vessel with tar, so that his mother would never know the difference; but all at once a terrible feeling didn't come over him, and something didn't seem to whisper to him, "Is it right to disobey my mother? Isn't it sinful to do this? Where do bad little boys go who gobble up their good kind mother's jam?" and then he didn't kneel down all alone and promise never to be wicked any more, and rise up with a light, happy heart, and go and tell his mother all about it, and beg her forgiveness, and be blessed by her with tears of pride and thankfulness in her eyes.

No; that is the way with all other bad boys in the books; but it happened otherwise with this Jim, strangely enough. He ate that jam, and said it was bully, in his sinful, vulgar way; and he put in the tar, and said that was bully also, and laughed, and observed "that the old woman would get up and snort" when she found it out; and when she did find it out, he denied knowing anything about it, and she whipped him severely, and he did the crying himself. Everything about this boy was curious—everything turned out differently with him from the way it does to the bad Jameses in the books.

Once he climbed up in Farmer Acorn's apple-tree to steal apples, and the limb didn't break, and he didn't fall and break his arm, and get torn by the farmer's great dog, and then languish on a sick bed for weeks, and repent and become good. Oh, no; he stole as many apples as he wanted, and came down all right; and he was all ready

for the dog, too, and knocked him endways with a brick
when he came to tear him.   It was very strange—nothing
like it ever happened in those mild little books with mar-
bled backs, and with pictures in them of men with swal-
low-tailed coats and bell-crowned hats, and pantaloons
that are short in the legs, and women with the waists of
their dresses under their arms, and no hoops on.   Nothing
like it in any of the Sunday school books.

Once he stole the teacher's pen-knife, and, when he was
afraid it would be found out and he would get whipped,
he slipped it into George Wilson's cap—poor widow Wilson's son, the moral boy, the good little boy of the village,
who always obeyed his mother, and never told an untruth,
and was fond of his lessons, and infatuated with Sunday
school.   And when the knife dropped from the cap, and
poor George hung his head and blushed, as if in conscious
guilt, and the grieved teacher charged the theft upon him,
and was just in the very act of bringing the switch down
upon his trembling shoulders, a white-haired, improbable
justice of the peace did not suddenly appear in their midst,
and strike an attitude and say, "Spare this noble boy—
there stands the cowering culprit!   I was passing the
school door at recess, and unseen myself, I saw the theft
committed!"   And then Jim didn't get whaled, and the
venerable justice didn't read the tearful school a homily,
and take George by the hand and say such a boy deserved
to be exalted, and then tell him to come and make his
home with him, and sweep out the office, and make fires,
and run errands, and chop wood, and study law, and help

his wife do household labours, and have all the balance of the time to play, and get forty cents a month, and be happy. No; it would have happened that way in the books, but it didn't happen that way to Jim. No meddling old clam of a justice dropped in to make trouble, and so the model boy George got thrashed, and Jim was glad of it because, you know, Jim hated moral boys. Jim said he was "down on them milksops." Such was the coarse language of this bad, neglected boy.

But the strangest thing that ever happened to Jim was the time he went boating on Sunday, and didn't get drowned, and that other time that he got caught out in the storm when he was fishing on Sunday, and didn't get struck by lightning. Why, you might look, and look, all through the Sunday school books from now till next Christmas, and you would never come across anything like this. Oh no; you would find that all the bad boys who go boating on Sunday invariably get drowned; and all the bad boys who get caught out in storms when they are fishing on Sunday, infallibly get struck by lightning. Boats with bad boys in them always upset on Sunday, and it always storms when bad boys go fishing on the Sabbath. How this Jim ever escaped is a mystery to me.

This Jim bore a charmed life—that must have been the way of it. Nothing could hurt him. He even gave the elephant in the menagerie a plug of tobacco, and the elephant didn't knock the top of his head off with his trunk. He browsed around the cupboard after essence of peppermint, and didn't make a mistake and drink *aqua fortis*.

He stole his father's gun and went hunting on the Sabbath, and didn't shoot three or four of his fingers off. He struck his little sister on the temple with his fist when he was angry, and she didn't linger in pain through long summer days; and die with sweet words of forgiveness upon her lips that redoubled the anguish of his breaking heart. No; she got over it. He ran off and went to sea at last, and didn't come back and find himself sad and alone in the world, his loved ones sleeping in the quiet churchyard, and the vine-embowered home of his boyhood tumbled down and gone to decay. Ah, no; he came home as drunk as a piper, and got into the station-house the first thing.

And he grew up and married, and raised a large family, and brained them all with an axe one night, and got wealthy by all manner of cheating and rascality; and now he is the infernalest wickedest scoundrel in his native village, and is universally respected, and belongs to the Legislature.

So you see there never was a bad James in the Sunday school books that had such a streak of luck as this sinful Tim with the charmed life.

THE STORY OF THE GOOD LITTLE BOY.

ONCE there was a good little boy by the name of Jacob Blivens. He always obeyed his parents, no matter how absurd and unreasonable their demands were; and he always learned his book, and never was late at Sabbath school. He would not play hookey, even when his sober judgment told him it was the most profitable thing he could do. None of the other boys could ever make that boy out, he acted so strangely. He wouldn't lie, no matter how convenient it was. He just said it was wrong to lie, and that was sufficient for him. And he was so honest that he was simply ridiculous. The curious ways that that Jacob had, surpassed everything. He wouldn't play marbles on Sunday, he wouldn't rob birds' nests, he wouldn't give hot pennies to organ-grinders' monkeys ; he didn't seem to take any interest in any kind of rational amusement. So the other boys used to try to reason it out and come to an understanding of him, but they couldn't arrive at any satisfactory conclusion. As I said before, they could only figure out a sort of vague idea that he was " afflicted," and so they took him under their protection, and never allowed any harm to come to him.

This good little boy read all the Sunday school books ;

they were his greatest delight. This was the whole
secret of it. He believed in the good little boys they put
in the Sunday school books; he had every confidence in
them. He longed to come across one of them alive, once;
but he never did. They all died before his time, maybe.
Whenever he read about a particularly good one he turned over quickly to the end to see what became of him,
because he wanted to travel thousands of miles and gaze
on him; but it wasn't any use; that good little boy
always died in the last chapter, and there was a picture
of the funeral, with all his relations and the Sunday
school children standing around the grave in pantaloons
that were too short, and bonnets that were too large, and
everybody crying into handkerchiefs that had as much as
a yard and a half of stuff in them. He was always headed
off in this way. He never could see one of those good little
boys on account of his always dying in the last chapter.

Jacob had a noble ambition to be put in a Sunday
school book. He wanted to be put in, with pictures representing him gloriously declining to lie to his mother,
and her weeping for joy about it; and pictures representing him standing on the doorstep giving a penny to a
poor beggar-woman with six children, and telling her to
spend it freely, but not to be extravagant, because extra-
vagance is a sin; and pictures of him magnanimously refusing to tell on the bad boy who always lay in wait for
him around the corner as he came from school, and welt-
ed him over the head with a lath, and then chased him
home, saying, "Hi! hi!" as he proceeded. That was the

ambition of young Jacob Blivens. He wished to be put in a Sunday school book. It made him feel a little uncomfortable sometimes when he reflected that the good little boys always died. He loved to live, you know, and this was the most unpleasant feature about being a Sunday school book boy. He knew it was not healthy to be good. He knew it was more fatal than consumption to be so supernaturally good as the boys in the books were; he knew that none of them had ever been able to stand it long, and it pained him to think that if they put him in a book he wouldn't ever see it, or even if they did get the book out before he died it wouldn't be popular without any picture of his funeral in the back part of it. It couldn't be much of a Sunday school book that couldn't tell about the advice he gave to the community when he was dying. So at last, of course, he had to make up his mind to do the best he could under the circumstances—to live right, and hang on as long as he could, and have his dying speech all ready when his time came.

But somehow nothing ever went right with this good little boy; nothing ever turned out with him the way it turned out with the good little boys in the books. They always had a good time, and the bad boys had the broken legs; but in his case there was a screw loose somewhere, and it all happened just the other way. When he found Jim Blake stealing apples, and went under the tree to read to him about the bad little boy who fell out of a neighbour's apple-tree and broke his arm, Jim fell out of the tree too, but he fell on *him*, and broke *his* arm, and

Jim wasn't hurt at all.   Jacob couldn't understand that.
There wasn't anything in the books like it.

And once, when some bad boys pushed a blind man
over in the mud, and Jacob ran to help him up and receive his blessing, the blind man did not give him any
blessing at all, but whacked him over the head with his
stick and said he would like to catch him shoving *him*
again, and then pretending to help him up.   This was not
in accordance with any of the books.   Jacob looked them
all over to see.

One thing that Jacob wanted to do was to find a lame
dog that hadn't any place to stay and was hungry and
persecuted, and bring him home and pet him and have
that dog's imperishable gratitude.   And at last he found
one and was happy; and he brought him home and fed
him, but when he was going to pet him the dog flew at
him and tore all the clothes off him except those that
were in front, and made a spectacle of him that was
astonishing.   He examined authorities, but he could not
understand the matter.   It was of the same breed of
dogs that was in the books, but it acted very differently.
Whatever this boy did he got into trouble.   The very
things the boys in the books got rewarded for turned out
to be about the most unprofitable things he could invest in.

Once, when he was on his way to Sunday-school, he
saw some bad boys starting off pleasuring in a sail-boat.
He was filled with consternation, because he knew from
his reading that boys who went sailing on Sunday invari-

ably got drowned. So he ran out on a raft to warn them, but a log turned with him and slid him into the river   A man got him out pretty soon, and the doctor pumped the water out of him, and gave him a fresh star with his bellows, but he caught cold and lay sick a-bed nine weeks.   But the most unaccountable thing about it was that the bad boys in the boat had a good time all day, and then reached home alive and well in the most surprising manner.   Jacob Blivens said there was nothing like these things in the books.   He was perfectly dumbfounded.

When he got well he was a little discouraged, but he resolved to keep on trying anyhow.   He knew that so far his experiences wouldn't do to go in a book, but he hadn't yet reached the allotted term of life for good little boys, and he hoped to be able to make a record yet if he could hold on till his time was fully up.   If everything else failed he had his dying speech to fall back on.

He examined his authorities, and found that it was now time for him to go to sea as a cabin-boy.   He called on a ship captain and made his application, and when the captain asked for his recommendations he proudly drew out a tract and pointed to the words, "To Jacob Blivens, from his affectionate teacher."   But the captain was a coarse, vulgar man, and he said, "Oh, that be blowed! *that* wasn't any proof that he knew how to wash dishes or handle a slush-bucket, and he guessed he didn't want him."   This was altogether the most extraordinary thing that ever happened to Jacob in all his life.   A compli-

ment from a teacher, on a tract, had never failed to move
the tenderest emotions of ship captains, and open the way
to all offices of honour and profit in their gift—it never
had in any book that ever *he* had read.   He could hardly
believe his senses.

The boy always had a hard time of it.   Nothing ever
came out according to the authorities with him.   At last,
one day, when he was around hunting up bad little boys
to admonish, he found a lot of them in the old iron
foundry fixing up a little joke on fourteen or fifteen dogs,
which they had tied together in long procession, and were
going to ornament with empty nitro-glycerine cans made
fast to their tails.   Jacob's heart was touched.   He sat
down on one of those cans (for he never minded grease
when duty was before him), and he took hold of the fore-
most dog by the collar, and turned his reproving eye upon
wicked Tom Jones.   But just at that moment Alderman
McWelter, full of wrath, stepped in.   All the bad boys
ran away, but Jacob Blivens rose in conscious innocence
and began one of those stately little Sunday-school-book
speeches which always commence with "Oh, sir!" in dead
opposition to the fact that no boy, good or bad, ever starts
a remark with "Oh, sir."   But the alderman never waited
to hear the rest.   He took Jacob Blivens by the ear and
turned him around, and hit him a whack in the rear with
the flat of his hand; and in an instant that good little
boy shot out through the roof and soared away towards
the sun, with the fragments of those fifteen dogs stringing
after him like the tail of a kite.   And there wasn't a sign

of that alderman or that old iron foundry left on the face of the earth; and, as for young Jacob Blivens, he never got a chance to make his last dying speech after all his trouble fixing it up, unless he made it to the birds; because, although the bulk of him came down all right in a tree-top in an adjoining county, the rest of him was apportioned around among four townships, and so they had to hold five inquests on him to find out whether he was dead or not, and how it occurred. You never saw a boy scattered so.*

Thus perished the good little boy who did the best he could, but didn't come out according to the books. Every boy who ever did as he did prospered except him. His case is truly remarkably. It will probably never be accounted for.

---

* This glycerine catastrophe is borrowed from a floating newspaper item, whose author's name I would give if I knew it.—[M. T.]

EXPERIENCE OF THE McWILLIAMSES WITH MEMBRANOUS CROUP.

AS RELATED TO THE AUTHOR OF THIS BOOK BY MR. MC-
WILLIAMS, A PLEASANT NEW YORK GENTLEMAN WHOM
THE SAID AUTHOR MET BY CHANCE ON A JOURNEY.

———

WELL, to go back to where I was before I digressed to explain to you how that frightful and incurable disease, membranous croup, was ravaging the town and driving all mothers mad with terror, I called Mrs. Mc-Williams' attention to little Penelope and said:

"Darling, I wouldn't let that child be chewing that pine stick if I were you."

"Precious, where is the harm in it?" said she, but at the same time preparing to take away the stick—for women cannot receive even the most palpably judicious suggestion without arguing it; that is, married women.

I replied:

"Love, it is notorious that pine is the least nutritious wood that a child can eat."

My wife's hand paused, in the act of taking the stick, and returned itself to her lap. She bridled perceptibly, and said:

"Hubby, you know better than that. You know you do. Doctors *all* say that the turpentine in pine wood is good for weak back and the kidneys."

"Ah—I was under a misapprehension. I did not know that the child's kidneys and spine were affected, and that the family physician had recommended—"

"Who said the child's spine and kidneys were affected?"

"My love, you intimated it."

"The idea! I never intimated anything of the kind."

"Why, my dear, it hasn't been two minutes since you said—"

"Bother what I said! I don't care what I did say. There isn't any harm in the child's chewing a bit of pine stick if she wants to, and you know it perfectly well. And she *shall* chew it, too. So there now!"

"Say no more, my dear. I now see the force of your reasoning, and I will go and order two or three cords of the best pine wood to-day. No child of mine shall want while I—"

"O *please* go along to your office and let me have some peace. A body can never make the simplest remark but you must take it up and go to arguing and arguing and arguing till you don't know what you are talking about, and you *never* do."

"Very well, it shall be as you say. But there is a want of logic in your last remark which—"

However she was gone with a flourish before I could finish, and had taken the child with her. That night at dinner she confronted me with a face as white as a sheet.

"O, Mortimer, there's another!   Little Georgie Gordon is taken."

"Membranous croup?"

"Membranous croup."

"Is there any hope for him?"

"None in the wide world.   Oh, what is to become of us!"

By and by a nurse brought in our Penelope to say good-night and offer the customary prayer at the mother's knee. In the midst of "Now I lay me down to sleep," she gave a slight cough!   My wife fell back like one stricken with death.   But the next moment she was up and brimming with the activities which terror inspires.

She commanded that the child's crib be removed from the nursery to our bed-room; and she went along to see the order executed.   She took me with her, of course. We got matters arranged with speed.   A cot bed was put up in my wife's dressing room for the nurse.   But now Mrs. McWilliams said we were too far away from the other baby, and what if he were to have the symptoms in the night—and she blanched again, poor thing.

We then restored the crib and the nurse to the nursery and put up a bed for ourselves in a room adjoining.

Presently, however, Mrs. McWilliams said, "Suppose the baby should catch it from Penelope?"   This thought struck a new panic to her heart, and the tribe of us could not get the crib out of the nursery again fast enough to satisfy my wife, though she assisted in her own person and well nigh pulled the crib to pieces in her frantic hurry.

We moved down stairs; but there was no place there

to stow the nurse, and Mrs. McWilliams said the nurse's experience would be an inestimable help. So we returned, bag and baggage, to our own bed-room once more, and felt a great gladness, like storm-buffeted birds that have found their nests again.

Mrs. McWilliams sped to the nursery to see how things were going on there. She was back in a moment with a new dread. She said:

"What *can* make Baby sleep so?"

I said:

"Why, my darling, Baby *always* sleeps like a graven image."

"I know. I know; but there's something peculiar about his sleep, now. He seems to—to—he seems to breathe so *regularly*. O, this is dreadful."

"But my dear he always breathes regularly."

"Oh, I know it, but there's something frightful about it now. His nurse is too young and inexperienced. Maria shall stay there with her, and be on hand if anything happens."

"That is a good idea, but who will help *you*?"

"You can help me all I want. I wouldn't allow anybody to do anything but myself, any how, at such a time as this."

I said I would feel mean to lie abed and sleep, and leave her to watch and toil over our little patient all the weary night.—But she reconciled me to it. So old Maria departed and took up her ancient quarters in the nursery.

Penelope coughed twice in her sleep.

"Oh, why *don't* that doctor come! Mortimer, this room is too warm. This room is certainly too warm. Turn off the register—quick!"

I shut it off, glancing at the thermometer at the same time, and wondering to myself if 70 *was* too warm for a sick child.

The coachman arrived from down town, now, with the news that our physician was ill and confined to his bed.— Mrs. McWilliams turned a dead eye upon me, and said in a dead voice:

"There is a Providence in it. It is foreordained. He never was sick before.—Never. We have not been living as we ought to live, Mortimer. Time and time again I have told you so. Now you see the result. Our child will never get well. Be thankful if you can forgive yourself; I never can forgive *myself*."

I said, without intent to hurt, but with heedless choice of words, that I could not see that we had been living such an abandoned life.

"*Mortimer!* Do you want to bring the judgment upon Baby, too!"

Then she began to cry, but suddenly exclaimed:

"The doctor must have sent medicines!"

I said:

"Certainly. They are here. I was only waiting for you to give me a chance."

"Well do give them to me! Don't you know that every moment is precious now? But what was the use in sending medicines, when he *knows* that the disease is incurable?"

I said that while there was life there was hope.

"Hope! Mortimer, you know no more what you are talking about than the child unborn. If you would—. As I live, the directions say give one teaspoonful once an hour! Once an hour!—as if we had a whole year before us to save the child in! Mortimer, please hurry. Give the poor perishing thing a table-spoonful, and *try* to be quick!"

"Why, my dear, a table-spoonful might—"

"*Don't* drive me frantic! . . . . There, there, there, my precious, my own; it's nasty bitter stuff, but it's good for Nelly—good for Mother's precious darling; and it will make her well. There, there, there, put the little head on Mamma's breast and go to sleep, and pretty soon—Oh, I know she can't live till morning! Mortimer, a table-spoonful every half hour will—. Oh, the child needs belladonna too; I know she does—and aconite. Get them, Mortimer. Now do let me have my way. You know nothing about these things."

We now went to bed, placing the crib close to my wife's pillow. All this turmoil had worn upon me, and within two minutes I was something more than half asleep. Mrs. McWilliams roused me:

"Darling, is that register turned on?"

"No."

"I thought as much. Please turn it on at once. This room is cold."

I turned it on, and presently fell asleep again. I was aroused once more:

"Dearie, would you mind moving the crib to your side of the bed?   It is nearer the register."

I moved it, but had a collision with the rug and woke up the child. I dozed off once more, while my wife quieted the sufferer.   But in a little while these words came murmuring remotely through the fog of my drowsiness:

"Mortimer, if we only had some goose-grease—will you ring?"

I climbed dreamily out, and stepped on a cat, which responded with a protest and would have got a convincing kick for it if a chair had not got it instead.

"Now, Mortimer, why do you want to turn up the gas and wake up the child again?"

"Because I want to see how much I am hurt, Caroline."

"Well look at the chair, too—I have no doubt it is ruined.   Poor cat, suppose you had—"

"Now I am not going to suppose anything about the cat.   It never would have occurred if Maria had been allowed to remain here and attend to these duties, which are in her line and are not in mine."

"Now Mortimer, I should think you would be ashamed to make a remark like that.   It is a pity if you cannot do the few little things I ask of you at such an awful time as this when our child—"

"There, there, I will do anything you want.   But I can't raise anybody with this bell.   They're all gone to bed.   Where is the goose-grease?"

"On the mantel-piece in the nursery.   If you'll step there and speak to Maria—"

I fetched the goose grease and went to sleep again:
Once more I was called:

"Mortimer, I so hate to disturb you, but the room is still too cold for me to try to apply this stuff. Would you mind lighting the fire? It is all ready to touch a match to."

I dragged myself out and lit the fire, and then sat down disconsolate.

"Mortimer, don't sit there and catch your death of cold. Come to bed."

As I was stepping in, she said:

"But wait a moment. Please give the child some more of the medicine."

Which I did. It was a medicine which made a child more or less lively; so my wife made use of its waking interval to strip it and grease it all over with goose-oil. I was soon asleep once more, but once more I had to get up.

"Mortimer, I feel a draft. I feel it distinctly. There is nothing so bad for this disease as a draft. Please move the crib in front of the fire."

I did it; and collided with the rug again, which I threw in the fire. Mrs. McWilliams sprang out of bed and rescued it and we had some words. I had another trifling interval of sleep, and then got up, by request, and constructed a flax-seed po 'tice. This was placed upon the child's breast and left there to do its healing work.

A wood fire is not a permanent thing. I got up every twenty minutes and renewed ours and this gave Mrs. Mc-Williams the opportunity to shorten the times of giving the medicines by ten minutes, which was a great satisfaction to her. Now and then, between times, I reorganized the flax-seed poultices, and applied sinapisms and other sorts of blisters where unoccupied places could be found upon the child. Well, toward morning the wood gave out and my wife wanted me to go down cellar and get some more. I said:

"My dear, it is a laborious job, and the child must be nearly warm enough, with her extra clothing. Now mightn't we put on another layer of poultices and—"

I did not finish, because I was interrupted. I lugged wood up from below for some little time, and then turned in and fell to snoring as only a man can whose strength is all gone and whose soul is worn out. Just at broad daylight I felt a grip on my shoulder that brought me to my senses suddenly.—My wife was glaring down upon me and gasping. As soon as she could command her tongue she said:

"It is all over! All over! The child's perspiring! What *shall* we do?"

"Mercy, how you terrify me! *I* don't know what we ought to do. Maybe if we scraped her and put her in the draft again—"

"O, idiot! There is not a moment to lose! Go for the doctor. Go yourself. Tell him he *must* come, dead or alive."

I dragged that poor sick man from his bed and brought him. He looked at the child and said she was not dying. This was joy unspeakable to me, but it made my wife as mad as if he had offered her a personal affront. Then he said the child's cough was only caused by some trifling irritation or other in the throat. At this I thought my wife had a mind to show him the door.—Now the doctor said he would make the child cough harder and dislodge the trouble. So he gave her something that sent her into a spasm of coughing, and presently up came a little wood splinter or so.

"This child has no membranous croup," said he. "She has been chewing a bit of pine shingle or something of the kind, and got some little slivers in her throat. They wont do her any hurt."

"No," said I, "I can well believe that. Indeed, the turpentine that is in them is very good for certain sorts of diseases that are peculiar to children. My wife will tell you so."

But she did not. She turned away in disdain and left the room ; and since that time there is one episode in our life which we never refer to. Hence the tide of our days flows by in deep and untroubled serenity.

[Very few married men have such an experience as McWilliams' and so the author of this book thought that maybe the novelty of it would give it a passing interest to the reader.]

SOME LEARNED FABLES, FOR GOOD OLD BOYS AND GIRLS.

In Three Parts.

PART FIRST.

HOW THE ANIMALS OF THE WOOD SENT OUT A SCIENTIFIC EXPEDITION.

ONCE the creatures of the forest held a great convention and appointed a commission consisting of the most illustrious scientists among them to go forth, clear beyond the forest and out into the unknown and unexplored world, to verify the truth of the matters already taught in their schools and colleges and also to make discoveries. It was the most imposing enterprise of the kind the nation had ever embarked in. True, the government had once sent Dr. Bull Frog, with a picked crew, to hunt for a north-westerly passage through the swamp to the right-hand corner of the wood, and had since sent out many expeditions to hunt for Dr. Bull Frog; but they never could find him, and so Government finally gave him up and en-nobled his mother to show its gratitude for the services her son had rendered to science. And once Government sent Sir Grass Hopper to hunt for the sources of the rill that emptied into the swamp; and afterwards sent out many expeditions to hunt for Sir Grass, and at last they were successful—they found his body, but if he had discovered the sources meantime, he did not let on. So Government acted handsomely by deceased and many envied his funeral.

But these expeditions were trifles compared with the present one; for this one comprised among its servants the very greatest among the learned ; and besides it was to go to the utterly unvisited regions believed to lie beyond the mighty forest—as we have remarked before. How the members were banqueted, and glorified, and talked about! Everywhere that one of them showed himself, straightway there was a crowd to gape and stare at him.

Finally they set off, and it was a sight to see the long procession of dry-land Tortoises heavily laden with savans, scientific instruments, Glow-Worms and Fire-Flies for signal-service, provisions, Ants and Tumble-Bugs to fetch and carry and delve, Spiders to carry the surveying chain and do other engineering duty, and so forth and so on; and after the Tortoises came another long train of iron-clads—stately and spacious Mud Turtles for marine transportation service; and from every Tortoise and every Turtle flaunted a flaming gladiolus or other splendid banner; at the head of the column a great band of Bumble-Bees, Mosquitoes, Katy-dids and Crickets discoursed martial music; and the entire train was under the escort and protection of twelve picked regiments of the Army Worm.

At the end of three weeks the expedition emerged from the forest and looked upon the great Unknown World. Their eyes were greeted with an impressive spectacle. A vast level plain stretched before them, watered by a sinuous stream; and beyond, there towered up against the sky a long and lofty barrier of some kind, they did not know what. The Tumble-Bug said he believed it was simply land tilted up on its edge, because he knew he could see trees on it. But Prof. Snail and the others said:

"You are hired to dig, sir—that is all. We need your muscle, not your brains. When we want your opinion on scientific matters, we will hasten to let you know. Your coolness is intolerable, too—loafing about here meddling with august matters of learning, when the other labourers are pitching camp. Go along and help handle the baggage."

The Tumble-Bug turned on his heel uncrushed, unabashed, observing to himself, "if it isn't land tilted up, let me die the death of the unrighteous."

Professor Bull Frog, (nephew of the late explorer,) said he believed the ridge was the wall that enclosed the earth. He continued:

"Our fathers have left us much learning, but they had not travelled far, and so we may count this a noble, new discovery. We are safe for renown, now, even though our labours began and ended with this single achievement. I wonder what this wall is built of? Can it be fungus? Fungus is an honourable good thing to build a wall of."

Professor Snail adjusted his field-glass and examined the rampart critically. Finally he said:

"The fact that it is not diaphanous, convinces me that it is a dense vapour formed by the calorification of ascending moisture dephlogisticated by refraction. A few endiometrical experiments would confirm this, but it is not necessary.—The thing is obvious."

So he shut up his glass and went into his shell to make a note of the discovery of the world's end, and the nature of it.

"Profound mind!" said Professor Angle-Worm to Professor Field-Mouse; "profound mind! nothing can long long remain a mystery to that august brain."

Night drew on apace, the sentinel crickets were posted, the Glow-Worm and Fire-Fly lamps were lighted, and the camp sang to silence and sleep. After breakfast in the morning, the expedition moved on. About noon a great avenue was reached, which had in it two endless parallel bars of some kind of hard black substance, raised the height of the tallest Bull Frog above the general level. The scientists climbed up on these and examined and tested them in various ways. They walked along them for a great distance, but found no end and no break in them. They could arrive at no decision. There was nothing in the records of science that mentioned anything of this kind. But at last the bald and venerable geographer, Professor Mud Turtle, a person who, born poor, and of a drudging low family, had, by his own native force raised himself to the headship of the geographers of his generation, said:

"My friends, we have indeed made a discovery here. We have found in a palpable, compact and imperishable state what the wisest of our fathers always regarded as a mere thing of imagination. Humble yourselves, my friends, for we stand in a majestic presence. These are parallels of latitude!"

Every heart and every head was bowed, so awful, so sublime was the magnitude of the discovery. Many shed tears.

The camp was pitched and the rest of the day given up to writing voluminous accounts of the marvel, and correcting astronomical tables to fit it. Toward midnight a demoniacal shriek was heard, then a clattering and rumbling noise, and the next instant a vast terrific eye shot by, with a long tail attached, and disappeared in the gloom, still uttering triumphant shrieks.

The poor camp labourers were stricken to the heart with fright, and stampeded for the high grass in a body. But not the scientists. They had no superstitions. They calmly proceeded to exchange theories. The ancient geographer's opinion was asked. He went into his shell and deliberated long and profoundly. When he came out at last, they all knew by his worshipping countenance that he brought light. Said he:

"Give thanks for this stupendous thing which we have been permitted to witness.—It is the Vernal Equinox!"

There was shoutings and great rejoicings.

"But," said the Angle-worm, uncoiling after reflection, "this is dead summer time."

"Very well," said the Turtle, "we are far from our region; the season differs with the difference of time between the two points."

"Ah, true. True enough. But it is night. How should the sun pass in the night?"

"In these distant regions he doubtless passes always in the night at this hour."

"Yes, doubtless that is true. But it being night, how is it that we could see him?"

"It is a great mystery. I grant that. But I am persuaded that the humidity of the atmosphere in these remote regions is such that particles of daylight adhere to the disk and it was by aid of these that we were enabled to see the sun in the dark."

This was deemed satisfactory, and due entry was made of the decision.

But about this moment those dreadful shriekings were heard again; again the rumbling and thundering came speeding up out of the night; and once more a flaming great eye flashed by and lost itself in gloom and distance.

The camp labourers gave themselves up for lost. The savants were sorely perplexed. Here was a marvel hard to account for. They thought and they talked, they talked and they thought.—Finally the learned and aged Lord Grand-Daddy-Longlegs, who had been sitting, in deep study, with his slender limbs crossed and his stemmy arms folded, said:

"Deliver your opinions, brethren, and then I will tell my thought—for I think I have solved this problem."

"So be it, good your lordship," piped the weak treble of the wrinkled and withered Professor Woodlouse, "for we shall hear from your lordship's lips naught but wisdom."—[Here the speaker threw in a mess of trite, thread-bare, exasperating quotations from the ancient poets and philosophers, delivering them with unction in the sounding grandeurs of the original tongues, they being from the Mastodon, the Dodo, and other dead languages]. "Perhaps I ought not to presume to meddle with matters pertaining to astronomy at all, in such a presence as this, I who have made it the business of my life to delve only among the riches of the extinct languages and unearth the opulence of their ancient lore; but still, as unacquainted as I am with the noble science of astronomy, I beg with deference and humility to suggest that inasmuch as the last of these wonderful apparitions proceeded in exactly the opposite direction from that pursued by the first, which you decide to be the Vernal Equinox, and greatly resembled it in all particulars, is it not possible, nay certain, that this last is the *Autumnal* Equi——"

"O-o-o!" "O-o-o! go to bed! go to bed!" with annoyed derision from everybody. So the poor old Woodlouse retreated out of sight, consumed with shame.

Further discussion followed, and then the united voice of the commission begged Lord Longlegs to speak. He said:

"Fellow-scientists, it is my belief that we have witnessed a thing which has occurred in perfection but once before in the knowledge of created beings. It is a phenomenon of inconceivable importance and interest, view it as one may, but its interest to us is vastly heightened by an added knowledge of its nature which no scholar has

heretofore possessed or even suspected. This great marvel which we have just witnessed, fellow-savants, (it
almost takes my breath away!) is nothing less than the
transit of Venus!"

Every scholar sprang to his feet pale with astonishment.
Then ensued tears, hand shakings, frenzied embraces, and
the most extravagant jubilations of every sort. But by
and by, as emotion began to retire within bounds, and
reflection to return to the front, the accomplished Chief
Inspector Lizard observed:

"But how is this?— Venus should traverse the sun's
surface, not the earth's."

The arrow went home. It carried sorrow to the breast
of every apostle of learning there, for none could deny
that this was a formidable criticism. But tranquilly the
venerable Duke crossed his limbs behind his ears and said:

"My friend has touched the marrow of our mighty discovery. Yes—all that have lived before us thought a
transit of Venus consisted of a flight across the sun's face;
they thought it, they maintained it, they honestly believed
it, simple hearts, and were justified in it by the limitations
of their knowledge; but to us has been granted the inestimable boon of proving that the transit occurs across
the earth's face, *for we have* SEEN *it!*"

The assembled wisdom sat in speechless adoration of
this imperial intellect. All doubts had instantly departed,
like night before the lightning.

The Tumble-Bug had just intruded, unnoticed. He
now came reeling forward among the scholars, familiarly

slapping first one and then another on the shoulder, saying
"Nice (ic!) nice old boy!" and smiling a smile of elaborate content. Arrived at a good position for speaking, he
put his left arm akimbo with his knuckles planted in his
hip just under the edge of his cut-away coat, bent his
right leg, placing his toe on the ground and resting his
heel with easy grace against his left shin, puffed out his
aldermanic stomach, opened his lips, leaned his right
elbow on Inspector Lizard's shoulder,—

But the shoulder was indignantly withdrawn and the
hard-handed son of toil went to earth. He floundered a
bit but came up smiling, arranged his attitude with the
same careful detail as before, only choosing Professor
Dogtick's shoulder for a support, opened his lips and—

Went to earth again. He presently scrambled up once
more, still smiling, made a loose effort to brush the dust
off his coat and legs, but a smart pass of his hand missed
entirely and the force of the unchecked impulse slewed
him suddenly around, twisted his legs together, and projected him limber and sprawling, into the lap of the Lord
Longlegs. Two or three scholars sprang forward, flung
the low creature head over heels into a corner and reinstated the patrician, smoothing his ruffled dignity with
many soothing and regretful speeches. Professor Bull
Frog roared out:

"No more of this, sirrah Tumble-Bug! Say your say
and then get you about your business with speed!—Quick,
what is your errand? Come move off a trifle; you smell
like a stable; what have you been at?"

"Please ('ic!) please your worship I chanced to light upon a find. But no m (*e-uck!*) matter 'bout that. There's b ('ic!) been another find which— —beg pardon yer honours, what was that th ('ic!) thing that ripped by here first?"

"It was the Vernal Equinox."

"Inf ('ic!) fernal equinox. 'At's all right.—D ('ic!) Dunno *him*. What's other one?"

"The transit of Venus."

"G ('ic!) Got me again. No matter. Las' one dropped something."

"Ah, indeed! Good luck! Good news! Quick—what is it?"

"M ('ic!) Mosey out 'n' see. It'll pay."

No more votes were taken for four and twenty hours. Then the following entry was made:

"The commission went in a body to view the find. It was found to consist of a hard, smooth, huge object with a rounded summit surmounted by a short upright projection resembling a section of a cabbage stalk divided transversely—This projection was not solid, but was a hollow cylinder plugged with a soft woody substance unknown to our region—that is, it had been so plugged, but unfortunately this obstruction had been heedlessly removed by Norway Rat, Chief of the Sappers and Miners, before our arrival. The vast object before us so mysteriously conveyed from the glittering domains of space, was found to be hollow and nearly filled with a pungent liquid of a brownish hue, like rain-water that has stood for some

time. And such a spectacle as met our view! Norway
Rat was perched upon the summit engaged in thrusting
his tail into the cylindrical projection, drawing it out
dripping, permitting the struggling multitude of labourers to suck the end of it, then straightway reinserting it
and delivering the fluid to the mob as before. Evidently
this liquor had strangely potent qualities; for all that
partook of it were immediately exalted with great and
pleasurable emotions, and went staggering about singing
ribald songs, embracing, fighting, dancing, discharging
irruptions of profanity, and defying all authority.
Around us struggled a massed and uncontrolled mob—
uncontrolled and likewise uncontrollable, for the whole
army, down to the very sentinels, were mad like the rest,
by reason of the drink. We were seized upon by these
reckless creatures, and within the hour, we, even we, were
undistinguishable from the rest—the demoralization was
complete and universal. In time the camp wore itself
out with its orgies and sank into a stolid and pitiable
stupor, in whose mysterious bonds rank was forgotten and
strange bed-fellows made, our eyes, at the resurrection,
being blasted and our souls petrified with the incredible
spectacle of that intolerable stinking scavenger, the Tum-
ble Bug, and the illustrious patrician my lord Grand
Daddy, Duke of Longlegs, lying soundly steeped in sleep,
and clasped lovingly in each other's arms, the like whereof hath not been seen in all the ages that tradition com-
passeth, and doubtless none shall ever in this world find
faith to master the belief of it save only we that have

beheld the damnable and unholy vision. Thus inscrutable be the ways of God, whose will be done.

"This day, by order, did the Engineer-in-Chief, Herr Spider, rig the necessary tackle for the overturning of the vast reservoir, and so its calamitous contents were discharged in a torrent upon the thirsty earth, which drank it up and now there is no more danger, we reserving but a few drops for experiment and scrutiny, and to exhibit to the king and subsequently preserve among the wonders of the museum. What this liquid is has been determined. It is without question that fierce and most destructive fluid called lightning. It was wrested, in its container, from its store-house in the clouds, by the resistless might of the flying planet, and hurled at our feet as she sped by. An interesting discovery here results. Which is, that lightning, kept to itself, is quiescent; it is the assaulting contact of the thunderbolt that releases it from captivity, ignites its awful fires and so produces an instantaneous combustion and explosion which spread disaster and desolation far and wide in the earth."

After another day devoted to rest and recovery, the expedition proceeded upon its way. Some days later it went into camp in a very pleasant part of the plain, and the savants sallied forth to see what they might find. Their reward was at hand. Professor Bull Frog discovered a strange tree, and called his comrades. They inspected it with profound interest.—It was very tall and straight, and wholly devoid of bark, limbs or foliage. By triangulation Lord Longlegs determined its altitude; Herr

Spider measured its circumference at the base and computed the circumference at its top by a mathematical demonstration based upon the warrant furnished by the uniform degree of its taper upward. It was considered a very extraordinary find; and since it was a tree of a hitherto unknown species, Professor Woodlouse gave it a name of a learned sound, being none other than that of Professor Bull Frog translated into the ancient Mastodon language, for it had always been the custom with discoverers to perpetuate their names and honour themselves by this sort of connection with their discoveries.

Now Professor Field-Mouse having placed his sensitive ear to the tree, detected a rich harmonious sound issuing from it. This surprising thing was tested and enjoyed by each scholar in turn, and great was the gladness and astonishment of all. Professor Woodlouse was requested to add to and extend the tree's name so as to make it suggest the musical quality it possessed—which he did, furnishing the addition *Anthem Singer*, done into the Mastodon tongue.

By this time Professor Snail was making some telescopic inspections. He discovered a great number of these trees, extending in a single rank, with wide intervals between, as far as his instrument would carry, both southward and northward. He also presently discovered that all these trees were bound together, near their tops, by fourteen great ropes, one above another, which ropes were continuous, from tree to tree, as far as his vision could reach. This was surprising. Chief Engineer

Spider ran aloft and soon reported that these ropes were simply a web hung there by some colossal member of his own species, for he could see its prey dangling here and there from the strands, in the shape of mighty shreds and rags that had a woven look about their texture and were no doubt discarded skins of prodigious insects which had been caught and eaten. And then he ran along one of the ropes to make a closer inspection, but felt a smart sudden burn on the soles of his feet, accompanied by a paralyzing shock, wherefore he let go and swung himself to the earth by a thread of his own spinning, and advised all to hurry at once to camp, lest the monster should appear and get as much interested in the savants as they were in him and his works. So they departed with speed, making notes about the gigantic web as they went. And that evening the naturalist of the expedition built a beautiful model of the colossal spider, having no need to see it in order to do this, because he had picked up a fragment of its vetebræ by the tree, and so knew exactly what the creature looked like and what its habits and its preferences were, by this simple evidence alone. He built it with a tail, teeth, fourteen legs and a snout, and said it ate grass, cattle, pebbles and dirt with equal enthusiasm. This animal was regarded as a very precious addition to science. It was hoped a dead one might be found, to stuff. Professor Woodlouse thought that he and his brother scholars, by lying hid and being quiet, might maybe catch a live one. He was advised to try it. Which was all the attention that was paid to his suggestion. The conference ended with the naming the monster after the naturalist, since he, after God, had created it.

"And improved it, mayhap," muttered the Tumble-Bug, who was intruding again, according to his idle custom and his unappeasable curiosity.

END OF PART FIRST.

SOME FABLES FOR GOOD OLD BOYS AND GIRLS.

PART SECOND.

HOW THE ANIMALS OF THE WOOD COMPLETED THEIR SCIENTIFIC LABOURS.

A WEEK later the expedition camped in the midst of a collection of wonderful curiosities. These were a sort of vast caverns of stone that rose singly and in bunches out of the plain by the side of the river which they had first seen when they emerged from the forest. These caverns stood in long straight rows on opposite sides of broad aisles that were bordered with single ranks of trees. The summit of each cavern sloped sharply both ways. Several horizontal rows of great square holes, obstructed by a thin, shiny, transparent substance, pierced the frontage of each cavern. Inside were caverns within caverns; and one might ascend and visit these minor compartments by means of curious winding ways consisting of continuous regular terraces raised one above another. There were many huge shapeless objects in each compartment which were considered to have been living creatures at one time, though now the thin brown skin was shrunken and loose, and rattled when disturbed. Spiders were here in great number, and their cobwebs, stretched in all directions and wreathing the great skinny dead together, were a pleasant spectacle, since they inspired with life and wholesome cheer a scene which would otherwise have brought to the mind only a sense of forsakenness and desolation. Information was sought of these spiders, but in vain. They were of a different nationality from those with the expedition, and their language seemed but a musical, meaningless jargon. They were a timid, gentle race, but ignorant, and heathenish worshippers of unknown gods. The expedition detailed a great detachment of missionaries to teach them the true religion, and in a week's time a precious work had been wrought among those darkened creatures, not three families being by that time at peace with each other or having a settled belief in any system of religion whatever. This encouraged the expedition to establish a colony of missionaries there permanently, that the work of grace might go on.

But let us not outrun our narrative. After close examination of the fronts of the caverns, and much thinking and exchanging of theories, the scientists determined the nature of these singular formations. They said that each belonged mainly to the Old Red Sandstone period; that the cavern fronts rose in innumerable and wonderfully regular strata high in the air, each stratum about five frog-spans thick, and that in the present discovery lay an overpowering refutation of all received geology; for between every two layers of Old Red Sandstone reposed a thin layer of decomposed limestone; so instead of there having been but one Old Red Sandstone period there had certainly been not less than a hundred and seventy-five! And by the same token it was plain that there had also been a hundred and seventy-five floodings of the earth and depositings of limestone strata! The unavoidable deduction from which pair of facts, was, the overwhelming truth that the world, instead of being only two hundred thousand years old, was older by millions upon millions of years! And there was another curious thing : every stratum of Old Red Sandstone was pierced and divided at mathematically regular intervals by vertical strata of limestone. Up-shootings of igneous rock through fractures in water formations were common; but here was the first instance where water-formed rock had been so projected. It was a great and noble discovery and its value to science was considered to be inestimable.

A critical examination of some of the lower strata demonstrated the presence of fossil ants and tumble-bugs, (the latter accompanied by their peculiar goods), and with high gratification the fact was enrolled upon the scientific record; for this was proof that these vulgar labourers belonged to the first and lowest orders of created beings, though at the same time there was something repulsive in the reflection that the perfect and exquisite creature of the modern uppermost order owed its origin to such ignominious beings through the mysterious law of Development of Species.

The Tumble-Bug, overhearing this discussion, said he

was willing that the parvenus of these new times should find what comfort they might in their wise-drawn theories, since as far as he was concerned he was content to be of the old first families and proud to point back to his place among the old original aristocracy of the land.

"Enjoy your mushroom dignity, stinking of the varnish of yesterday's veneering, since you like it," said he; "suffice it for the Tumble-Bugs that they come of a race that rolled their fragrant spheres down the solemn aisles of antiquity, and left their imperishable works embalmed in the Old Red Sandstone to proclaim it to the wasting centuries as they file along the highway of Time!"

"O, take a walk!" said the chief of the expedition, with derision.

The summer passed, and winter approached. In and about many of the caverns were what seemed to be inscriptions. Most of the scientists said they were inscriptions, a few said they were not. The chief philologist, Professor Woodlouse, maintained that they were writings, done in a character utterly unknown to scholars, and in a language equally unknown. He had early ordered his artists and draughtsmen to make fac-similes of all that were discovered; and had set himself about finding the key to the hidden tongue. In this work he had followed the method which had always been used by decipherers previously. That is to say, he placed a number of copies of inscriptions before him and studied them both collectively and in detail. To begin with, he placed the following copies together:

The American Hotel.	Meals at all Hours.
The Shades.	No Smoking.
Boats for Hire Cheap.	Union Prayer Meeting, 4 P. M.
Billiards.	The Waterside Journal.
The A 1 Barber Shop.	Telegraph Office.
Keep off the Grass.	Try Brandreth's Pills.
Cottages for Rent during the Watering Season.	
For Sale Cheap.	For Sale Cheap.
For Sale Cheap.	For Sale Cheap.

At first it seemed to the Professor that this was a sign-language, and that each word was represented by a distinct sign; further examination convinced him that it was a written language, and that every letter of its alphabet was represented by a character of its own; and finally, he decided that it was a language which conveyed itself partly by letters, and partly by signs or hieroglyphics.

He observed that certain inscriptions were met with in greater frequency than others. Such as "For Sale Cheap;" "Billiards;" "S. T.—1860—X;" "Keno;" "Ale on Draught." Naturally, then, these must be religious maxims. But this idea was cast aside, by and by, as the mystery of the strange alphabet began to clear itself. In time, the Professor was enabled to translate several of the inscriptions with considerable plausibility, though not to the perfect satisfaction of all the scholars. Still, he made constant and encouraging progress.

Finally a cavern was discovered with these inscriptions upon it:

WATERSIDE MUSEUM.

Open at all Hours.   *Admission 50 cents.*

Wonderful Collection of Wax-Works, Ancient Fossils, etc,

Professor Woodlouse affirmed that the word "Museum" was equivalent to the phrase "*lungath molo,*" or "Burial-Place." Upon entering, the scientists were well astonished. But what they saw may be best conveyed in the language of their own official report:

"Erect, and in a row, were a sort of rigid great figures which struck us instantly as belonging to the long extinct species of reptile called MAN, described in our ancient records. This was a peculiarly gratifying discovery, because of late times it has become fashionable to regard this creature as a myth and a superstition, a work of the inventive imaginations of our remote ancestors. But here, indeed, was Man, perfectly preserved, in a fossil state. And this was his burial place, as already ascertained by the inscription. And now it began to be suspected that the caverns we had been inspecting had been his ancient haunts in that old time that he roamed the earth—for upon the breast of each of these tall fossils was an inscription in the character heretofore noticed. One read, 'CAPTAIN KIDD, THE PIRATE;' another, 'QUEEN VICTORIA;' another, 'ABE LINCOLN;' another, 'GEORGE WASHINGTON,' etc.

"With feverish interest we called for our ancient scientific records to discover if perchance the description of Man there set down would tally with the fossils before us. Professor Woodlouse read it aloud in its quaint and musty phraseology, to wit:

"'In ye time of our fathers Man still walked ye earth, as by tradition we know. It was a creature of exceeding

great size, being compassed about with a loose skin, sometimes of one colour, sometimes of many, the which it was
able to cast at will; which being done, the hind legs were
discovered to be armed with short claws like to a mole's but
broader, and ye fore-legs with fingers of a curious slimness
and a length much more prodigious than a frog's, armed
also with broad talons for scratching in ye earth for its
food.   It had a sort of feathers upon its head such as hath
a rat, but longer, and a beak suitable for seeking its food
by ye smell thereof.   When it was stirred with happiness
it leaked water from its eyes; and when it suffered or was
sad, it manifested it with a horrible hellish cackling
clamour that was exceeding dreadful to hear and made one
long that it might rend itself and perish, and so end its
troubles.   Two Mans being together, they uttered noises
at each other like to this: 'Haw-haw-haw—dam good,
dam good,' together with other sounds of more or less
likeness to these, wherefore ye poets conceived that they
talked, but poets be always ready to catch at any frantic
folly, God he knows.   Sometimes this creature goeth about
with a long stick ye which it putteth to its face and bloweth
fire and smoke through ye same with a sudden and most
damnable bruit and noise that doth fright its prey to
death, and so seizeth it in its talons and walketh away to
its habitat, consumed with a most fierce and devilish joy.'

"Now was the description set forth by our ancestors
wonderfully endorsed and confirmed by the fossils before
us, as shall be seen.   The specimen marked 'Captain
Kidd' was examined in detail.   Upon its head and part

of its face was a sort of fur like that upon the tail of a
horse. With great labour its loose skin was removed,
whereupon its body was discovered to be of a polished
white texture, thoroughly petrified. The straw it had
eaten, so many ages gone by, was still in its body, undi-
gested—and even in its legs.

"Surrounding these fossils were objects that would
mean nothing to the ignorant, but to the eye of science
they were a revelation. They laid bare the secrets of
dead ages. These musty Memorials told us when Man
lived, and what were his habits. For here, side by side
with Man, were the evidences that he had lived in the
earliest ages of creation, the companion of the other low
orders of life that belonged to that forgotten time.—Here
was the fossil nautilus that sailed the primeval seas; here
was the skeleton of the mastodon, the ichthyosaurus, the
cave bear, the prodigious elk. Here, also, were the charred
bones of some of these extinct animals and of the young
of Man's own species, split lengthwise, showing that to
his taste the marrow was a toothsome luxury. It was
plain that Man had robbed those bones of their contents,
since no tooth-mark of any beast was upon them—albeit
the Tumble-Bug intruded the remark that 'no beast could
mark a bone with its teeth, anyway.' Here were proofs
that Man had vague, grovelling notions of art; for this fact
was conveyed by certain things marked with the untranslatable words, 'FLINT HATCHETS, KNIVES, ARROW-HEADS,
AND BONE-ORNAMENTS OF PRIMEVAL MAN.' Some of these
seemed to be rude weapons chipped out of flint, and in a

secret place was found some more in process of construc-
tion, with this untranslatable legend on a thin flimsy
material, lying by :

'*Jones, if you don't want to be discharged from the
Musseum, make the next primeaveal weppons more care-
ul—you couldn't even fool one of those sleapy old syen-
tiffic grannys from the Coledge with the last ones.   And
mind you the animlesyou carved on some of the Bone Orna-
ments is a blame sight too good for any primeaveal man
that was ever fooled.—Varnum, Manager.*"

"Back of the burial place was a mass of ashes, showing
that Man always had a feast at a funeral—else why
the ashes in such a place ? and showing, also, that he believed in God and the immortality of the soul—else why
these solemn ceremonies ?

"To sum up. —We believe that Man had a written language.   We *know* that he indeed existed at one time, and is
not a myth ; also, that he was the companion of the cave
bear, the mastodon, and other extinct species ; that he
cooked and ate them and likewise the young of his own
kind ; also, that he bore rude weapons, and knew something of art ; that he imagined he had a soul, and pleased
himself with the fancy that it was immortal.   But let us
not laugh ; there may be creatures in existence to whom we
and our vanities and profundities may seem as ludicrous."

END OF PART SECOND.

SOME FABLES FOR GOOD OLD BOYS AND GIRLS.

PART THIRD

NEAR the margin of the great river the scientists presently found a huge, shapely stone, with this inscription:

"*In 1847, in the spring, the river overflowed its banks and covered the whole township.   The depth was from two to six feet.   More than 900 head of cattle were lost, and many homes destroyed.   The Mayor ordered this memorial to be erected to perpetuate the event.   God spare us the repetition of it.*"

With infinite trouble, Professor Woodlouse succeeded in making a translation of this inscription, which was sent home and straightway an enormous excitement was created about it.   It confirmed, in a remarkable way, certain treasured traditions of the ancients.   The translation was slightly marred by one or two untranslatable words, but these did not impair the general clearness of the meaning.   It is here presented:

"*One thousand eight hundred and forty-seven years ago, the (fires?) descended and consumed the whole city. Only some nine hundred souls were saved, all others des-*

*troyed.   The (king?) commanded this stone to be set up
to . . . . (untranslatable) . . . . prevent the repetition of it."*

This was the first successful and satisfactory translation
that had been made of the mysterious character left behind him by extinct man, and it gave Professor Woodlouse
such reputation that at once every seat of learning in his
native land conferred a degree of the most illustrious
grade upon him, and it was believed that if he had been
a soldier and had turned his splendid talents to the exter-
mination of a remote tribe of reptiles, the king would have
ennobled him and made him rich.   And this, too, was the
origin of that school of scientists called Manologists, whose
specialty is the deciphering of the ancient records of the
extinct bird termed Man.   [For it is now decided that
Man was a bird and not a reptile].   But Professor Woodlouse began and remained chief of these, for it was
granted that no translations were ever so free from error
as his.   Others made mistakes—he seemed incapable of
it.   Many a memorial of the lost race was afterward
found, but none ever attained to the renown and venera-
tion achieved by the "Mayoritish Stone"—it being so
called from the word "Mayor" in it, which, being translated "King," "Mayoritish Stone" was but another way
of saying "King Stone."

Another time the expedition made a great "find."   It
was a vast round flattish mass, ten frog-spans in diameter,
and five or six high.   Professor Snail put on his spectacles
and examined it all around, and then climbed up and inspected the top.   He said:

"The result of my perlustration and perscontation of this isoperimetrical protuberance is a belief that it is one of those rare and wonderful creations left by the Mound Builders. The fact that this one is lamelli-branchiate in its formation, simply adds to its interest as being possibly of a different kind from any we read of in the records of science, but yet in no manner marring its authenticity. Let the megalophonous grasshopper sound a blast and summon hither the perfunctory and circumforaneous Tumble-Bug, to the end that excavations may be made and learning gather new treasures."

Not a Tumble-Bug could be found on duty, so the Mound was excavated by a working party of ants. Nothing was discovered. This would have been a great disappointment, had not the venerable Longlegs explained the matter.—He said:

"It is now plain to me that the mysterious and forgotten race of Mound Builders did not always erect these edifices as mausoleums, else in this case, as in all previous cases, their skeletons would be found here, along with the rude implements which the creatures used in life. Is not this manifest?"

"True! true!" from everybody.

"Then we have made a discovery of peculiar value here; a discovery which greatly extends our knowledge of this creature in place of diminishing it; a discovery which will add lustre to the achievements of this expedition and win for us the commendations of scholars everywhere. For the absence of the customary relics here means nothing less than this: The Mound Builder, instead of being the ignorant, savage reptile we have been taught to consider him, was a creature of cultivation and high intelligence, capable of not only appreciating worthy achievements of the great and noble of his species, but of commemorating them! Fellow-scholars, this stately Mound is not a sepulchre, it is a monument!"

A profound impression was produced by this.

But it was interrupted by rude and derisive laughter— and the Tumble-Bug appeared.

"A monument!" quoth he. "A monument set up by a Mound Builder! Aye, so it is! So it is, indeed, to the shrewd keen eye of science; but to an ignorant poor devil who has never seen a college, it is not a Monument, strictly speaking, but is yet a most rich and noble property; and with your worships' good permission I will proceed to manufacture it into spheres of exceeding grace and—"

The Tumble-Bug was driven away with stripes, and the draughtsmen of the expedition were set to making views of the Monument from different standpoints, while Professor Woodlouse, in a frenzy of scientific zeal, travelled all over it and all around it hoping to find an inscription. But if there had ever been one it had decayed or been removed by some vandal as a relic.

The views having been completed, it was now considered safe to load the precious Monument itself upon the backs of four of the largest Tortoises and send it home to the King's museum, which was done; and when it arrived it was received with enormous *eclat* and escorted to its future abiding-place by thousands of enthusiastic citizens, King Bullfrog XVI, himself attending and condescending to sit enthroned upon it throughout the progress.

The growing rigour of the weather was now admonishing the scientists to close their labours for the present, so they made preparations to journey homeward. But even their last day among the Caverns bore fruit; for one of the scholars found in an out-of-the-way corner of the Museum or "Burial-Place" a most strange and extraordinary thing. It was nothing less than a double Man-Bird lashed together breast to breast by a natural ligament, and labelled with the untranslatable words, "*Siamese Twins.*" The official report concerning this thing closed thus:

" Wherefore it appears that there were in old times two distinct species of this majestic fowl, the one being single and the other double. Nature has a reason for all things. It is plain to the eye of science that the Double-Man originally inhabited a region where dangers abounded; hence he was paired together to the end that while one part slept the other might watch; and likewise that danger being discovered, there might always be a double instead of a single power to oppose it. All honour to the mystery-dispelling eye of godlike science!"

And near the Double Man-Bird was found what was plainly an ancient record of his, marked upon numberless sheets of a thin white substance and bound together. Almost the first glance that Professor Woodlouse threw into it revealed this following sentence, which he instantly translated and laid before the scientists, in a tremble, and it uplifted every soul there with exultation and astonishment:

"*In truth it is believed by many that the lower animals reason and talk together.*"

When the great official report of the expedition appeared, the above sentence bore this comment:

"Then there are lower animals than Man! This remarkable passage can mean nothing else. Man himself is extinct, but *they* may still exist. What can they be? Where do they inhabit? One's enthusiasm bursts all bounds in the contemplation of the brilliant field of discovery and investigation here thrown open to science. We close our labours with the humble prayer that your Majesty will immediately appoint a commission and command it to rest not nor spare expense until the search for this hitherto unsuspected race of the creatures of God shall be crowned with success."

The expedition then journeyed homeward after its long absence and its faithful endeavours, and was received with a mighty ovation by the whole grateful country.

There were vulgar, ignorant carpers, of course, as there always are and always will be; and naturally one of those was the obscene Tumble-Bug. He said that all he had learned by his travels was that science only needed a spoonful of supposition to build a mountain of demonstrated fact out of; and that for the future he meant to be content with the knowledge that nature had made free to all creatures and not go prying into the august secrets of the Deity.

THE "JUMPING FROG."

IN ENGLISH. THEN IN FRENCH. THEN CLAWED BACK
INTO A CIVILIZED LANGUAGE ONCE MORE BY PATIENT,
UNREMUNERATED TOIL.

———

EVEN a criminal is entitled to fair play; and certainly
when a man who has done no harm has been unjustly
treated, he is privileged to do his best to right himself.
My attention has just been called to an article some three
years old in a French Magazine entitled " Revue des Deux
Mondes" (Review of some two worlds), wherein the
writer treats of " Les Humoristes Americanes" (These
Humourists Americans). I am one of these humourists
Americans dissected by him, and hence the complaint I
am making.

This gentleman's article is an able one (as articles go
in the French, where they always tangle up everything
to that degree that when you start into a sentence you
never know whether you are going to come out alive or
not). It is a very good article, and the writer says all manner of kind and complimentary things about me—for which
I am sure I thank him with all my heart ; but then why
should he go and spoil all his praise by one unlucky
experiment ? What I refer to is this : he says my Jump-

ing Frog is a funny story, but still he can't see why it should ever really convulse any one with laughter—and straightway proceeds to translate it into French in order to prove to his nation that there is nothing so very extravagantly funny about it. Just there is where my complaint originates. He has not translated it at all; he has simply mixed it all up; it is no more like the Jumping Frog when he gets through with it than I am like a meridian of longitude. But my mere assertion is not proof; wherefore I print the French version, that all may see that I do not speak falsely; furthermore, in order that even the unlettered may know my injury and give me their compassion, I have been at infinite pains and trouble to re-translate this French version back into English; and to tell the truth I have well nigh worn myself out at it, having scarcely rested from my work during five days and nights. I cannot speak the French language, but I can translate very well, though not fast, I being self-educated. I ask the reader to run his eye over the original English version of the Jumping Frog, and then read the French or my re-translation, and kindly take notice how the Frenchman has riddled the grammar. I think it is the worst I ever saw; and yet the French are called a polished nation. If I had a boy that put sentences together as they do, I would polish him to some purpose. Without further introduction, the Jumping Frog, as I originally wrote it, was as follows—[after it will be found the French version, and after the latter my re-translation from the French]:

THE NOTORIOUS JUMPING FROG OF CALAVERAS* COUNTY.

In compliance with the request of a friend of mine, who wrote me from the East, I called on good-natured, garrulous old Simon Wheeler, and inquired after my friend's friend, Leonidas W. Smiley, as requested to do, and I hereunto append the result. I have a lurking suspicion that *Leonidas W.* Smiley is a myth; that my friend never knew such a personage; and that he only conjectured that if I asked old Wheeler about him, it would remind him of his infamous *Jim* Smiley, and he would go to work and bore me to death with some exasperating reminiscence of him as long and as tedious as it should be useless to me. If that was the design it succeeded.

I found Simon Wheeler dozing comfortably by the bar-room stove of the dilapidated tavern in the decayed mining camp of Engel's, and I noticed that he was fat and bald-headed, and had an expression of winning gentleness and simplicity upon his tranquil countenance. He roused up and gave me good-day. I told him a friend of mine had commissioned me to make some inquiries about a cherished companion of his boyhood named *Leonidas W.* Smiley—*Rev. Leonidas W.* Smiley, a young minister of the Gospel, who he had heard was at one time a resident of Angel's Camp. I added that if Mr. Wheeler could tell me anything about this Rev. Leonidas W. Smiley, I would feel under many obligations to him.

Simon Wheeler backed me into a corner and blockaded me there with his chair, and then sat down and reeled off the monotonous narrative which follows this paragraph. He never smiled, he never frowned, he never changed his voice from the gentle-flowing key to which he tuned his initial sentence, he never betrayed the slightest suspicion of enthusiasm; but all through the interminable narrative there ran a vein of impressive earnestness and sincerity, which showed me plainly that, so far from his imagining that there was anything ridiculous or funny about his story, he regarded it as a really important matter, and admired its two heroes as men of transcendant genius in *finesse*. I let him go on in his own way, and never interrupted him once.

"Rev. Leonidas W. H'm, Reverend Le—well, there was a feller here once by the name of *Jim* Smiley, in the winter of '49—or maybe it was the spring of '50—I don't recollect exactly, somehow, though what makes me think it was one or the other is because I remember the big flume warn't finished when he first come to the camp; but any way he was the curiosest man about always betting on anything that turned up you ever see, if he could get anybody to bet on the other side; and if he couldn't he'd change

---

      Pronounced Cal-e-*va*-ras,

sides. Any way that suited the other man would suit *him*—any way just so's he got a bet, *he* was satisfied. But still he was lucky, uncommon lucky; he most always come out winner. He was always ready and laying for a chance; there couldn't be no solit'ry thing mentioned but that feller'd offer to bet on it, and take ary side you please as I was just telling you. If there was a horse-race, you'd find him flush or you'd find him busted at the end of it; if there was a dog-fight, he'd bet on it; if there was a cat-fight he'd bet on it; if there was a chicken-fight he'd bet on it; why, if there was two birds sitting on a fence, he would bet you which one would fly first; or if there was a camp-meeting, he would be there reg'lar to bet on Parson Walker, which he judged to be the best exhorter about here, and so he was too, and a good man. If he even see a straddle-bug start to go anywheres, he would bet you how long it would take him to get to—to wherever he was going to, and if you took him up he would foller that straddle-bug to Mexico but what he would find out where he was bound for and how long he was on the road. Lots of the boys here has seen that Smiley, and can tell you about him. Why, it never made no difference to *him*—he'd bet on *any* thing—the dangdest feller. Parson Walker's wife laid very sick once, for a good while, and it seemed as if they warn't going to save her; but one morning he come in, and Smiley up and asked him how she was, and he said she was consider-able better—thank the Lord for his inf'nit mercy—and coming on so smart that with the blessing of Prov'dence she'd get well yet; and Smiley, before he thought, says, "Well, I'll resk two-and-a-half she don't anyway."

Thish-yer Smiley had a mare—the boys called her the fifteen minute nag, but that was only in fun, you know, because of course she was faster than that—and he used to win money on that horse, for all she was so slow and always had the asthma, or the distemper, or the consumption, or something of that kind. They used to give her two or three hundred yards' start, and then pass her under way; but always at the fag end of the race she'd get excited and desperate-like, and come cavorting and straddling up and scattering her legs around limber, sometimes in the air, and sometimes out to one side amongst the fences, and kicking up m-o-r-e dust and raising m-o-r-e racket with her coughing and sneezing and blowing her nose—and *always* fetch up at the stand just about a neck ahead, as near as you could cipher it down.

And he had a little small bull-pup that to look at him you'd think he warn't worth a cent but to set around and look ornery and lay for a chance to steal something. But as soon as money was up on him he was a different dog; his under jaw began to stick out like the fo'castle of a steamboat, and his teeth would uncover and shine like the furnaces. And a dog might tackle him and bullyrag him, and bite him, and throw him over his shoulder two or three times, and Andrew Jackson—which was the name of the pup—Andrew Jackson would never let on but what *he* was satisfied, and hadn't expected nothing else—and the bets being doubled and doubled on the other side all the time, till the money was all up; and then all of a sudden he would grab that other dog jest by the j'int of his hind leg and freeze to it—not chaw, you understand, but only just grip and hang on till they throwed up the sponge, if it was a year. Smiley always come out winner on that pup, till he harnessed a dog once that did'nt have no hind legs, because they'd been sawed off in a circular saw, and when the thing had gone along far enough, and the money was all up, and he come to make a snatch for his pet holt, he see in a minute how he'd been imposed on, and how the other dog had him in the door, so to speak, and he 'peared surprised, and then he looked sorter discouraged-like, and didn't try no more to win the fight, and so he got shucked out bad. He give Smiley a look, as much as to say his heart was broke, and it was *his* fault, for putting up a dog that hadn't no hind legs for him to take holt of, which was his main dependence in a fight, and then he limped off a piece and laid down and died. It was a good pup was that Andrew Jackson, and would have made a name for hisself if he'd lived, for the stuff was in him and he had genius—I know it, because he hadn't no opportunities to speak of, and it don't stand to reason that a dog could make such a fight as he could under them circumstances if he hadn't no talent. It always makes me feel sorry when I think of that last fight of his'n, and the way it turned out.

Well, thish-yer Smiley had rat-tarriers, and chicken cocks, and tom-cats and all them kind of things, till you couldn't rest, and you couldn't fetch nothing for him to bet on but he'd match you. He ketched a frog one day, and took him home, and said he cal'lated to educate him; and so he never done nothing for three months but set in his back yard and learn that frog to jump. And you bet you he *did* learn him, too. He'd give him a little punch behind, and the next minute you'd see that frog whirling in the air like a doughnut—see him turn one summerset, or maybe a couple, if he got a good start, and come down flat-footed and all right, like a cat. He got him up so in the matter of catching flies, and kep' him in practice so constant, that he'd nail a fly every time as fur as he could see him. Smiley said all a frog wanted was education and he could do 'most anything—and I believe him. Why, I've seen him set Dan'l Webster down here on this floor—Dan'l Webster was the name of the frog—and sing out, "Flies Dan'l, flies!" and quicker'n you could wink he'd spring straight up and snake a fly off'n the counter there, and flop down on the floor ag'in as solid as a gob of mud, and fall to scratching the side of his head with his hind foot as indifferent as if he hadn't no idea he'd been doin' any more'n any frog might do. You never see a frog so modest and straightfor'ard as he was, for all he was so gifted. And when it come to fair and square jumping on a dead level, he could get over more ground at one straddle than any animal of his breed you ever see. Jumping on a dead level was his strong suit, you understand; and when it come to that, Smiley would ante up money on him as long as he had a red,

Smiley was monstrous proud of his frog, and well he might be, for fellers that had travelled and been everywhere, all said he laid over any frog that ever *they* see.

Well, Smiley kep' the beast in a little lattice box, and he used to fetch him down town sometimes and lay for a bet. One day, a feller—a stranger in the camp, he was—come acrost him with his box, and says:

"What might it be that you've got in the box?"

And Smiley says, sorter indifferent-like, "It might be a parrot, or it might be a canary, maybe, but it ain't—it's only just a frog."

And the feller took it, and looked at it careful, and turned it round this way and that, and says, "H'm—so 'tis. Well, what's *he* good for?"

"Well," Smiley, says, easy and careless, "he's good enough for *one* thing, I should judge—he can outjump any frog in Calaveras county."

The feller took the box again, and took another long, particular look, and gave it back to Smiley, and says, very deliberate, "Well," he says, "I don't see no p'ints about that frog that's any better'n any other frog."

"Maybe you don't," Smiley says. "Maybe 'you understand frogs and maybe you don't understand 'em; maybe you've had experience, and maybe you ain't only a amature, as it were. Anyways, I've got *my* opinion and I'll resk forty dollars that he can outjump any frog in Calaveras county."

And the feller studied a minute, and then says, kinder sad like, "Well, I'm only a stranger here, and I aint got no frog; but if I had a frog, I'd bet you."

And then Smiley says, "That's all right—that's all right—if you'll hold my box a minute, I'll go and get you a frog." And so the feller took the box, and put up his forty dollars along with Smiley's, and set down to wait.

So he sat there a good while thinking and thinking to hisself, and then he got the frog out and prized his mouth open and took a teaspoon and filled him full of quail shot—filled him pretty near up to his chin—and set him on the floor. Smiley he went to the swamp and slopped around in the mud for a long time, and finally he ketched a frog, and fetched him in, and gave him to this feller and says:

"Now, if you're ready, set him alongside of Dan'l, with his fore-paws just even with Dan'l's, and I'll give the word." Then he says, "One—two—three—*git!*" and him and the feller touched up the frogs from behind, and the new frog hopped off lively, but Dan'l gave a heave, and hysted up his shoulders—so—like a Frenchman, but it warn't no use—he couldn't budge; he was planted as solid as a church, and he couldn't no more stir than if he was anchored out. Smiley was a good deal surprised, and he was disgusted too, but he didn't have no idea what the matter was, of course.

The feller took the money and started away; and when he was going out at the door, he sorter jerked his thumb over his shoulder—so—at Dan'l, and says again, very deliberate, "Well," he says, "*I* don't see no p'ints about that frog that's any better'n any other frog."

Smiley he stood scratching his head and looking down at Dan'l a long time. and at last he says, "I do wonder what in the nation that frog throw'd off for—I wonder if there ain't something the matter with him—he 'pears to look mighty baggy, somehow." And he ketched Dan'l by the nap of the neck, and hefted him, and says, "Why, blame my cats if he don't weigh five pound!" and turned him upside down and he belched out a double handful of shot. And then he see how it was, and he was the maddest man—he set the frog down and took out after that feller, but he never ketched him. And——"

[Here Simon Wheeler heard his name called from the front yard, and got up to see what was wanted.] And turning to me as he moved away, he said: "Just set where you are, stranger, and rest easy—I ain't going to be gone a second."

But, by your leave, I did not think that a continuation of the history of the enterprising vagabond *Jim* Smiley would be likely to afford me much information concerning the Rev. *Leonidas W.* Smiley, and so I started away.

At the door I met the sociable Wheeler returning, and he button-holed me and re-commenced :

"Well, thish-yer Smiley had a yaller one-eyed cow that didn't have no tail, only jest a short stump like a bannanner, and ——"

However, lacking both time and inclination, I did not wait to hear about the afflicted cow, but took my leave.

————

Now let the learned look upon this picture and say if iconoclasm can further go:

[From the *Revue des Deux Mondes*, of July 15th, 1872.]

LA GRENOUILLE SANTEUSE DU COMTE DE CALAVERAS.

——

—Il y avait une fois ici un individu connu sous le nom de Jim Smiley : c'était dans l'hiver de 49, peut-être bien au printemps de 50, je ne me rappelle pas exactement. Ce qui me fait croire que c'était l'un ou l'autre, c'est que je me souviens que le grand bief n'était pas achevé lorsqu'il arriva au camp pour la première fois, mais de toutes façons il était l'homme le lus friand de paris qui se pût voir, pariant sur tout ce qui se présantait, quand il pouvait trouver un adversaire, et, quand il n'en trouvait pas il passa it du côté opposé. Tout ce que convenait à l'autre lui convenait ; pourvu qu'il eût un pari, Smiley était satisfait. Et il avait une chance ! une chance inouïe : presque toujours il gagnait. Il faut dire qu'il était toujours prêt à s' exposer, qu' on nepouvait mentionner la moindre chose sans que ce gaillard offrét de parier làdessus n'importe quoi et de prendre le côté que l'on voudrait, comme je vous le disais tout à l'heure. S'il y avait des courses, vous le trouviez riche ou ruiné à la fin ; s'il yavait un combat de chiens il apportait son enjue ; il l'ap, portait pour un combat de chats, pour un combat de coqs ;—parbleu ! si vous aviez vu deux oiseaux sur une haie, il vous aurait offert de parier lequel s'envolerait le premier, et, s'il y avait *meeting* au camp, il venait parier régulièrement pour le curé Walker, qu'il jugeat être le meilleur prédicateur des environs, et qui l'était en effet, et en brave homme. Il aurait rencontré une punaise de bois en chemin, qu'il aurait parié sur le temps qu'il lui faudrait pour aller où elle vaudrait aller, et, si vous l'aviez pris au mot, il aurait suivi la punaise jusqu'au Mexique, sans se soucier d'aller si loin, ni du temps qu'il y perdrait. Une fois la femme du curé Walker fut trés malade pendant longtemps, il semblait qu'on ne la sauverait pas ; mais un matin le curé arrive, et Smiley lui demande comment elle va, et il dit qu'elle est bien mieux, grâce à l'infinie miséricorde, tellement mieux qu'avec la bénédiction de la providence elle s'en tirerait, et voilà que, sans y penser, Smiley répond :—Eh bien ! je gage deux et demi qu'elle mourra tout de même.

"Ce Smiley avait une jument que les gars appelaient le bidet du quart d'heure, mais seulement pour plaisanter, vous comprenez, parce que, bien entendu, elle était plus *vite* que ça ! Et il avait coutume de gagner de l'argent avec cette bête, quoiqu'elle fût poussive, cornarde, toujours prise d'asthme, de coliques ou de consumption, ou de quelque chose d'approchant. On lui donnait 2 ou 300 *yards* au départ, puis on la dépassait sans peine ; mais jamais à la fin elle ne manquait de s'échauffer, des exaspérer, et elle arrivait, s'écartant, se défendant, ses jambes grêles en l'air devant les obstacles, quelquefois les évitant et faisant avec cela plus de poussiére qu'aucun cheval, plus de bruit surtout avec ses éternumens et reniflemens, —crac ! elle arrivait donc toujours première d'une tête, aussi juste qu'on peut le mesurer. Et il avait un petit bouledogue qui, à le voir, ne valait pas un sue ; on aurait cru que parier contre lui c'était voler, tant il était ordinaire ; mais aussitôt les enjeux faits, il devinait un autre chien. Sa mâchoire inférieure commençait à ressortir comme un gaillard d'avant, ses dentes se découvraient brillantes comme des fournaises, et un chien pouvait le ta quiner, l'exciter, lo mordre, le jeter deux ou trois fois par-dessus son épaule, André Jackson, c'était le nom du chien, André Jackson prenait cela tranquillement, comme s'il ne se fût jamais attendu à autre chose, et quand les paris étaient doublés et redoublés contre lui, il vous saisissait l'autre chien juste à l'articulation de la jambe de derrière, et il ne la lâchait plus, non pas qu'il la mâchât, vous concevez, mais il s'y serait tenu pendu jusqu'à ce qu'on jetât l'eponge en l'air, fallût-il attendre un an. Smiley gagnait toujours avec cette bête-là; malheureusement ils ont fini par dresser un chien qui n'avait pas de pattes de derrière, parce qu'on les avait sciées, et quand les choses furent au point qu'il voulait, et qu'il en vint à se jeter sur son morceau favori, le pauvre chien comprit en un instant qu'on s'était moqué de lui, et que l'autre le tenait. Vous n'avez jamais vu personne avoir l'air plus penaud et plus découragé; il ne fit aucun effort pour gagner le combat et fut rudement secoué, de sorte que, regardant Smiley comme pour lui dire:—Mon cœur est brisé, c'est ta faute; pourquoi m'avoir livré à un chien qui n'a pas de pattes de derrière, puisque c'est par là que je les bats?—il s'en alla en clopinant, et se coucha pour mourir. Ah! c'était un bon chien, cet André Jackson, et il se serait fait un nom, s'il avait vécu, car il y avait de l'etoffe en lui, il avait du génie, je le sais, bien que de grandes occasions lui aient manqué; mais il est impossible de supposer qu'un chien capable de se battre comme lui, certaines circonstances étant données, ait manqué de talent. Je me sens triste toutes les fois que je pense à son dernier combat et au dénoûment qu'il a lu. Eh bien! ce Smiley nourrissait des terriers à rats, et des coqs de combat, et des chats, et toute sorte de choses, au point qu'il était toujours en mesure de vous tenir tête, et qu'avec sa rage de paris on n'avait plus de repos. Il attrapa un jour une grenouille et l'emporta chez lui, disant qu'il prétendait faire son éducation; vous me croirez si vous voulez, mais pendant trois mois il n'a rien fait que lui apprendre à sauter dans une cour retirée de sa maison. Et je vous réponds qu'il avait réussi. Il lui donnait un petit coup par derrière, et l'instant d'après vous voyiez la grenouille tourner en l'air comme un beignet au-dessus de la poêle, faire une culbute, quelquefois deux, lorsqu'elle était bein partie, et retomber sur ses pattes comme un chat. Il l'avait dressée dans l'art de gober des mouches, et l'y exerçait continuellement, si bien qu'une mouche, du plus loin qu'elle apparaissait, était une mouche perdue. Smiley avait contume de dire que tout ce qui manquait à une grenouille, c'était l'éducation, qu'avec l'éducation elle pouvait faire presque tout, et je le crois. Tenez, je l'ai vu poser Daniel Webster là sur ce plancher.—Daniel Webster était le nom de la grenouille,—et lui chanter:—Des mouches! Daniel, des mouches!—En un clin d'œil, Daniel avait bondi et saisi une mouche ici sur le comptoir, puis sauté de nouveau par terre, où il restait vraiment à se gratter la tête avec sa patte de derrière, comme s'il n'avait pas eu la moindre idée de sa supériorité. Jamais vous n'avez grenouille vu de aussi modeste, aussi naturelle, douée comme elle l'était! Et quand il s'agissait de sauter purement et simplement sur terrain plat, elle faisait plus de chemin en un saut qu'aucune bête de son espèce que vous puissiez connaitre. Sauter à plat, c'était son fort! Quand il s'agissait de cela, Smiley entassait les enjeux sur elle tant qu'il lui, restait un rouge liard. Il faut le reconnaitre, Smiley était monstrueusement fier de sa grenouille, et il en avait le droit, car des gens qui avaient voyagé, qui avaient tout vu, disaient qu'on lui ferait injure de la comparer a une autre; de façon

que Smiley gardait Daniel dans une petite boîte à claire-voie qu'il emporta
it parfois à la ville pour quelque pari.

"Un jour, un individu, étranger au camp l'arrête avec sa boîte et lui dit:
—Qu'est-ce que vous avez donc serré là dedans ?

"Smiley dit d'un air indifférent:—Cela puorrait être un perroquet ou un
serin, mais ce n'est rien de pareil, ce n'est qu'une grenouille.

"L'individu la prend, la regarde avec soin, la tourne d'un côté et de l'autre puis il dit.—Tiens ! en effet ! A quoi est-elle bonne ?

"—Mon Dieu ! répond Smiley, toujours d'un air dégagé, elle est bonne
pour une chose à mon avis, elle peut battre en sautant toute grenouille du
comté de Calaveras.

"L'individu reprend la boîte, l'examine de nouveau longuement, et la
rend à Smiley en disant d'un air délibéré:—Eh bien ! je ne vois pas que cette
grenouille ait rien de mieux qu'aucune grenouille.

"—Possible que vous ne le voyiez pas, dit Smiley, possible que vous vous
entendiez en grenouilles, possible que vous ne vous y entendez point, possible
que vous ayez de l'expérience, et possible que vous ne soyez qu'un amateur.
De toute manière, je parie quarante dollars qu'elle battra en sautant n'importe
qu'elle grenouille du comté de Calaveras.

"L'individu réfléchit une seconde et dit comme attristé:—Je ne suis qu'un
étranger ici, je n'ai pas de grenouille; mais, si j'en avis une, je tiendrais le
pari.

"—Fort bien ! répond Smiley. Rien de plus facile. Si vous voulez tenir
ma boîte une minute, j'irai vous chercher une grenouille.—Voilà donc l'individu qui garde la boîte, qui met ses quarante dollars sur ceux de Smiley et
qui attend. Il attend assez longtemps, réfléchissant tout seul, et figurez-vous
qu'il prend Daniel, lui ouvre la bouche de force et avec une cuiller à thé
l'emplit de menu plomb de chasse, mais l'emplit jusqu'au menton, puis il le
pose par terre. Smiley pendant ce temps était à barboter dans une mare.
Finalement il attrape une grenouille, l'apporte à cet individu et dit:—Main-
tenant, si vous êtes prêt, mettez-la tout contre Daniel, avec leurs pattes de
devant sur la même ligne, et je donnerai le signal;—puis il ajoute:—Un, deux,
rois, sautez !

"Lui et l'individu touchent leurs grenouilles par derrière, et la grenouille
neuve se met à sautiller, mais Daniel se soulève lourdement, hausse les
épaules ainsi, comme un Français; à quoi bon? il ne pouvait bouger, il était
planté solide comme une enclume, il n'avançait pas puls que si on l'eût mis
à l'ancre. Smiley fut surpris et dégoûté, mais il ne se doutait pas du tour,
bien entendu. L'individu empoche l'argent, s'en va, et en s'en allant est-ce
qu'il ne donne pas un coup de pouce par-dessus l'épaule, comme ça, au pauvre
Daniel, en disant de son air délibéré:—Eh bien! je ne vois pas que cette
grenouille ait rien de mieux qu'une autre.

"Smiley se gratta longtemps la tête, les yeux fixés sur Daniel, jusqu'à ce qu'enfin il dit:—Je me demande comment diable il se fait que cette bête ait refusé...Est-ce qu'elle aurait quelque chose?...On croirait qu'elle est enflée.

"Il empoigne Daniel par la peau du cou, le soulève et dit:—Le loup me croque, s'il ne pèse pas cinq livres.

"Il le retourne, et le malheureux crache deux poignées de plomb. Quand Smiley reconnut ce qui en était, il fut comme fou. Vous le voyez d'ici poser sa grenouille par terre et courir après cet individu, mais il ne le rattrapa jamais, et..."

[Translation of the above back from the French.]

THE FROG JUMPING OF THE COUNTY OF CALAVERAS.

It there was one time here an individual known under the name of Jim Smiley: it was in the winter of '49, possibly well at the spring of '50, I no me recollect not exactly. This which me makes to believe that it was the one or the other, it is that I shall remember that the grand flume is not achieved when he arrives at the camp for the first time, but of all sides he was the man the most fond of to bet which one have seen, betting upon all that which is presented, when he could find an adversary; and when he not of it could not, he passed to the side opposed. All that which convenienced to the other, to him convenienced also; seeing that he had a bet, Smiley was satisfied. And he had a chance! a chance even worthless: nearly always he gained. It must to say that he was always near to himself expose, but one no could mention the least thing without that this gaillard offered to bet the

bottom, no matter what, and to take the side that one him
would, as I you it said all at the hour (tout à l'heure). If
it there was of races, you him find rich or ruined at the
end; if it there is a combat of dogs, he bring his bet; he
himself laid always for a combat of cats, for a combat of
cocks;—by-blue! if you have see two birds upon a fence,
he you should have offered of to bet which of those birds
shall fly the first; and if there is *meeting* at the camp
(*meeting* au camp) he comes to bet regularly for the curé
Walker, which he judged to be the best predicator of the
neighburhood (prédicateur des environs) and which he was
in effect, and a brave man. He would encounter a bug of
wood in the road, whom he will bet upon the time which he
shall take to go where she would go—and if you him have
take at the word, he will follow the bug as far as Mexique,
without himself caring to go so far; neither of the time
which he there lost. One time the woman of the curé
Walker is very sick during long time, it seemed that one not
her saved not; but one morning the curé arrives, and Smiley
him demanded how she goes, and he said that she is well
better, grace to the infinite misery (lui demande comment
elle va, et il dit qu'elle est bien mieux, grâce à l'infini
misèricorde) so much better that with the benediction of
the Providence she herself of it would pull out (elle s'en
tirerait); and behold that without there thinking Smiley
responds: "Well, I gage two-and-half that she will die
all of same."

This Smiley had an animal which the boys called the
nag of the quarter of hour, but solely for pleasantry, you

comprehend, because, well understand, she was more fast
as that! [Now why that exclamation ?—M. T.] And it
was custom of to gain of the silver with this beast, notwithstanding she was poussive, cornarde, always taken of
asthma, of colics, or of consumption, or something of approaching. One him would give two or three hundred
yards at the departure, then one him passed without pain;
but never at the last she not fail of herself èchauffer, of
herself exasperate, and she arrives herself écartant, se dè-
fendant, her legs grêles in the air before the obstacles,
sometimes them elevating and making with this more of
dust than any horse, more of noise above with his éternumens and reniflemens—crac! she arrives then always first
by one head, as just as one can it measure. And he had
a small bull dog (boule dogue!) who, to him see, no value,
not a cent; one would believe that to bet against him it
was to steal, so much he was ordinary; but as soon as the
game made, she becomes another dog. Her jaw inferior
commence to project like a deck of before, his teeth themselves discover brilliant like some furnaces, and a dog
could him tackle (le taquiner), him excite, him murder
(le mordre), him throw two or three times over his shoulder, André Jackson—this was the name of the dog—
André Jackson takes that tranquilly, as if he not himself
was never expecting other thing, and when the bets were
doubled and redoubled against him, he you seize the other
dog just at the articulation of the leg of behind, and he
not it leave more, not that he it masticate, you conceive,
but he himself there shall be holding during until that

one **throws** the sponge in the air, must he wait a year.
Smiley gained always with this beast-là; unhappily they
have finished by elevating a dog who no had not of feet
of behind, because one them had sawed; and when things
were at the point that he would, and that he came to
himself throw upon his morsel favourite, the poor dog comprehended in an instant that he himself was deceived in
him, and that the other dog him had.   You no have
never see person having the air more penaud and more
discouraged; he not made no effort to gain the combat,
and was rudely shucked.

Eh bien! this Smiley nourished some terriers a rats, and
some cocks of combat, and some cats, and all sort of things;
and with his rage of betting one no had more of repose.
He trapped one day a frog and him imported with him
(et l'emporta chez lui) saying that he pretended to make
his education.   You me believe if you will, but during
three months he not has nothing done but to him appre-
hend to jump (apprendre a sauter) in a court retired of her
mansion (de sa maison).   And I you respond that he have
succeeded.   He him gives a small blow by behind, and
the instant after you shall see the frog turn in the air like
a grease-biscuit, make one summersault, sometimes two,
when she was well started, and refall upon his feet like a
cat.   He him had accomplished in the art of to gobble the
flies (gober des mouches), and him there exercised con-
tinually—so well that a fly at the most far that she appeared was a fly lost.   Smiley had custom to say that all
which lacked to a frog it was the education, but with the

education she could do nearly all—and I him believe.
Tenez, I him have seen pose Daniel Webster there upon
this plank—Daniel Webster was the name of the frog—
and to him sing, "Some flies, Daniel, some flies!"—in a
flash of the eye Daniel had bounded and seized a
fly here upon the counter, then jumped anew at the earth,
where he rested truly to himself, scratch the head with his
behind-foot, as if he no had not the least idea of his
superiority.   Never you not have seen frog as modest, as
natural, sweet as she was.   And when he himself agitated
to jump purely and simply upon plain earth, she does
more ground in one jump than any beast of his species
than you can know.   To jump plain—this was his
strong.   When he himself agitated for that, Smiley
multiplied the bets upon her as long as there to him remained a red.   It must to know, Smiley was monstrously
proud of his frog, and he of it was right, for some men
who were travelled, who had all seen, said that they to
him would be injurious to him compare to another frog.
Smiley guarded Daniel in a little box latticed which he
carried bytimes to the village for some bet.

One day an individual stranger at the camp him arrested with his box and him said:

"What is this that you have then shut up there within?"

Smiley said, with an air indifferent:

"That could be a paroquet, or a syringe (ou un serin),
but this no is nothing of such, it not is but a frog."

The individual it took, it regarded with care, it turned
from one side and from the other then he said:

"Tiens! in effect!—At what is she good?"

"My God!" respond Smiley, always with an air dis-engaged, "she is good for one thing, to my notice, (a mor avis) she can batter in jumping (elle peut batter en sautant) all frogs of the county of Calaveras."

The individual re-took the box, it examined of new longly, and it rendered to Smiley in saying with an air deliberate:

"Eh bien! I no saw not that that frog had nothing of better than each frog. (Je ne vois pas que cette grenouille ait rien de mieux qu'aucune grenouille). [If that isn't grammar gone to seed, then I count myself no judge. M. T.]

"Possible that you not it saw not," said Smiley, "possible that you—you comprehend frogs; possible that you not you there comprehend nothing; possible that you had of the experience and possible that you not be but an amateur. Of all manner, (De toute maniere) I bet forty dollars that she batter in jumping no matter which frog of the county of Calaveras."

The individual reflected a second, and said like sad:

"I not am but a stranger here, I no have not a frog; but if I of it had one, I would embrace the bet."

"Strong well!" respond Smiley; "nothing of more facility. If you will hold my box a minute, I go you to search a frog (j' irai vous chercher)."

Behold, then the individual, who guards the box, who put his forty dollars upon those of Smiley, and who attends, (et qui attend). He attended enough longtimes reflecting all solely. And figure you that he takes Daniel, him opens the mouth by force and with a tea-spoon him fills with shot of the hunt, even him fills just to the chin, then he him puts by the earth. Smiley during these times was at slopping in a swamp. Finally he trapped (attrape) a frog, him carried to that individual, and said:

"Now if you be ready, put him all against Daniel, with their before-feet upon the same line, and I give the signal;" then he added: "One, two, three,—advance!"

Him and the individual touched their frogs by behind, and the frog new put to jump smartly, but Daniel himself lifted ponderously, exalted the shoulders thus, like a Frenchman—to what good? he not could budge, he is planted solid like a church, he not advance no more than if one him had put at the anchor.

Smiley was surprised and disgusted, but he not himself doubted not one of the turn being intended (mais il ne se doutait pas du tour, bien entendu). The individual empocketed the silver, himself with it went, and of it himself in going is it that he no gives not a jerk of thumb over the shoulder—like that—at the poor Daniel, in saying with his air deliberate—(L' individu empoche l'argent, s'en va et en s'en allant est ce qu'il ne donne pas un coup de pouce par-dessus l'epaule, comme ca, au pauvre Daniel, endisant de son air delibere):

"Eh bien! *I no see not that that frog has nothing of better than another.*"

Smiley himself scratched longtimes the head, the eyes fixed upon Daniel, until that which at last he said:

"I me demand how the devil it makes itself that this beast has refused. Is it that she had something? One would believe that she is stuffed."

He grasped Daniel by the skin of the neck, him lifted and said:

"The wolf me bite if he no weigh not five pounds."

He him reversed and the unhappy belched two handfuls of shot (et le malhereus, etc).—When Smiley recognized how it was, he was like mad. He deposited his frog by the earth and ran after that individual, but he not him caught never.

Such is the Jumping Frog, to the distorted French eye. I claim that I never put together such an odious mixture of bad grammar and delirium tremens in my life. And what has a poor foreigner like me done, to be abused and misrepresented like this? When I say, "Well, I don't see no p'ints about that frog that's any better'n any other frog," is it kind, is it just, for this Frenchman to try to make it appear that I said, "Eh bien! I no saw not that that frog had nothing of better than each frog?" I have no heart to write more. I never felt so about anything before.

MY WATCH.

AN INSTRUCTIVE LITTLE TALE.

———

MY beautiful new watch had run eighteen months without loosing or gaining, and without breaking any
part of its machinery or stopping.   I had come to believe
it infallible in its judgments about the time of day, and to
consider its constitution and its anatomy imperishable.
But at last, one night, I let it run down.   I grieved
about it as if it were a recognized messenger and forerun-
ner of calamity.   But by-and-by I cheered up, set the
watch by guess, and commanded my bodings and superstitions to depart.   Next day I stepped into the chief
jeweller's to set it by the exact time, and the head of the
establishment took it out of my hand and proceeded to
set it for me.   Then he said, " She is four minutes slow—
regulator wants pushing up."   I tried to stop him—tried
to make him understand that the watch kept perfect
time.   But no; all this human cabbage could see was
that the watch was four minutes slow, and the regulator
must be pushed up a little; and so, while I danced
around him in anguish, and implored him to let the watch
alone, he calmly and cruelly did the shameful deed.   My

watch began to gain. It gained faster and faster day by day. Within the week it sickened to a raging fever, and its pulse went up to a hundred and fifty in the shade. At the end of two months it had left all the timepieces of the town far in the rear, and was a fraction over thirteen days ahead of the almanac. It was away into November enjoying the snow, while the October leaves were still turning. It hurried up house rent, bills payable, and such things, in such a ruinous way that I could not abide it. I took it to the watchmaker to be regulated. He asked me if I had ever had it repaired. I said no, it had never needed any repairing. He looked a look of vicious happiness and eagerly pried the watch open, and then put a small dice box into his eye and peered into its machinery. He said it wanted cleaning and oiling, besides regulating—come in a week. After being cleaned and oiled, and regulated, my watch slowed down to that degree that it ticked like a tolling bell. I began to be left by trains, I failed all appointments, I got to missing my dinner; my watch strung out three days' grace to four and let me go to protest; I gradually drifted back into yesterday, then day before, then into last week, and by-and-by the comprehension came upon me that all solitary and alone I was lingering along in week before last, and the world was out of sight. I seemed to detect in myself a sort of sneaking fellow-feeling for the mummy in the museum, and a desire to swap news with him. I went to a watchmaker again. He took the watch all to pieces while I waited, and then said the barrel was "swelled."

He said he could reduce it in three days. After this the watch *averaged* well, but nothing more. For half a day it would go like the very mischief, and keep up such a barking and wheezing, and whooping and sneezing and snorting, that I could not hear myself think for the disturbance; and as long as it held out there was not a watch in the land that stood any chance against it. But the rest of the day it would keep on slowing down and fooling along until all the clocks it had left behind caught up again. So at last, at the end of twenty-four hours, it would trot up to the judges' stand all right and just in time. It would show a fair and square average, and no man could say it had done more or less than its duty. But a correct average is only a mild virtue in a watch, and I took this instrument to another watchmaker. He said the kingbolt was broken. I said I was glad it was nothing more serious. To tell the plain truth, I had no idea what the kingbolt was, but I did not choose to appear ignorant to a stranger. He repaired the kingbolt, but what the watch gained in one way it lost in another. It would run awhile and then stop awhile, and then run awhile again, and so on, using its own discretion about the intervals. And every time it went off it kicked back like a musket. I padded my breast for a few days, but finally took the watch to another watchmaker. He picked it all to pieces, and turned the ruin over and over under his glass; and then he said there appeared to be something the matter with the hair-trigger. He fixed it, and gave it a fresh start. It did well now, except that

always at ten minutes to ten the hands would shut together like a pair of scissors, and from that time forth
they would travel together. The oldest man in the world
could not make head or tail of the time of day by such a
watch, and so I went again to have the thing repaired.
This person said that the crystal had got bent, and that
the main-spring was not straight. He also remarked that
part of the works needed half-soling. He made these
things all right, and then my timepiece performed unex-
ceptionably, save that now and then, after working along
quietly for nearly eight hours, everything inside would
let go all of a sudden and begin to buzz like a bee, and
the hands would straightway begin to spin round and
round so fast that their individuality was lost completely,
and they simply seemed a delicate spider's web over the
face of the watch. She would reel off the next twenty-
four hours in six or seven minutes, and then stop with a
bang. I went with a heavy heart to one more watchmaker, and looked on while he took her to pieces. Then
I prepared to cross-question him rigidly, for this thing
was getting serious. The watch had cost two hundred
dollars originally, and I seemed to have paid out two or
three thousand for repairs. While I waited and looked
on I presently recognized in this watchmaker an old
acquaintance—a steamboat engineer of other days, and
not a good engineer either. He examined all the parts
carefully, just as the other watchmakers had done, and
then delivered his verdict with the same confidence of
manner.

He said—

"She makes too much steam—you want to hang the monkey-wrench on the safety-valve!"

I brained him on the spot, and had him buried at my own expense.

My uncle William (now deceased, alas!) used to say that a good horse was a good horse until it had run away once, and that a good watch was a good watch until the repairers got a chance at it. And he used to wonder what became of all the unsuccessful tinkers, and gun-smiths, and shoemakers, and engineers, and blacksmiths; but nobody could ever tell him.

POLITICAL ECONOMY.

———

POLITICAL ECONOMY is the basis of all good government. The wisest men of all ages have brought to bear upon this subject the—

[Here I was interrupted and informed that a strangei wished to see me down at the door. I went and confronted him, and asked to know his business, struggling all the time to keep a tight rein on my seething political economy ideas, and not let them break away from me or get tangled in their harness. And privately I wished the stranger was in the bottom of the canal with a cargo of wheat on top of him. I was all in a fever, but he was cool. He said he was sorry to disturb me, but as he was passing he noticed that I needed some lightning-rods. I said, "Yes, yes—go on—what about it?" He said there was nothing about it, in particular—nothing except that he would like to put them up for me. I am new to housekeeping; have been used to hotels and boarding-houses all my life. Like anybody else of similar experience, I try to appear (to strangers) to be an old housekeeper; consequently I said in an off-hand way that I had been intending for some time to have six or eight lightning-rods put up, but—— The stranger started, and looked inquiringly at me, but I was serene. I thought that if I chanced to make any mistakes, he would not catch me by my countenance. He said he would rather have my custom than any man's in town. I said, "All right," and started off to wrestle with my great subject again, when he called me back and said it would be necessary to know exactly how many "points" I wanted put up, what parts of the house I wanted them on, and what quality of rod I preferred. It was close quarters for a man not used to the exigencies of housekeeping; but I went through creditably, and he probably never suspected that I was a novice. I told him to put up eight "points," and put them all on the roof, and use the best quality of rod. He said he could furnish the "plain" article at 20 cents a foot; "coppered," 25 cents; "zinc-plated spiral-twist," at 30 cents, that would stop a streak of lightning any time, no matter where it was bound, and "render its errand harmless and its further progress apocryphal." I said apocryphal was no slouch of a word, emanating from the source it did, but, philology aside, I liked the spiral-twist and would take that brand. Then he said he *could* make two hundred and fifty feet answer; but to do it right, and make the best job in town of it, and attract the admiration of the just and the unjust alike, and compel all parties to say they never saw a more symmetrical and hypothetical display of lightning-rods since they were born, he supposed he really couldn't get along without four hundred, though he was not vindictive, and trusted he was willing to try. I said, go ahead and use four hundred, and make any kind of a job he pleased out of it, but let me get back to my work. So I got rid of him at last; and now, after half-an-hour spent in getting my train of political economy thoughts coupled together again, I am ready to go on once more.]

richest treasures of their genius, their experience of life, and their learning. The great lights of commercial jurisprudence, international confraternity, and biological deviation, of all ages, all civilizations, and all nationalities, from Zoroaster down to Horace Greeley, have——

[Here I was interrupted again, and required to go down and confer further with that lightning-rod man. I hurried off, boiling and surging with prodigious thoughts wombed in words of such majesty that each one of them was in itself a straggling procession of syllables that might be fifteen minutes passing a given point, and once more I confronted him—he so calm and sweet, I so hot and frenzied. He was standing in the contemplative attitude of the Colossus of Rhodes, with one foot on my infant tube-rose, and the other among my pansies, his hands on his hips, his hat-brim tilted forward, one eye shut and the other gazing critically and admiringly in the direction of my principal chimney. He said now *there* was a state of things to make a man glad to be alive; and added, "I leave it to *you* if you ever saw anything more deliriously picturesque than eight lightning-rods on one chimney?" I said I had no present recollection of anything that transcended it. He said that in his opinion nothing on earth but Niagara Falls was superior to it in the way of natural scenery. All that was needed now, he verily believed, to make my house a perfect balm to the eye, was to kind of touch up the other chimneys a little, and thus "add to the generous *coup d'œil* a soothing uniformity of achievement which would allay the excitement naturally consequent upon the first *coup d'etat.*" I asked him if he learned to talk out of a book, and if I could borrow it anywhere? He smiled pleasantly, and said that his manner of speaking was not taught in books, and that nothing but familiarity with lightning could enable a man to handle his conversational style with impunity. He then figured up an estimate, and said that about eight more rods scattered about my roof would about fix me right, and he guessed five hundred feet of stuff would do it; and added that the first eight had got a little the start of him, so to speak, and used up a mere trifle of material more than he had calculated on—a hundred feet or along there. I said I was in a dreadful hurry, and I wished we could get this business permanently mapped out, so that I could go on with my work. He said, "I *could* have put up those eight rods, and marched off about my business—some men *would* have done it. But no: I said to myself, this man is a stranger to me, and I will die before I'll wrong him; there ain't lightning-rods enough on that house, and for one I'll never stir out of my tracks till I've done as I would be done by, and told him so. Stranger, my duty is accomplished; if the recalcitrant and dephlogistic messenger of heaven strikes your"——"There, now, there," I said, "put on the other eight—add five hundred feet of spiral-twist—do anything and everything you want to do· but calm your sufferings, and try to keep

your feelings where you can reach them with the diction-
ary. Meanwhile, if we understand each other now, I will
go to work again."

I think I have been sitting here a full hour, this time,
trying to get back to where I was when my train of thought
was broken up by the last interruption; but I believe I
have accomplished it at last, and may venture to proceed
again.]

wrestled with this great subject, and the greatest among them have found
it is a worthy adversary, and one that always comes up fresh and smiling after
every throw. The great Confucius said that he would rather be a profound
political economist than chief of police. Cicero frequently said that political economy was the grandest consummation that the human mind was capable of consuming; and even our own Greely has said vaguely but forcibly
that "*Political*——

[Here the lightning-rod man sent up another call for
me I went down in a state of mind bordering on im-
patience. He said he would rather have died than inter-
rupt me, but when he was employed to do a job, and that
job was expected to be done in a clean, workmanlike
manner, and when it was finished and fatigue urged him
to seek the rest and recreation he stood so much in need
of, and he was about to do it, but looked up and saw at a
glance that all the calculations had been a little out, and
if a thunder storm were to come up, and that house, which
he felt a personal interest in, stood there with nothing on
earth to protect it but sixteen lightning-rods—— " Let
us have peace!" I shrieked. "Put up a hundred and
fifty! Put some on the kitchen! Put a dozen on the
barn! Put a couple on the cow!—Put one on the cook!

—scatter them all over the persecuted place till it looks like a zinc-plated, spiral-twisted, silver-mounted cane-break! Move! Use up all the material you can get your hands on, and when you run out of lightning-rods put up ram-rods, cam-rods, stair-rods, piston-rods—*any-thing* that will pander to your dismal appetite for artificial scenery, and bring respite to my raging brain, and healing to my lacerated soul!" Wholly unmoved—further than to smile sweetly—this iron being simply turned back his wristbands daintily, and said, " He would now proceed to hump himself." Well, all that was nearly three hours ago. It is questionable whether I am calm enough yet to write on the noble theme of political economy, but I cannot resist the desire to try, for it is the one subject that is nearest to my heart and dearest to my brain of all this world's philosophy.]

"——*economy is heaven's best boon to man.*" When the loose but gifted Byron lay in his Venetian exile he observed that, if it could be granted him to go back and live his misspent life over again, he would give his lucid and unintoxicated intervals to the composition, not of frivolous rhymes, but of essays upon political economy. Washington loved this exquisite science ; such names as Baker, Beckwith, Judson, Smith, are imperishably linked with it ; and even imperial Homer, in the ninth book of the Iliad, has said :—

Fiat justitia, ruat cœlum,
Post mortem unum, ante bellum,
Hic jacet hoc, ex-parte res,
Politicum e-conomico est.

The grandeur of these conceptions of the old poet, together with the felicity of the wording which clothes them, and the sublimity of the imagery whereby they are illustrated, have singled out that stanza, and make it more celebrated than any that ever——

[" Now, not a word out of you—not a single word.

Just state your bill and relapse into impenetrable silen
for ever and ever on these premises. Nine hundred dollars? Is that all? This cheque for the amount will be
honoured at any respectable bank in America. What is
that multitude of people gathered in the street for?
How?—'looking at the lightning-rods!' Bless my life,
did they never see any lightning-rods before? Never saw
'such a stack of them on one establishment,' did I understand you to say? I will step down and critically observe this popular ebullition of ignorance."]

THREE DAYS LATER.—We are all about worn out. For
four-and-twenty hours our bristling premises were the
talk and wonder of the town. The theatres languished,
for their happiest scenic inventions were tame and com-
monplace compared with my lightning-rods. Our street
was blocked night and day with spectators, and among
them were many who came from the country to see. It
was a blessed relief on the second day, when a thunder-
storm came up and the lightning began to "go for" my
house, as the historian Josephus quaintly phrases it. It
cleared the galleries, so to speak. In five minutes there
was not a spectator within half a mile of my place; but
all the high houses about that distance away were full,
windows, roof, and all. And well they might be, for all
the falling stars and Fourth-of-July fireworks of a generation, put together and rained down simultaneously out
of heaven in one brilliant shower upon one helpless roof,
would not have any advantage of the pyrotechnic display

that was making my house so magnificently conspicuous in the general gloom of the storm. By actual count, the lightning struck at my establishment seven hundred and sixty-four times in forty minutes, but tripped on one of those faithful rods every time, and slid down the spiral twist and shot into the earth before it probably had time to be surprised at the way the thing was done. And through all that bombardment only one patch of slates was ripped up, and that was because, for a single instant, the rods in the vicinity were transporting all the lightning they could possibly accommodate. Well, nothing was ever seen like it since the world began. For one whole day and night not a member of my family stuck his head out of the window but he got the hair snatched off it as smooth as a billiard-ball; and if the reader will believe me, not one of us ever dreamt of stirring abroad. But at last the awful siege came to an end—because there was absolutely no more electricity left in the clouds above us within grappling distance of my insatiable rods. Then I sallied forth, and gathered daring workmen together, and not a bite or a nap did we take till the premises were utterly stripped of all their terrific armament except just three rods on the house, one on the kitchen, and one on the barn—and behold these remain there even unto this day. And then, and not till then, the people ventured to use our street again. I will remark here, in passing, that during that fearful time I did not continue my essay upon political economy. I am not even yet settled enough in nerve and brain to resume it.

To Whom it May Concern.—Parties having need of three thousand two hundred and eleven feet of best quality zinc-plated spiral-twist lightning-rod stuff, and sixteen hundred and thirty-one silver-tipped points, all in tolerable repair (and, although much worn by use, still equal to any ordinary emergency), can hear of a bargain by addressing the publisher.

JOURNALISM IN TENNESSEE.

The editor of the Memphis *Avalanche* swoops thus mildly down upon a correspondent who posted him as a Radical:—"While he was writing the first word, the middle, dotting his i's, crossing his t's, and punching his period, he knew he was concocting a sentence that was saturated with infamy and reeking with falsehood."—*Exchange.*

I WAS told by the physician that a Southern climate would improve my health, and so I went down to Tennessee, and got a berth on the *Morning Glory and Johnson County War-Whoop* as associate editor. When I went on duty I found the chief editor sitting tilted back in a three-legged chair with his feet on a pine table. There was another pine table in the room and another afflicted chair, and both were half buried under newspapers and scraps and sheets of manuscript. There was a wooden box of sand, sprinkled with cigar stubs and "old soldiers," and a stove with a door hanging by its upper hinge. The chief editor had a long-tailed black cloth frock coat on, and white linen pants. His boots were small and neatly blacked. He wore a ruffled shirt, a large seal ring, a standing collar of obsolete pattern, and a chequered neckerchief with the ends hanging down. Date of costume about 1848. He was smoking a cigar, and trying

to think of a word, and in pawing his hair he had rumpl-
ed his locks a good deal.   He was scowling fearfully, and
I judged that he was concocting a particularly knotty
editorial.   He told me to take the exchanges and skim
through them and write up the "Spirit of the Tennessee
Press," condensing into the article all of their contents
that seemed of interest.

I wrote as follows :—

"SPIRIT OF THE TENNESSEE PRESS.

"The editors of the *Semi-Weekly Earthquake* evidently labour under a
misapprehension with regard to the Ballyhack railroad.   It is not the object
of the company to leave Buzzardville off to one side.   On the contrary, they
consider it one of the most important points along the line, and consequently
can have no desire to slight it.   The gentlemen of the *Earthquake* will, of
course, take pleasure in making the correction.

"John W. Blossom, Esq., the able editor of the Higginsville *Thunderbolt
and Battle Cry of Freedom*, arrived in the city yesterday.   He is stopping at
the Van Buren House.

"We observe that our contemporary of the Mud Springs *Morning Howl*,
has fallen into the error of supposing that the election of Van Werter is not
an established fact, but he will have discovered his mistake before this re-
minder reaches him, no doubt.   He was doubtless misled by incomplete
election returns.

"It is pleasant to note that the city of Blathersville is endeavouring to
contract with some New York gentleman to pave its well-nigh impassable
streets with the Nicholson pavement.   The *Daily Hurrah* urges the measure
with ability, and seems confident of ultimate success."

I passed my manuscript over to the chief editor for
acceptance, alteration, or destruction.   He glanced at it
and his face clouded.   He ran his eye down the pages,
and his countenance grew portentous.   It was easy to see
that something was wrong.   Presently he sprang up and
said—

"Thunder and lightning!   Do you suppose I am going

to speak of those cattle that way? Do you suppose my subscribers are going to stand such gruel as that. Give me the pen!"

I never saw a pen scrape and scratch its way so viciously, or plough through another man's verbs and adjectives so relentlessly. While he was in the midst of his work, somebody shot at him through the open window, and marred the symmetry of my ear.

"Ah," said he, "that is that scoundrel Smith, of the *Moral Volcano*—he was due yesterday." And he snatched a navy revolver from his belt and fired. Smith dropped shot in the thigh. The shot spoiled Smith's aim, who was just taking a second chance, and he crippled a stranger. It was me. Merely a finger shot off.

Then the chief editor went on with his erasures and interlineations. Just as he finished them a hand-grenade came down the stove-pipe, and the explosion shivered the stove into a thousand fragments. However it did no further damage, except that a vagrant piece knocked a couple of my teeth out.

"That stove is utterly ruined," said the chief editor.

I said I believed it was.

"Well, no matter—don't wan't it this kind of weather. I know the man that did it. I'll get him. Now, *here* is the way this stuff ought to be written."

I took the manuscript. It was scarred with erasures and interlineations till its mother wouldn't have known it if it had had one. It now read as follows:—

"SPIRIT OF THE TENNESSEE PRESS.

"The inveterate liars of the *Semi-Weekly Earthquake* are evidently endeavouring to palm off upon a noble and chivalrous people another of their vile and brutal falsehoods with regard to that most glorious conception of the nineteenth century, the Ballyhack railroad. The idea that Buzzardville was to be left off at one side originated in their own fulsome brains—or rather in the settlings which *they* regard as brains. They had better swallow this lie if they want to save their abandoned reptile carcasses the cowhiding they so richly deserve.

"That ass, Blossom, of the Higginsville *Thunderbolt and Battle Cry of Freedom*, is down here again sponging at the Van Buren.

"We observe that the besotted blackguard of the Mud Spring *Morning Howl* is giving out, with his usual propensity for lying, that Van Werter is not elected. The heaven-born mission of journalism is to disseminate truth; to eradicate error; to educate, refine and elevate the tone of public morals and manners, and make all men more gentle, more virtuous, more charitable, and in all ways better, and holier, and happier; and yet this black-hearted scoundrel degrades his great office persistently to the dissemination of falsehood, calumny, vituperation, and vulgarity.

"Blathersville wants a Nicholson pavement—it wants a jail and a poorhouse more. The idea of a pavement in a one-horse town composed of two gin mills, a blacksmith's shop, and that mustard-plaster of a newspaper, the *Daily Hurrah!* The crawling insect, Buckner, who edits the *Hurrah*, is braying about this business with his customary imbecility, and imagining that he is talking sense."

"Now *that* is the way to write—peppery and to the point. Mush-and-milk journalism gives me the fan-tods."

About this time a brick came through the window with a splintering crash, and gave me a considerable of a jolt in the back. I moved out of range—I began to feel in the way.

The chief said, "That was the Colonel, likely. I've been expecting him for two days. He will be up, now, right away."

He was correct. The Colonel appeared in the door a moment afterward with a dragoon revolver in his hand.

He said, "Sir, have I the honour of addressing the pol-
troon who edits this mangy sheet?"

"You have. Be seated, sir. Be careful of the chair,
one of its legs is gone. I believe I have the honour of
addressing the putrid liar, Col. Blatherskite Tecumseh?"

"Right, sir. I have a little account to settle with you.
If you are at leisure we will begin."

"I have an article on the 'Encouraging Progress of
Moral and Intellectual Development in America,' to finish,
but there is no hurry. Begin."

Both pistols rang out their fierce clamour at the same
instant. The chief lost a lock of his hair, and the Colonel's
bullet ended its career in the fleshy part of my thigh.

The Colonel's left shoulder was clipped a little. They
fired again. Both missed their men this time, but I got
my share, a shot in the arm. At the third fire both
gentlemen were wounded slightly, and I had a knuckle
chipped. I then said I believed I would go out and take
a walk, as this was a private matter, and I had a delicacy
about participating in it further. But both gentleman
begged me to keep my seat, and assured me that I was
not in the way.

They then talked about the elections and the crops
while they reloaded, and I fell to tying up my wounds.
But presently they opened fire again with animation, and
every shot took effect—but it is proper to remark that five
out of the six fell to my share. The sixth one mortally
wounded the Colonel, who remarked, with fine humour,
that he would have to say good morning now, as he had

business up town. He then enquired the way to the undertaker's and left.

The chief turned to me and said, "I am expecting company to dinner, and shall have to get ready. It will be a favour to me if you will read proof and attend to the customers."

I winced a little at the idea of attending to the customers, but I was too bewildered by the fusilade that was still ringing in my ears to think of anything to say.

He continued, "Jones will be here at 3—cowhide him. Gillespie will call earlier, perhaps—throw him out of the window. Ferguson will be along about 4—kill him. That is all for to day, I believe. If you have any odd time, you may write a blistering article on the police— give the Chief Inspector rats. The cowhides are under the table; weapons in the drawer—ammunition there in the corner—lint and bandages up there in the pigeon-holes. In case of accident, go to Lancet, the surgeon, down-stairs. He advertises—we take it out in trade."

He was gone. I shuddered. At the end of the next three hours I had been through perils so awful that all peace of mind and all cheerfulness were gone from me. Gillespie had called and thrown *me* out **of** the window. Jones arrived promptly, and when I got ready to do the cowhiding he took the job off my hands. In an encounter with a stranger, not in the bill of fare, I had lost my scalp. Another stranger, by the name of Thompson, left me a mere wreck and ruin of chaotic rags. And at last, at bay in the corner, and beset by an infuriated mob

of editors, blacklegs, politicians, and desperadoes, who
raved and swore and flourished their weapons about
my head till the air shimmered with glancing flashes of
steel, I was in the act of resigning my berth on the paper,
when the chief arrived, and with him a rabble of charmed
and enthusiastic friends.   Then ensued a scene of riot and
carnage such as no human pen, or steel one either, could
describe.   People were shot, probed, dismembered, blown
up, thrown out of the window.   There was a brief tornado
of murky blasphemy, with a confused and frantic war-
dance glimmering through it, and then all was over.   In
five minutes there was silence, and the gory chief and I
sat alone and surveyed the sanguinary ruin that strewed
the floor around us.

He said, "You'll like this place when you get used to it."

I said, "I'll have to get you to excuse me; I think maybe I might write to suit you after a while; as soon as I
had had some practice and learned the language I am confident I could.   But, to speak the plain truth, that sort of
energy of expression has its inconveniences, and a man is
liable to interruption.   You see that yourself.   Vigorous
writing is calculated to elevate the public, no doubt, but
then I do not like to attract so much attention as it calls
forth.   I can't write with comfort when I am interrupted
so much as I have been to-day.   I like this berth well
enough, but I don't like to be left here to wait on the
customers.   The experiences are novel, I grant you, and
entertaining too, after a fashion, but they are not judiciously distributed.   A gentleman shoots at you through

the window and cripples *me ;* a bomb-shell comes down
the stove-pipe for your gratification and sends the stove-
door down *my* throat ; a friend drops in to swap compli-
ments with you, and freckles *me* with bullet-holes till my
skin won't hold my principles ; you go to dinner, and
Jones comes with his cowhide, Gillespie throws me out of
the window, Thompson tears all my clothes off. and an
entire stranger takes my scalp with the easy freedom of
an old acquaintance ; and in less than five minutes all the
blackguards in the country arrive in their war-paint, and
proceed to scare the rest of me to death with their toma-
hawks. Take it altogether, I never had such a spirited time
in all my life as I have had to-day.   No ; I like you, and I
like your calm unruffled way of explaining things to the
customers, but you see I am not used to it.   The Southern
heart is too impulsive ; Southern hospitality is too lavish
with the stranger.   The paragraphs which I have written
to-day, and into whose cold sentences your masterly hand
has infused the fervent spirit of Tenneseean journalism,
will wake up another nest of hornets.   All that mob of
editors will come—and they will come hungry, too, and
want somebody for breakfast.   I shall have to bid you
adieu.   I decline to be present at these festivities. I came
South for my health, I will go back on the same errand,
and suddenly.   Tenneseean journalism is too stirring for
me."

After which we parted with mutual regret, and I took
apartments at the hospital.

A COUPLE OF POEMS BY TWAIN AND MOORE.

THOSE EVENING BELLS.

BY THOMAS MOORE.

Those evening bells! those evening bells!
How many a tale their music tells
Of youth, and home, and that sweet time
When last I heard their soothing chime.

Those joyous hours are passed away;
And many a heart that then was gay,
 Within the tomb now darkly dwells,
 And hears no more those evening bells.

And so 'twill be when I am gone—
That tuneful peal will still ring on;
While other bards shall walk these dells,
And sing your praise, sweet evening bells.

THOSE ANNUAL BILLS.

BY MARK TWAIN.

These annua bills! these annual bills!
How many a song their discord trills
Of "truck" consumed, enjoyed, forgot,
Since I was skinned by last year's lot.

Those joyous beans are passed away ;
Those onions blithe, O where are they !
Once loved, lost, mourned—*now* vexing ILLS
Your shades troop back in annual bills !

And so 'twill be when I'm aground—
These yearly duns will still go round,
While other bards, with frantic quills,
Shall damn and *damn* these annual bills !

TO RAISE POULTRY. *

SERIOUSLY, from early youth I have taken an especial
    interest in the subject of poultry-raising, and so this
membership touches a ready sympathy in my breast.
Even as a school-boy, poultry raising was a study with
me, and I may say without egotism that as early as the
age of seventeen I was acquainted with all the best and
speediest methods of raising chickens, from raising them
off a roost by burning lucifer matches under their noses,
down to lifting them off a fence on a frosty night by insinuating the end of a warm board under their heels.
By the time I was twenty years old, I really suppose I
had raised more poultry than any one individual in all
the section round about there.   The very chickens came
to know my talent, by and by.   The youth of both sexes
ceased to paw the earth for worms, and old roosters that
came to crow, " remained to pray," when I passed by.

I have had so much experience in the raising of fowls
that I cannot but think that a few hints from me might be
useful to the Society.   The two methods I have already
touched upon are very simple, and are only used in the

---

* Being a letter written to a Poultry Society that had conferred a complimentary membership upon the author.

raising of the commonest class of fowls ; one is for summer,
the other for winter. In the one case you start out with
a friend along about eleven o'clock on a summer's night
(not later,—because in some States—especially in
California and Oregon—chickens always rouse up just
at midnight and crow from ten to thirty minutes, according to the ease or difficulty they experience in getting
the public waked up) and your friend carries with him
a sack. Arrived at the hen-roost (your neighbour's,
not your own), you light a match and hold it under first
one and then another pullet's nose until they are willing to go into that bag without making any trouble about
it. You then return home, either taking the bag with
you or leaving it behind, according as circumstances shall
dictate. *N. B.* I *have* seen the time when it was eligible
and appropriate to leave the sack behind and walk off
with considerable velocity, without ever leaving any word
where to send it.

In the case of the other method mentioned for raising
poultry, your friend takes along a covered vessel with a
charcoal fire in it, and you carry a long slender plank.
This is a frosty night understand. Arrived at the tree,
or fence, or other hen-roost (your own if you are an idiot),
you warm the end of your plank in your friend's fire
vessel, and then raise it aloft and ease it up gently against
a slumbering chicken's foot. If the subject of your atten-
tions is a true bird, he will infallibly return thanks with
a sleepy cluck or two, and step out and take up quarters
on the plank, thus becoming so conspicuously accessory

before the fact to his own murder as to make it a grave question in our minds, as it once was in the mind of Blackstone, whether he is not really and deliberatly committing suicide in the second degree. [But you enter into a contemplation of these legal refinements subsequently—not then].

When you wish to raise a fine, large, donkey-voiced Shanghai rooster, you do it with a lasso, just as you would a bull. It is because he must be choked, and choked effectually, too. It is the only good, certain way, for whenever he mentions a matter which he is cordially interested in, the chances are ninety-nine in a hundred that he secures somebody else's immediate attention to it too, whether it be day or night.

The Black Spanish is an exceedingly fine bird and a costly one. Thirty-five dollars is the usual figure, and fifty a not uncommon price for a specimen. Even its eggs are worth from a dollar to a dollar and a half a-piece, and yet are so unwholesome that the city physician seldom or never orders them for the workhouse. Still I have once or twice procured as high as a dozen at a time for nothing, in the dark of the moon. The best way to raise the Black Spanish fowl is to go late in the evening and raise coop and all. The reason I recommend this method is, that the birds being so valuable, the owners do not permit them to roost around promiscuously, but put them in a coop as strong as a fire-proof safe, and keep it in the kitchen at night. The method I speak of is not always a bright and satisfying success, and yet there are so many little articles of *vertu* about a kitchen, that if you fail on the coop you can generally bring away something else. I brought away a nice steel trap one night, worth ninety cents.

But what is the use in my pouring out my whole intellect on this subject?   I have shown the Western New York Poultry Society that they have taken to their bosom a party who is not a spring chicken by any means, but a man who knows all about poultry, and is just as high up in the most efficient methods of raising it as the President of the institution himself.   I thank these gentlemen for the honorary membership they have conferred upon me, and shall stand at all times ready and willing to testify my good feeling and my official zeal by deeds as well as by this hastily penned advice and information. Whenever they are ready to go to raising poultry, let them call for me any evening after eleven o'clock, and I shall be on hand promptly.

10

MY FIRST LITERARY VENTURE.

I WAS a very smart child at the age of thirteen—an un-usually smart child, I thought at the time. It was then that I did my first newspaper scribbling, and most unexpectedly to me it stirred up a fine sensation in the community. It did, indeed, and I was very proud of it, too. I was a printer's "devil," and a progressive and aspiring one. My uncle had me on his paper *(the Weekly Hannibal Journal*, two dollars a year in advance—five hundred subscribers, and they paid in cordwood, cabbages, and unmarketable turnips), and on a lucky summer's day he left town to be gone a week, and asked me if I thought I could edit one issue of the paper judiciously. Ah! didn't I want to try! Higgins was the editor on the rival paper. He had lately been jilted, and one night a friend found an open note on the poor fellow's bed, in which he stated that he could no longer endure life and had drowned him-self in Bear Creek. The friend ran down there and dis-covered Higgins wading back to shore! He had concluded he wouldn't. The village was full of it for several days, but Higgins did not suspect it. I thought this was a fine opportunity. I wrote an elaborately wretched account of the whole matter, and then illustrated it with villainous

cuts engraved on the bottoms of wooden type with a jack-
knife—one of them a picture of Higgins wading out into
the creek in his shirt, with a lantern, sounding the depth
of the water with a walking stick. I thought it was
desperately funny, and was densely unconscious that there
was any moral obliquity about such a publication. Being
satisfied with this effort I looked around for other worlds
to conquer, and it struck me that it would make good, interesting matter to charge the editor of a neighbouring
country paper with a piece of gratuitous rascality and " see
him squirm."

I did it, putting the article into the form of a parody
on the " Burial of Sir John Moore "—and a pretty crude
parody it was, too.

Then I lampooned two prominent citizens outrageously
—not because they had done anything to deserve it, but
merely because I thought it was my duty to make the
paper lively.

Next I gently touched up the newest stranger—the lion
of the day, the gorgeous journeyman tailor from Quincy.
He was a simpering coxcomb of the first water, and the
" loudest" dressed man in the state. He was an inveterate woman-killer. Every week he wrote lushy " poetry "
for the " Journal," about his newest conquest. His rhymes
for my week were headed, " To MARY IN H——L," meaning to Mary in Hannibal, of course. But while setting up
the piece I was suddenly riven from head to heel by what
I regarded as a perfect thunderbolt of humour, and I com-
pressed it into a snappy foot-note at the bottom—thus :—

" We will let this thing pass, just this once; but we wish
Mr. J. Gordon Runnels to understand distinctly that we
have a character to sustain, and from this time forth when
he wants to commune with his friends in h—l, he must
select some other medium than the columns of this journal !"

The paper came out, and I never knew any little thing
attract so much attention as those playful trifles of mine.

For once the Hannibal Journal was in demand—a
novelty it had not experienced before. The whole town
was stirred. Higgins dropped in with a double-barrelled
shot-gun early in the forenoon. When he found it was
an infant (as he called me) that had done him the damage,
he simply pulled my ears and went away; but he threw
up his situation that night and left town for good. The
tailor came with his goose and a pair of shears; but he
despised me too, and departed for the south that night.
The two lampooned citizens came with threats of libel,
and went away incensed at my insignificance. The
country editor pranced in with a warwhoop next day,
suffering for blood to drink; but he ended by forgiving
me cordially and inviting me down to the drug store to
wash away all animosity in a friendly bumper of " Fahne-
stock's Vermifuge." It was his little joke. My uncle was
very angry when he got back—unreasonably so, I thought,
considering what an impetus I had given the paper, and
considering also that gratitude for his preservation ought
to have been uppermost in his mind, inasmuch as by his
delay he had so wonderfully escaped dissection, tomahawk-

ing, libel, and getting his head shot off. But he softened when he looked at the accounts and saw that I had actually booked the unparalleled number of thirty-three new subscribers, and had the vegetables to show for it, cordwood, cabbage, beans, and unsaleable turnips enough to run the family for two years!

THE FACTS IN THE CASE OF THE GREAT BEEF CONTRACT.

———

IN as few words as possible I wish to lay before the nation what share, howsoever small, I have had in this matter—this matter which has so exercised the public mind, engendered so much ill-feeling, and so filled the newspapers of both continents with distorted statements and extravagant comments.

The origin of this distressful thing was this—and I assert here that every fact in the following *resume* can be amply proved by the official records of the General Government :—

John Wilson Mackenzie, of Rotterdam, Chemung county, New Jersey, deceased, contracted with the General Government, on or about the 10th day of October. 1861, to furnish to General Sherman the sum total of thirty barrels of beef.

Very well.

He started after Sherman with the beef, but when he got to Washington Sherman had gone to Manassas ; so he took the beef and followed him there, but arrived too late; he followed him to Nashville, and from Nashville to Chattanooga, and from Chattanooga to Atlanta—but he never could overtake him. At Atlanta he took a fresh start and followed him clear through his march to the sea. He arrived too late again·by a few days ; but hearing that Sherman was going out in the *Quaker City* excursion to the Holy Land, he took shipping for Beirut, calculating to head off the other vessel. When he arrived in Jerusalem with his beef, he learned that Sherman had not sailed in the *Quaker City*, but had gone to the Plains to fight the Indians. He returned to America, and started for the Rocky Mountains. After sixty-eight days of arduous travel on the Plains, and when he had got within four miles of Sherman's head-quarters, he was tomahawked and scalped, and the Indians got the beef. They got all of it but one barrel. Sherman's army captured that, and so even in death, the bold navigator partly fulfilled his contract. In his will, which he had kept like a journal, he bequeathed the contract to his son Bartholomew W. Bartholomew W. made out the following bill, and then died :—

THE UNITED STATES

In account with JOHN WILSON MACKENZIE, of New Jersey, deceased. Dr.

To thirty barrels of beef for General Sherman, at $100...... $3,000
To travelling expenses and transportation................. 14,000

Total..............$17,000

Rec'd Pay't.

He died then ; but he left the contract to Wm. J. Martin, who tried to collect it, but died before he got through. He left it to Barker J. Allen, and he tried to collect it also. He did not survive. Barker J. Allen left it to

Anson G. Rogers, who attempted to collect it, and got along as far as the Ninth Auditor's Office, when Death the great Leveller, came all unsummoned, and foreclosed on *him* also. He left the bill to a relative of his in Connecticut, Vengeance Hopkins by name, who lasted four weeks and two days, and made the best time on record, coming within one of reaching the Twelfth Auditor. In his will he gave the contract bill to his uncle, by the name of O-be-joyful Johnson. It was too undermining for Joyful. His last words were: "Weep not for me—*I* am willing to go." And so he was, poor soul. Seven people inherited the contract after that; but they all died. So it came into my hands at last. It fell to me through a relative by the name of Hubbard—Bethlehem Hubbard, of Indiana. He had a grudge against me for a long time; but in his last moments he sent for me, and forgave me everything, and, weeping, gave me the beef contract.

This ends the history of it up to the time that I succeeded to the property. I will now endeavour to set myself straight before the nation in everything that concerns my share in the matter. I took this beef contract, and the bill for mileage and transportation, to the President of the United States.

He said, " Well sir, what can I do for you ? "

I said, " Sire, on or about the 10th day of October, 1861. John Wilson Mackenzie, of Rotterdam, Chemung county, New Jersey, deceased, contracted with the General Government to furnish to General Sherman the sum total of thirty barrels of beef——"

He stopped me there, and dismissed me from his presence—kindly, but firmly. The next day I called on the Secretary of State.

He said, " Well, sir ?"

I said, " Your Royal Highness, on or about the 10th day of October, 1861, John Wilson Mackenzie, of Rotterdam, Chemung county, New Jersey, deceased, contracted with the General Government to furnish to General Sherman the sum total of thirty barrels of beef——"

" That will do, sir—that will do; this office has nothing to do with contracts for beef."

I was bowed out. I thought the matter all over, and finally, the following day, I visited the Secretary of the Navy, who said, " Speak quickly, sir; do not keep me waiting."

I said, " Your Royal Highness, on or about the 10th day of October, 1861, John Wilson Mackenzie, of Rotterdam, Chemung county, New Jersey, deceased, contracted with the General Government to furnish to General Sherman the sum total of thirty barrels of beef——"

Well, it was as far as I could get. *He* had nothing to do with beef contracts for General Sherman either. I began to think it was a curious kind of a Government. It looked somewhat as if they wanted to get out of paying for that beef. The following day I went to the Secretary of the Interior.

I said, " Your Imperial Highness, on or about the 10th day of October—"

" That is sufficient, sir. I have heard of you before.

Go, take your infamous beef contract out of this establishment. The Interior Department has nothing whatever to do with subsistence for the army."

I went away. But I was exasperated now. I said I would haunt them ; I would infest every department of this iniquitous Government till that contract business was settled. I would collect that bill, or fall, as fell my predecessors, trying. I assailed the Postmaster-General ; I besieged the Agricultural Department ; I waylaid the Speaker of the House of Representatives. *They* had nothing to do with army contracts for beef. I moved upon the Commissioner of the Patent Office.

I said, "Your August Excellency, on or about——"

"Perdition ! have you got *here* with your incendiary beef contract, at last ? We have *nothing* to do with beef contracts for the army, my dear sir."

" Oh, that is all very well—but *somebody* has got to pay for that beef. It has got to be paid *now*, too, or I'll confiscate this old Patent Office and everything in it."

" But, my dear sir——"

"It don't make any difference, sir. The Patent Office is liable for that beef, I reckon ; and, liable or not liable, the Patent Office has got to pay for it."

Never mind the details. It ended in a fight. The Patent Office won. But I found out something to my advantage. I was told that the Treasury Department was the proper place for me to go to. I went there. I waited two hours and a half, and then I was admitted to the First Lord of the Treasury.

I said, " Most noble, grave, and reverend Signor, on or
about the 10th day of October, 1861, John Wilson Mac-
ken——"

" That is sufficient, sir.   I have heard of you.   Go to
the First Auditor of the Treasury."

I did so.   He sent me to the Second Auditor.   The
Second Auditor sent me to the Third, and the Third sent
me to the First Comptroller of the Corn-Beef Division.
This began to look like business.   He examined his books
and all his loose papers, but found no minute of the beef
contract.   I went to the Second Comptroller of the Corn-
Beef Division.   He examined his books and his loose
papers, but with no success.   I was encouraged.   During
that week I got as far as the Sixth Comptroller in that
division; the next week I got through the Claims Department; the third week I began and completed the Mis-
laid Contracts Department, and got a foothold in the
Dead Reckoning Department.   I finished that in three
days.   There was only one place left for it now.   I laid
siege to the Commissioner of Odds and Ends.   To his Clerk
rather,—he was not there himself.   There were sixteen
beautiful young ladies in the room, writing in books, and
there were seven well-favoured young clerks showing
them how.   The young women smiled up over their
shoulders, and the clerks smiled back at them, and all
went merry as a marriage bell.   Two or three clerks that
were reading the newspapers looked at me rather hard,
but went on reading, and nobody said anything.   However, I had been used to this kind of alacrity from

Fourth-Assistant-Junior Clerks all through my eventful
career, from the very day I entered the first office of the
Corn-Beef Bureau clear till I had passed out of the last
one in the Dead Reckoning Division.   I had got so accomplished by this time that I could stand on one foot from
the moment I entered an office till a clerk spoke to me,
without changing more than two, or maybe three times.

So I stood there till I had changed four different times.
Then I said to one of the clerks who was reading—

"Illustrious Vagrant, where is the Grand Turk?"

"What do you mean, sir, whom do you mean?   If you
mean the Chief of the Bureau, he is out."

"Will he visit the harem to-day?"

The young man glared upon me awhile, and then went
on reading his paper.   But I knew the ways of those clerks.
I knew I was safe if he got through before another New
York mail arrived.   He only had two more papers left.
After a while he finished them, and then he yawned and
asked me what I wanted.

"Renowned and honoured Imbecile: On or about——"

"You are the beef contract man.   Give me your papers."

He took them, and for a long time he ransacked his
odds and ends.   Finally he found the North-West Passage, as *I* regarded it—he found the long-lost record of
that beef contract—he found the rock upon which so
many of my ancestors had split before they ever got to
it.   I was deeply moved.   And yet I rejoiced—for I had
survived.   I said with emotion, "Give it me.   The Govern-

ment will settle now." He waved me back, and said there was something yet to be done first.

"Where is this John Wilson Mackenzie?" said he.

" Dead."

"When did he die?"

"He didn't die at all—he was killed."

"How?"

"Tomahawked."

" Who tomahawked him?"

" Why, an Indian, of course. You didn't suppose it was the superintendent of a Sunday-school, did you?"

" No. An Indian, was it?"

" The same."

" Name of the Indian?"

" His name? *I* don't know his name."

" *Must* have his name. Who saw the tomahawking done?"

" I don't know."

" You were not present yourself, then?"

" Which you can see by my hair. I was absent."

" Then how do you know that Mackenzie is dead?"

" Because he certainly died at that time, and I have every reason to believe that he has been dead ever since. I *know* he has, in fact."

" We must have proofs. Have you got the Indian?"

" Of course not."

" Well, you must get him. Have you got the tomahawk?"

" I never thought of such a thing."

"You must get the tomahawk. You must produce the Indian and the tomahawk. If Mackenzie's death can be proven by these, you can then go before the commission appointed to audit claims with some show of getting your bill under such headway that your children may possibly live to receive the money and enjoy it. But that man's death *must* be proven. However, I may as well tell you that the Government will never pay that transportation and those travelling expenses of the lamented Mackenzie. It *may* possibly pay for the barrel of beef that Sherman's soldiers captured, if you can get a relief bill through Congress making an appropriation for that purpose; but it will not pay for the twenty-nine barrels the Indians ate."

"Then there is only a hundred dollars due me, and *that* isn't certain! After all Mackenzie's travels in Europe, Asia, and America with that beef; after all his trials and tribulations and transportation; after the slaughter of all those innocents that tried to collect that bill! Young man, why didn't the First Comptroller of the Corn-Beef Division tell me this?"

"He didn't know anything about the genuineness of your claim."

"Why didn't the Second tell me? why didn't the Third? why didn't all those divisions and departments tell me?"

"None of them knew. We do things by routine here. You have followed the routine and found out what you wanted to know. It is the best way. It is the only way. It is very regular, and very slow, but it is very certain."

"Yes, certain death. It has been, to the most of our tribe. I begin to feel that I, too, am called. Young man, you love the bright creature yonder with the gentle blue eyes and the steel pens behind her ears—I see it in your soft glances; you wish to marry her—but you are poor. Here, hold out you hand—here is the beef contract; go, take her and be happy! Heaven bless you, my children!"

This is all I know about the great beef contract, that has created so much talk in the community. The clerk to whom I bequeathed it died. I know nothing further about the contract, or any one connected with it. I only know that if a man lives long enough he can trace a thing through the Circumlocution Office of Washington, and find out, after much labour and trouble and delay, that which he could have found out on the first day if the business of the Circumlocution Office were as ingeniously systematized as it would be if it were a great private mercantile institution.

THE CASE OF GEORGE FISHER.*

THIS is history. It is not a wild extravaganza, like
"John Wilson Mackenzie's Great Beef Contract,"
but is a plain statement of facts and circumstances with
which the Congress of the United States has interested
itself from time to time during the long period of half a
century.

I will not call this matter of George Fisher's a great
deathless and unrelenting swindle upon the Government
and people of the United States—for it has never been
decided, and I hold that it is a grave and solemn wrong
for a writer to cast slurs or call names when such is the
case—but will simply present the evidence and let the
reader deduce his own verdict. Then we shall do nobody
injustice, and our consciences shall be clear.

On or about the 1st day of September 1813, the Creek

* Some years ago, when this was first published, few people believed it,
but considered it a mere extravaganza. In these latter days it seems hard to
realize that there was ever a time when the robbing of our government was
a novelty. The very man who showed me where to find the documents for
this case was at that very time spending hundreds of thousands of dollars
in Washington for a mail steamship concern, in the effort to procure a sub-
sidy for the company—a fact which was a long time coming to the surface,
but leaked out at last and underwent Congressional investigation.

war being then in progress in Florida, the crops, herds, and houses of Mr. George Fisher, a citizen, were destroyed, either by the Indians or by the United States troops in pursuit of them. By the terms of the law, if the *Indians* destroyed the property, there was no relief for Fisher; but if the *troops* destroyed it, the Government of the United States was debtor to Fisher for the amount involved.

George Fisher must have considered that the *Indians* destroyed the property, because, although he lived several years afterward, he does not appear to have ever made any claim upon the Government.

In the course of time Fisher died, and his widow married again. And by and by, nearly twenty years after that dimly-remembered raid upon Fisher's cornfields, *the widow Fisher's new husband* petitioned Congress for pay for the property, and backed up the petition with many depositions and affidavits which purported to prove that the troops, and not the Indians, destroyed the property; that the troops, for some inscrutable reason, deliberately burned down "houses" (or cabins) valued at $600, the same belonging to a peaceable private citizen, and also destroyed various other property belonging to the same citizen. But Congress declined to believe that the troops were such idiots (after overtaking and scattering a band of Indians proved to have been found destroying Fisher's property) as to calmly continue the work of destruction themselves, and make a complete job of what the Indians had only commenced. So Congress denied the petition

11

of the heirs of George Fisher in 1832, and did not pay them a cent.

We hear no more from them officially until 1848, sixteen years after their first attempt on the Treasury, and a full generation after the death of the man whose fields were destroyed. The new generation of Fisher heirs then came forward and put in a bill for damages. The Second Auditor awarded them $8,873, being half the damage sustained by Fisher. The Auditor said the testimony showed that at least half the destruction was done by the Indians *"before the troops started in pursuit,"* and of course the Government was not responsible for that half.

2. That was in April, 1848. In December, 1848, the heirs of George Fisher, deceased, came forward and pleaded for a " revision " of their bill of damages. The revision was made, but nothing new could be found in their favour except an error of $100 in the former calculation. However, in order to keep up the spirits of the Fisher family, the Auditor concluded to go back and allow *interest* from the date of the first petition (1832) to the date when the bill of damages was awarded. This sent the Fishers home happy with sixteen years' interest on $8,873 —the same amounting to $8,997.94. Total, $17,870.94.

3. For an entire year the suffering Fisher family remained quiet—even satisfied, after a fashion. Then they swooped down upon Government with their wrongs once more. That old patriot, Attorney-General Toucey, burrowed through the musty papers of the Fishers and discovered one more chance for the desolate orphans—in-

terest on that original award of $8,873 from date of de-
structio.· of the property (1813) up to 1832! Result, $10,-
004.89 for the indigent Fishers.   So now we have :—First,
$8,873 damages ; second, interest on it from 1832 to 1848,
$8,997.94 ; third, interest on it dated back to 1813. $10,-
004.89.   Total, $27,875.83 !   What better investment for
a great-grandchild than to get the Indians to burn a corn-
field for him sixty or seventy years before his birth, and
plausibly lay it on lunatic United States troops ?

4. Strange as it may seem, the Fishers let Congress
alone for five years—or, what is perhaps more likely, failed to make themselves heard by Congress for that length
of time.   But at last in 1854, they got a hearing.   They
persuaded Congress to pass an act requiring the Auditor
to re-examine their case.   But this time they stumbled
upon the misfortune of an honest Secretary of the Treasury (Mr. James Guthrie), and he spoiled everything.   He
said in very plain language that the Fishers were not only
not entitled to another cent, but that those children of
many sorrows and acquainted with grief *had been paid
too much already,*

5. Therefore another interval of rest and silence ensued
—an interval which lasted four years—viz., till 1858.   The
"right man in the right place" was then Secretary of War
—John B. Floyd, of peculiar renown !   Here was a master
intellect ; here was the very man to succour the suffering
heirs of dead and forgotten Fisher.   They came up from
Florida with a rush—a great tidal wave of Fishers freighted with the same old musty documents about the same

immortal cornfields of their ancestor. They straightway got an Act passed transferring the Fisher matter from the dull Auditor to the ingenious Floyd. What did Floyd do? He said, "IT WAS PROVED *that the Indians destroyed everything they could before the troops entered in pursuit.*" He considered, therefore, that what they destroyed must have consisted of "*the houses with all their contents, and the liquor*" (the most trifling part of the destruction, and set down at only $3,200 all told), and that the Government troops then drove them off and calmly proceeded to destroy—

Two hundred and twenty acres of corn in the field, thirty-five acres of wheat, and nine hundred and eighty-six head of live stock! [What a singularly intelligent army we had in those days, according to Mr. Floyd—though not according to the Congress of 1832.]

So Mr. Floyd decided that the Government was not responsible for that $3,200 worth of rubbish which the Indians destroyed, but was responsible for the property destroyed by the troops—which property consisted of (I quote from the printed United States Senate document)—

Corn at Bassett's Creek	3,000
Cattle	5,000
Stock hogs	1,050
Drove hogs	1,204
Wheat	350
Hides	4,000
Corn on the Alabama River	3,500
Total	18,104

That sum, in his report, Mr. Floyd calls the "*full value of the property destroyed by the troops.*" He allows that

sum to the starving Fishers, TOGETHER WITH INTEREST
FROM 1813. From this new sum total the amounts already paid to the Fishers were deducted, and then the
cheerful remainder (a fraction under *forty thousand dollars*) was handed to them, and again they retired to Florida in a condition of temporary tranquility. Their ancestor's farm had now yielded them, altogether, nearly *sixty-
seven thousand dollars* in cash.

6. Does the reader suppose that that was the end of it ?
Does he suppose those diffident Fishers were satisfied ?
Let the evidence show. The Fishers were quiet just two
years.—Then they came swarming up out of the fertile
swamps of Florida with their same old documents, and
besieged Congress once more. Congress capitulated on
the first of June, 1860, and instructed Mr. Floyd to over-
haul those papers again and pay that bill. A Treasury
clerk was ordered to go through those papers and report
to Mr. Floyd what amount was still due the emaciated Fishers. This clerk (I can produce him whenever he is wanted)
discovered what was apparently a glaring and recent
forgery in the papers, whereby a witness's testimony as
to the price of corn in Florida in 1813 was made to
name double the amount which that witness had originally specified as the price ! The clerk not only called his
superior's attention to this thing, but in making up his
brief of the case called particular attention to it in writing. That part of the brief *never got before Congress*, nor
has Congress ever yet had a hint of a forgery existing
among the Fisher papers. Nevertheless, on the basis of the

double prices (and totally ignoring the clerk's assertion
that the figures were manifestly and unquestionably a
recent forgery,) Mr. Floyd remarks in his new report that
the "testimony, *particularly in regard to the corn crops*
DEMANDS A MUCH HIGHER ALLOWANCE than any *heretofore*
made by the Auditor or myself." So he estimates the
crop at *sixty bushels* to the acre (double what Florida
acres produce), and then virtuously allows pay for only
half the crop, *but* allows *two dollars and a half* a bushel
for that half, when there are rusty old books and documents in the Congressional library to show just what the
Fisher testimony showed before the forgery—viz., that in
the fall of 1813 corn was only worth from $1.25 to $1.50
a bushel. Having accomplished this, what does Mr.
Floyd do next? Mr. Floyd ("with an earnest desire to
execute truly the legislative will," as he piously remarks)
goes to work and makes out an entirely new bill of Fisher
damages, and in this new bill he placidly *ignores the
Indians* altogether—puts no particle of the destruction
of the Fisher property upon them, but, even repenting
him of charging them with burning the cabins and drinking the whiskey and breaking the crockery, lays the *entire*
damage at the door of the imbecile United States troops,
down to the very last item! And not only that, but uses
the forgery to double the loss of corn at "Bassett's Creek,"
and uses it again to absolutely *treble* the loss of corn on
the "Alabama River." This new and ably conceived and
executed bill of Mr. Floyd's figures up as follows (I copy
again from the printed U. S. Senate document):—

The United States in account with the legal representatives of George Fisher, deceased.

	Dol.	C.
1813.—To 550 head of cattle, at 10 dollars..........	5,500	00
To 80 heads of drove hogs.......	1,204	00
To 350 head of stock hogs..................,......	1,750	00
To 100 ACRES OF CORN ON BASSETT'S CREEK...	6,000	00
To 8 barrels of whiskey.........	350	00
To 2 barrels of brandy.............................. .	280	00
To 1 barrel of rum..................................	70	00
To dry goods and merchandise in store.................	1,100	00
To 35 acres of wheat...........	350	00
To 2,000 hides	4,000	00
To furs and hats in store........	600	00
To crockery ware in store...........	100	00
To smiths' and carpenters' tools......................	250	00
To houses burned and destroyed......................	600	00
To 4 dozen bottles of wine..........................	48	00
1814.—To 120 acres of corn on Alabama River..............	9,500	00
To crops of peas, fodder, etc....................,....	3,250	00
Total...	34,952	00
To interest on $22,202, July 1813 to November 1860, 47 years and 4 months....................... ..	63,053	63
To interest on $12,750, from September 1814 to November 1860, 46 years and 2 months..............	35,317	50
Total...............	133,323	18

He puts everything in this time. He does not even allow that the Indians destroyed the crockery or drank the four dozen bottles of (currant) wine. When it came to supernatural comprehensiveness in "gobbling," John B. Floyd was without his equal, in his own or any other generation. Subtracting from the above total the $67,- 000 already paid to George Fisher's implacable heirs, Mr. Floyd announced that the Government was still indebted to them in the sum of *sixty-six thousand five hundred and nineteen dollars and eighty-five cents*, "which" Mr.

Floyd complacently remarks, "will be paid, accordingly, to the administrator of the estate of George Fisher, deceased, or to his attorney in fact."

But sadly enough for the destitute orphans, a new President came in just at this time, Buchanan and Floyd went out, and they never got their money. The first thing Congress did in 1861 was to rescind the resolution of June 1, 1860, under which Mr. Floyd had been ciphering. Then Floyd (and doubtless the heirs of George Fisher likewise) had to give up financial business for a while, and go into the Confederate army and serve their country.

Were the heirs of George Fisher killed? No. They are back now at this very time (July 1870), beseeching Congress through that blushing and diffident creature, Garrett Davis, to commence making payments again on their interminable and insatiable bill of damages for corn and whiskey destroyed by a gang of irresponsible Indians, so long ago that even government red-tape has failed to keep consistent and intelligent track of it.

Now, the above are facts. They are history. Any one who doubts it can send to the Senate Document Department of the Capitol for H. R. Ex. Doc. No. 21, 36th Congress, 2nd Session, and for S. Ex. Doc. No. 106, 41st Congress, 2nd Session, and satisfy himself. The whole case is set forth in the first volume of the Court of Claims Reports.

It is my belief that as long as the continent of America holds together, the heirs of George Fisher, deceased, will still make pilgrimages to Washington from the swamps of Florida, to plead for just a little more cash on their bill of damages (even when they received the last of that sixty-seven thousand dollars, they said it was only *one-fourth* what the Government owed them on that fruitful corn-field), and as long as they choose to come, they will find Garrett Davises to drag their vampire schemes before Congress. This is not the only hereditary fraud (if fraud it is—which I have before repeatedly remarked is not proven) that is being quietly handed down from generation to generation of fathers and sons, through the perse cuted Treasury of the United States.

THE JUDGE'S "SPIRITED WOMAN."

"I WAS sitting here," said the judge, "in this old pul-
pit, holding court, and we were trying a big, wicked-
looking Spanish desperado for killing the husband of a
bright, pretty Mexican woman.   It was a lazy summer
day, and an awfully long one, and the witnesses were
tedious.   None of us took any interest in the trial except that nervous, uneasy devil of a Mexican woman—
because you know how they love and how they hate, and
this one had loved her husband with all her might, and
now she had boiled it all down into hate, and stood there
spitting it at that Spaniard with her eyes; and I tell you
she would stir *me* up, too, with a little of her summer
lightning occasionally.   Well, I had my coat off and my
heels up, lolling and sweating, and smoking one of those
cabbage cigars the San Francisco people used to think
were good enough for us in those times; and the lawyers
they all had their coats off, and were smoking and whit-
tling, and the witnesses the same, and so was the prisoner.
Well, the fact is, there warn't any interest in a murder
trial then, because the fellow was always brought in
"not guilty," the jury expecting him to do as much for
them some time; and, although the evidence was straight

and square against this Spaniard, we knew we could not convict him without seeming to be rather high handed and sort of reflecting on every gentleman in the community; for there warn't any carriages and liveries then, and so the only 'style' there was, was to keep your private graveyard. But that woman seemed to have her heart set on hanging that Spaniard; and you'd ought to have seen how she would glare on him a minute, and then look up at me in her pleading way, and then turn and for the next five minutes search the jury's faces, and by and by drop her face in her hands for just a little while as if she was most ready to give up; but out she'd come again directly, and be as live and anxious as ever. But when the jury announced the verdict—Not Guilty, and I told the prisoner he was acquitted and free to go, that woman rose up till she appeared to be as tall and grand as a seventy-four-gun-ship, and says she—

"'Judge, do I understand you to say that this man is not guilty, that murdered my husband without any cause before my own eyes and my little children's, and that all has been done to him that ever justice and the law can do?'

"'The same,' says I.

"And then what do you reckon she did? Why, she turned on that smirking Spanish fool like a wild cat, and out with a 'navy' and shot him dead in open court!"

"That *was* spirited, I am willing to admit."

"Wasn't it, though?" said the judge, admiringly. "I wouldn't have missed it for anything. I adjourned court right on the spot, and we put on our coats and went out and took up a collection for her and her cubs, and sent them over the mountains to their friends. Ah, she was a spirited wench!"

MY LATE SENATORIAL SECRETARYSHIP.

I AM not a private secretary to a senator any more, now. I held the berth two months in security and in great cheerfulness of spirit, but my bread began to return from over the waters, then—that is to say, my works came back and revealed themselves. I judged it best to resign. The way of it was this. My employer sent for me one morning tolerably early, and, as soon as I had finished inserting some conundrums clandestinely into his last great speech upon finance, I entered the presence. There was something portentous in his appearance. His cravat was untied, his hair was in a state of disorder, and his countenance bore about it the signs of a suppressed storm. He held a package of letters in his tense grasp, and I knew that the dreaded Pacific mail was in. He said—

"I thought you were worthy of confidence."

I said, "Yes, sir."

He said, "I gave you a letter from certain of my constituents in the State of Nevada, asking the establishment of a post-office at Baldwin's Ranch, and told you to answer it, as ingeniously as you could, with arguments which should persuade them that there was no real necessity for an office at that place."

I felt easier. "Oh, if that is all, sir, I *did* do that."

"Yes, you *did*. I will read your answer, for your own humiliation :

" WASHINGTON, Nov. 24.

"'*Messrs. Smith, Jones, and others.*

"'GENTLEMEN : What the mischief do you suppose you want with a post-office at Baldwin's Ranch? It would not do you any good. If any letters came there, you couldn't read them, you know ; and, besides, such letters as ought to pass through, with money in them, for other localities, would not be likely to *get* through, you must perceive at once; and that would make trouble for us all. No, don't bother about a post-office in your camp. I have your best interests at heart, and feel that it would only be an ornamental folly. What you want is a nice jail, you know—a nice, substantial jail and a free school. These will be a lasting benefit to you. These will make you really contented and happy. I will move in the matter at once.

" 'Very truly, etc.,

" 'MARK TWAIN,

"'For James W. N**, U. S. Senator.'

"That is the way you answered that letter. Those people say they will hang me, if I ever enter that district again; and I am perfectly satisfied they *will*, too."

"Well, sir, I did not know I was doing any harm. I only wanted to convince them."

"Ah. Well you *did* convince them, I make no manner of doubt. Now, here is another specimen. I gave you a petition from certain gentleman of Nevada, praying that I would get a bill through Congress incorporating the Methodist Episcopal Church of the State of Nevada. I told you to say, in reply, that the creation of such a law came more properly within the province of the State Legislature; and to endeavour to show them that, in the present feebleness of the religious element in that new commonwealth, the expediency of incorporating the church was questionable. What did you write ?

> "'WASHINGTON, Nov. 24.
>
> "'*Rev. John Halifax and others.*
>
> "'GENTLEMEN: You will have to go to the State Legislature about that speculation of yours—Congress don't know anything about religion. But don't you hurry to go there, either; because this thing you propose to do out in that new country isn't expedient—in fact, it is ridiculous. Your religious people there are too feeble, in intellect, in morality, in piety—in everything, pretty much. You had better drop this—you can't make it work. You can't issue stock on an incorporation like that—or if you could, it would only keep you in trouble all the time. The other denominations would abuse it, and "bear" it, and "sell it short," and break it down. They would do with it just as they would with one of your silver mines out there—they would try to make all the world believe it was "wildcat." You ought not to do anything that is calculated to bring a sacred thing into disrepute. You ought to be ashamed of yourselves—that is what *I* think about it. You close your petition with the words: "And we will ever pray." I think you had better—you need to do it.
>
> "'Very truly, etc.,
>
> "'MARK TWAIN,
>
> "'For James W. N**, U. S. Senator.'

"*That* luminous epistle finishes me with the religious element among my constituents. But that my political murder might be made sure, some evil instinct prompted me to hand you this memorial from the grave company of elders composing the Board of Aldermen of the city of San Francisco, to try your hand upon—a memorial praying that the city's right to the water-lots upon the city front might be established by law of Congress. I told you this was a dangerous matter to move in. I told you to write a non-committal letter to the Aldermen—an ambiguous letter that should avoid, as far as possible, all real consideration and discussion of the water-lot ques-

tion. If there is any feeling left in you—any shame—
surely this letter you wrote, in obedience to that order,
ought to evoke it, when its words fall upon your ears:

WASHINGTON, NOV. 27.

" ' *The Hon. Board of Aldermen, etc.*

" 'GENTLEMEN : George Washington, the revered Father of his Country
is dead. His long and brilliant career is closed, alas! forever. He was
greatly respected in this section of the country, and his untimely decease
cast a gloom over the whole community. He died on the 14th day of December, 1799. He passed peacefully away from the scene of his honours and
his great achievements, the most lamented hero and the best beloved that
ever earth hath yielded unto Death. At such a time as this, *you* speak of
water-lots!—what a lot was his!

" 'What is fame? Fame is an accident. Sir Isaac Newton discovered
an apple falling to the ground—a trivial discovery, truly, and one which a
million men had made before him—but his parents were influential, and so
they tortured that small circumstance into something wonderful, and, lo!
the simple world took up the shout and, in almost the twinkling of an eye,
the man was famous. Treasure these thoughts.

" 'Poesy, sweet poesy, who shall estimate what the world owes to thee!

" Mary had a little lamb, its fleece was white as snow,
    And everywhere that Mary went the lamb was sure to go."

" Jack and Gill went up the hill
    To draw a pail of water ;
    Jack fell down and broke his crown,
    And Gill came tumbling after."

For simplicity, elegance of diction, and freedom from immoral tendencies,
I regard those two poems in the light of gems. They are suited to all grades
of intelligence, to every sphere of life — to the field, to the nursery, to the
guild. Especially should no Board of Aldermen be without them.

" 'Venerable fossils! write again. Nothing improves one so much as
friendly correspondence. Write again—and if there is anything in this memorial of yours that refers to anything in particular, do not be backward
about explaining it. We shall always be happy to hear you chirp.

" 'Very truly, etc.

" 'MARK TWAIN,

" 'For James W. N**, U. S. Senator.

"That is an atrocious, a ruinous epistle! Distraction!"

"Well, sir, I am really sorry if there is anything wrong about it—but—but it appears to me to dodge the water-lot question."

"Dodge the mischief! Oh!—but never mind. As long as destruction must come now, let it be complete. Let it be complete—let this last of your performances, which I am about to read, make a finality of it. I am a ruined man. I *had* my misgivings when I gave you the letter from Humboldt, asking that the post route from Indian Gulch to Shakespeare Gap and intermediate points, be changed partly to the old Mormon trail. But I told you it was a delicate question, and warned you to deal with it deftly—to answer it dubiously, and leave them a little in the dark. And your fatal imbecility impelled you to make *this* disastrous reply. I should think you would stop your ears, if you are not dead to all shame:

WASHINGTON, Nov. 30.

"'*Messrs. Perkins, Wagner, et al.*

"'GENTLEMEN: It is a delicate question about this Indian trail, but, handled with proper deftness and dubiousness, I doubt not we shall succeed in some measure or otherwise, because this place where the route leaves the Lassen Meadows, over beyond where those two Shawnee chiefs, Dilapidated-Vengeance and Biter-of-the-Clouds, were scalped last winter, this being the favourite direction to some, but others preferring something else in consequence of things, the Mormon trail leaving Mosby's at three in the morning, and passing through Jawbone Flat to Blucher, and then down by Jug-Handle, the road passing to the right of it, and naturally leaving it on the right, too, and Dawson's on the left of the trail where it passes to the left of said Dawson's and onward thence to Tomahawk, thus making the route cheaper, easier of access to all who can get at it, and compassing all the desirable objects so considered by others, and therefore, conferring the most good upon the greatest number, and, consequently, I am encouraged to hope we shall. However, I shall be ready, and happy, to afford you still further information npon the subject, from time to time, as you may desire it and the Post-office Department be enabled to furnish it to me.

"'Very truly, etc.

"'MARK TWAIN,

"'For James W. N**, U. S. Senator.'

"There—now *what* do you think of that?"

"Well, I don't know, sir.   It — well, it appears to me —to be dubious enough."

"Du—leave the house! I am a ruined man. Those Humboldt savages never will forgive me for tangling their brains up with this inhuman letter. I have lost the respect of the Methodist Church, the Board of Aldermen——"

"Well, I haven't anything to say about that, because I may have missed it a little in their cases, but I *was* too many for the Baldwin's Ranch people, General!"

"Leave the house!   Leave it for ever and for ever, too!"

I regarded that as a sort of covert intimation that my services could be dispensed with, and so I resigned.   I never will be a private secretary to a senator again.   You can't please that kind of people.   They don't know anything.   They can't appreciate a party's efforts.

RILEY—NEWSPAPER CORRESPONDENT.

———

ONE of the best men in Washington—or elsewhere—
is RILEY, correspondent of one of the great San
Francisco dailies.

Riley is full of humour, and has an unfailing vein of
irony, which makes his conversation to the last degree
entertaining (as long as the remarks are about somebody
else).   But, notwithstanding the possession of these qualities, which should enable a man to write a happy and an
appetizing letter, Riley's newspaper letters often display
a more than earthly solemnity, and likewise an unimagi-
native devotion to petrified facts, which surprise and distress all men who know him in his unofficial character.
He explains this curious thing by saying that his employ-
ers sent him to Washington to write facts, not fancy, and
that several times he has come near losing his situation
by inserting humorous remarks which, not being looked for at headquarters, and consequently not understood,
were thought to be dark and bloody speeches intended to
convey signals and warnings to murderous secret societies,
or something of that kind, and so were scratched out with
a shiver and a prayer and cast into the stove.   Riley says
that sometimes he is so afflicted with a yearning to write

a sparkling and absorbingly readable letter, that he simply cannot resist it, and so he goes to his den and revels
in the delight of untrammelled scribbling ; and then with
suffering such as only a mother can know, he destroys the
pretty children of his fancy and reduces his letter to the
required dismal accuracy. Having seen Riley do this very
thing more than once, I know whereof I speak. Often
I have laughed with him over a happy passage, and
grieved to see him plough his pen through it.   He
would say, "I had to write that or die; and I've got
to scratch it out or starve. *They* wouldn't stand it, you
know."

l think Riley is about the most entertaining company
I ever saw.   We lodged together in many places in Washington during the winter of '67-8, moving comfortably
from place to place, and attracting attention by paying
our board—a course which cannot fail to make a person
conspicuous in Washington.   Riley would tell all about
his trip to California in the early days, by way of the
Isthmus and the San Juan River ; and about his baking
bread in San Francisco to gain a living, and setting up
ten-pins, and practising law, and opening oysters, and
delivering lectures, and teaching French, and tending
bar, and reporting for the newspapers, and keeping dancing schools, and interpreting Chinese in the courts—
which latter was lucrative, and Riley was doing handsomely and laying up a little money, when people began
to find fault because his translations were too "free," a
thing for which Riley considered he ought not to be held

responsible, since he did not know a word of the Chinese
tongue, and only adopted interpreting as a means of gaining an honest livelihood.   Through the machinations of
enemies he was removed from the position of official in-
terpreter, and a man put in his place who was familiar
with the Chinese language, but did not know any English.   And Riley used to tell about publishing a newspaper up in what is Alaska now, but was only an iceberg
then, with a population composed of bears, walruses,
Indians, and other animals; and how the iceberg got
adrift at last, and left all his paying subscribers behind,
and as soon as the commonwealth floated out of the jur-
isdiction of Russia the people rose and threw off their
allegiance and ran up the English flag, calculating to hook
on and become an English colony as they drifted along
down the British Possessions; but a land breeze and a
crooked current carried them by, and they ran up the
Stars and Stripes and steered for California, missed the
connection again and swore allegiance to Mexico, but it
wasn't any use; the anchors came home every time, and
away they went with the north-east trades drifting off
side-ways toward the Sandwich Islands, whereupon they
ran up the Cannibal flag and had a grand human barba-
cue in honour of it, in which it was noticed that the better a man liked a friend the better he enjoyed him; and
as soon as they got fairly within the tropics the weather
got so fearfully hot that the iceberg began to melt, and it
got so sloppy under foot that it was almost impossible for
ladies to get about at all; and at last, just as they came in

sight of the islands, the melancholy remnant of the once majestic iceberg canted first to one side and then to the other, and then plunged under for ever, carrying the national archives along with it—and not only the archives and the populace, but some eligible town lots which had increased in value as fast as they diminished in size in the tropics, and which Riley could have sold at thirty cents a pound and made himself rich if he could have kept the province afloat ten hours longer and got her into port.

Riley is very methodical, untiringly accommodating, never forgets anything that is to be attended to, is a good son, a staunch friend, and a permanent reliable enemy. He will put himself to any amount of trouble to oblige a body, and therefore always has his hands full of things to be done for the helpless and shiftless. And he knows how to do nearly everything, too. He is a man whose native benevolence is a well-spring that never goes dry. He stands always ready to help whoever needs help, as far as he is able—and not simply with his money, for that is a cheap and common charity, but with hand and brain, and fatigue of limb and sacrifice of time. This sort of men is rare.

Riley has a ready wit, a quickness and aptness at se-lecting and applying quotations, and a countenance that is as solemn and as blank as the back side of a tombstone when he is delivering a particularly exasperating joke. One night a negro woman was burned to death in a house next door to us, and Riley said that our landlady would be oppressively emotional at breakfast, because she generally made use of such opportunities as offered, being of a morbidly sentimental turn, and so we should find it best to let her talk along and say nothing back— it was the only way to keep her tears out of the gravy. Riley said there never was a funeral in the neighbourhood but that the gravy was watery for a week.

And sure enough, at breakfast the landlady was down in the very sloughs of woe—entirely broken-hearted. Everything she looked at reminded her of that poor old negro woman, and so the buckwheat cakes made her sob, the coffee forced a groan, and when the beef-steak came on she fetched a wail that made our hair rise. Then she got to talking about deceased, and kept up a steady drizzle till both of us were soaked through and through.   Presently she took a fresh breath and said, with a world of sobs—

"Ah, to think of it, only to think of it!—the poor old faithful creature.   For she was *so* faithful.   Would you believe it, she had been a servant in that self-same house and that self-same family for twenty-seven years come Christmas, and never a cross word and never a lick! And, oh, to think she should meet such a death at last!—a-sitting over the red hot stove at three o'clock in the morning and went to sleep and fell on it and was actually *roasted* ! Not just frizzled up a bit, but literally roasted to a crisp! Poor faithful creature, how she *was* cooked ! I am but a poor woman, but even if I have to scrimp to do it, I will put up a tombstone over that lone sufferer's grave—and Mr. Riley if you would have the goodness to think up a little epitaph to put on it which would sort of describe the awful way in which she met her—"

"Put it, '*Well done*, good and faithful servant,'" said Riley, and never smiled.

SCIENCE vs. LUCK.

———

A T that time, in Kentucky, (said the Hon. Mr. K——),
the law was very strict against what is termed
"games of chance." About a dozen of the boys were detected playing "seven-up" or "old sledge" for money,
and the grand jury found a true bill against them. Jim
Sturgis was retained to defend them when the case came
up, of course. The more he studied over the matter, and
looked into the evidence, the plainer it was that he
must lose a case at last—there was no getting around
that painful fact. Those boys had certainly been betting
money on a game of chance. Even public sympathy was
roused in behalf of Sturgis. People said it was a pity to
see him mar his successful career with a big prominent
case like this, which must go against him.

But after several restless nights an inspired idea flashed
upon Sturgis, and he sprang out of bed delighted. He
thought he saw his way through. The next day he whispered around a little among his clients and a few friends,
and then when the case came up in court he acknowledged
the seven-up and the betting, and, as his sole defence, had
the astounding effrontery to put in the plea that old sledge
was not a game of chance! There was the broadest sort

of a smile all over the faces of that sophisticated audience. The judge smiled with the rest. But Sturgis maintained a countenance whose earnestness was even severe. The opposite counsel tried to ridicule him out of his position, and did not succeed. The judge jested in a ponderous judicial way about the thing, but did not move him. The matter was becoming grave. The judge lost a little of his patience, and said the joke had gone far enough. Jim Sturgis said he knew of no joke in the matter—his clients could not be punished for indulging in what some people chose to consider a game of chance until it was *proven* that it was a game of chance. Judge and counsel said that would be an easy matter, and forthwith called Deacons Job, Peters, Burke, and Johnson, and Dominies Wirt and Miggles, to testify; and they unanimously and with strong feeling put down the legal quibble of Sturgis by pronouncing that old sledge *was* a game of chance.

"What do you call it *now?*" said the judge.

"I call it a game of science!" retorted Sturgis; "and I'll prove it, too!"

They saw his little game.

He brought in a cloud of witnesses, and produced an overwhelming mass of testimony, to show that old sledge was not a game of chance but a game of science.

Instead of being the simplest case in the world, it had somehow turned out to be an excessively knotty one. The judge scratched his head over it a while, and said there was no way of coming to a determination, because just as many men could be brought into court who would testify on one side as could be found to testify on the other. But he said he was willing to do the fair thing by all parties, and would act upon any suggestion Mr. Sturgis would make for the solution of the difficulty.

Mr. Sturgis was on his feet in a second.

"Impanel a jury of six of each, Luck *versus* Science. Give them candles and a couple of decks of cards. Send them into a jury room, and just abide by the result!"

There was no disputing the fairness of the proposition. The four deacons and the two dominies were sworn in as the "chance" jurymen, and six inveterate old seven-up professors were chosen to represent the "science" side of the issue. They retired to the jury room.

In about two hours Deacon Peters sent into court to borrow three dollars from a friend. [Sensation.] In about two hours more Dominic Miggles sent into court to borrow a "stake" from a friend. [Sensation.] During the next three or four hours the other dominie and the other deacons sent into court for small loans. And still the packed audience waited, for it was a prodigious occasion in Bull's Corners, and one in which every father of a family was necessarily interested.

The rest of the story can be told briefly. About daylight the jury came in, and Deacon Job, the foreman, read the following

VERDICT.

We, the jury in the case of the Commonwealth of Kentucky vs. John Wheeler *et al.*, have carefully considered the points of the case, and tested the merits of the several theories advanced, and do hereby unanimously decide that the game commonly known as old sledge or seven-up is eminently a game of science and not of chance. In demonstration whereof it is hereby and herein stated, iterated, reiterated, set forth, and made manifest that, during the entire night, the " chance " men never won a game or turned a jack, although both feats were common and frequent to the opposition ; and furthermore, in support of this our verdict, we call attention to the significant fact that the " chance " men are all busted, and the " science " men have got the money. It is the deliberate opinion of this jury, that the " chance " theory concerning seven-up is a pernicious doctrine, and calculated to inflict untold suffering and pecuniary loss upon any community that takes stock in it.

" That is the way that seven-up came to be set apart and particularized in the statute-books of Kentucky as being a game not of chance but of science, and therefore not punishable under the law," said Mr. K——. " That verdict is of record, and holds good to this day."

THE KILLING OF JULIUS CÆSAR "LOCALIZED."

BEING THE ONLY TRUE AND RELIABLE ACCOUNT EVER PUBLISHED; TAKEN FROM THE ROMAN "DAILY EVENING FASCES," OF THE DATE OF THAT TREMENDOUS OCCURRENCE.

——

NOTHING in the world affords a newspaper reporter so much satisfaction as gathering up the details of a bloody and mysterious murder, and writing them up with aggravating circumstantiality. He takes a living delight in this labour of love—for such it is to him, especially if he knows that all the other papers have gone to press, and his will be the only one that will contain the dreadful intelligence. A feeling of regret has often come over me that I was not reporting in Rome when Cæsar was killed —reporting on an evening paper, and the only one in the city, and getting at least twelve hours ahead of the morning paper boys with this most magnificent "item" that ever fell to the lot of the craft. Other events have happened as startling as this, but none possessed so peculiarly all the characteristics of the favourite "item" of the present day, magnified into grandeur and sublimity by the high rank, fame, and social and political standing of the actors in it.

However, as I was not permitted to report Cæsar's assassination in the regular way, it has at least afforded me rare satisfaction to translate the following able account of it from the original Latin of the *Roman Daily Evening Fasces* of that date—second edition.

"Our usually quiet city of Rome was thrown into a state of wild excitement yesterday by the occurrence of one of those bloody affrays which sicken the heart and fill the soul with fear, while they inspire all thinking men with forebodings for the future of a city where human life is held so cheaply, and the gravest laws are so openly set at defiance. As the result of that affray, it is our painful duty, as public journalists, to record the death of one of our most esteemed citizens—a man whose name is known wherever this paper circulates, and whose fame it has been our pleasure and our privilege to extend, and also to protect from the tongue of slander and falsehood, to the best of our poor ability. We refer to Mr. J. Cæsar, the Emperor-elect.

"The facts of the case, as nearly as our reporter could determine them from the conflicting statements of eye-witnesses, were about as follows :—The affair was an election row, of course. Nine-tenths of the ghastly butcheries that disgrace the city now-a-days grow out of the bickerings and jealousies and animosities engendered by these accursed elections. Rome would be the gainer by it if her very constables were elected to serve a century ; for in our experience we have never even been able to choose a dog-pelter without celebrating the event with a dozen knock-downs and a general cramming of the station-house with drunken vagabonds over-night. It is said that when the immense majority for Cæsar at the polls in the market was declared the other day, and the crown was offered to that gentleman, even his amazing unselfishness in refusing it three times was not sufficient to save him from the whispered insults of such men as Casca, of the Tenth Ward, and the other hirelings of the disappointed candidate, hailing mostly from the Eleventh and Thirteenth and other outside districts, who were overheard speaking ironically and contemptuously of Mr. Cæsar's conduct upon that occasion.

"We are further informed that there are many among us who think they are justified in believing that the assassination of Julius Cæsar was a put-up thing —a cut-and-dried arrangement, hatched by Marcus Brutus and a lot of his hired roughs, and carried out only too faithfully according to the programme. Whether there be good grounds for this suspicion or not, we leave the people to judge for themselves, only asking that they will read the following account of the sad occurrence carefully and dispassionately before they render that judgment.

"The Senate was already in session, and Cæsar was coming down street towards the capitol, conversing with some personal friends, and followed as usual, by a large number of citizens. Just as he was passing in front of Demosthenes and Thucydides' drug-store, he was observing casually to a gentleman, who, our informant thinks, is a fortune-teller, that the Ides of March were come. The reply was, 'Yes, they are come, but not gone yet.' At this moment Artemidorus stepped up and passed the time of day, and asked Cæsar to read a schedule or a tract or something of the kind, which he had brought for his perusal. M. Decius Brutus also said something about an 'humble suit' which *he* wanted read. Artemidorus begged that attention might be paid to his first, because it was of personal consequence to Cæsar. The latter replied that what concerned himself should be read last, or words to that effect. Artemidorus begged and beseeched him to read the paper instantly.* However, Cæsar shook him off, and refused to read any petition in the street. He then entered the capitol and the crowd followed him.

"About this time the following conversation was overheard, and we consider that, taken in connection with the events which succeeded it, it bears an appalling significance : Mr. Papilius Lena remarked to George W. Cassius (commonly known as the 'Nobby Boy of the Third Ward'), a bruiser in the pay of the Opposition, that he hoped his enterprise to-day might thrive ; and when Cassius asked 'What enterprise ?' he only closed his left eye temporarily and said with simulated indifference, 'Fare you well,' and sauntered towards Cæsar. Marcus Brutus who is suspected of being the ringleader of the band that killed Cæsar, asked what it was that Lena had said. Cassius told him, and added in a low tone, '*I fear our purpose is discovered.*'

"Brutus told his wretched accomplice to keep an eye on Lena, and a moment after Cassius urged that lean and hungry vagrant, Casca whose reputation here is none of the best, to be sudden, for *he feared prevention.* He then turned to Brutus, apparently much excited, and asked what should be done, and swore that either he or Cæsar *should never turn back*—he would kill himself first. At this time Cæsar was talking to some of the back-country members about the approaching fall elections, and paying little attention to what was going on around him. Billy Trebonius got into conversation with the people's friend and Cæsar's—Mark Antony—and under some pretence or other got him away, and Brutus, Decius, Casca, Cinna, Metellus Cimber, and others of the gang of infamous desperadoes that infest Rome at present,

---

* Mark that: it is hinted by William Shakespeare, who saw the beginning and the end of the unfortunate affray, that this "schedule" was simply a note discovering to Cæsar that a plot was brewing to take his life.

closed around the doomed Cæsar.   Then Metellus Cimber knelt down and
begged that his brother might be recalled from banishment, but Cæsar re-
buked him for his fawning conduct, and refused to grant his petition.   Immediately, at Cimber's request, first Brutus and then Cassius begged for the
return of the banished Publius ; but Cæsar still refused.   He said he could
not be moved ; that he was as fixed as the North Star, and proceeded to speak
in the most complimentary terms of the firmness of that star, and its steady
character.   Then he said he was like it, and he believed he was the only man
in the country that was ; therefore, since he was 'constant' that Cimber
should be banished, he was also 'constant' that he should stay banished,
and he'd be hanged if he didn't keep him so !

"Instantly seizing upon this shallow pretext for a fight, Casca sprang at
Cæsar and struck him with a dirk, Cæsar grabbing him by the arm with his
right hand, and launching a blow straight from the shoulder with his left,
that sent the reptile bleeding to the earth.   He then backed up against
Pompey's statue, and squared himself to receive his assailants.   Cassius and
Cimber and Cinna rushed upon him with their daggers drawn, and the
former succeeded in inflicting a wound upon his body ; but before he could
strike again, and before either of the others could strike at all, Cæsar
stretched the three miscreants at his feet with as many blows of his powerful fist.   By this time the Senate was in an indescribable uproar ; the throng of
citizens in the lobbies had blockaded the doors in their frantic efforts to escape
from the building, the sergeant-at-arms and his assistants were struggling
with the assassins, venerable senators had cast aside their encumbering robes,
and were leaping over benches and flying down the aisles in wild confusion
towards the shelter of the committee-rooms, and a thousand voices were
shouting 'Po-lice ! Po-lice !' in discordant tones that rose above the frightful
din like shrieking winds above the roaring of the tempest.   And amid it all,
great Cæsar stood with his back against the statue, like a lion at bay, and
fought his assailants, weaponless and hand to hand, with the defiant bearing
and the unwavering courage which he had shown before on many a bloody
field.   Billy Trebonius and Caius Legarius struck him with their daggers
and fell, as their brother-conspirators before them had fallen.   But at last,
when Cæsar saw his old friend Brutus step forward armed with a murderous
knife, it is said he seemed utterly overpowered with grief and amazement,
and dropping his invincible left arm by his side, he hid his face in the folds
of his mantle and received the treacherous blow without an effort to stay
the hand that gave it.   He only said, ' *Et tu, Brute !*' and fell lifeless, on the
marble pavement.

"We learn that the coat deceased had on when he was killed was the
same he wore in his tent on the afternoon of the day he overcame the Nervii,
and that when it was removed from the corpse it was found to be cut and
gashed in no less than seven different places.   There was nothing in the

pockets. It will be exhibited at the coroner's inquest, and will be damning proof of the fact of the killing. These latter facts may be relied on, as we get them from Mark Antony, whose position enables him to learn every item of news connected with the one subject of absorbing interest of to-day.

"LATER.—While the coroner was summoning a jury, Mark Antony and other friends of the late Cæsar got hold of the body, and lugged it off to the Forum, and at last accounts Antony and Brutus were making speeches over it and raising such a row among the people that, as we go to press, the chief of police is satisfied there is going to be a riot, and is taking measures accordingly.

13

MR. BLOKE'S ITEM.

———

OUR esteemed friend, Mr. John William Bloke, of Virginia City, walked into the office where we are sub-editor at a late hour last night, with an expression of profound and heartfelt suffering upon his countenance, and sighing heavily, laid the following item reverently upon the desk, and walked slowly out again. He paused a moment at the door, and seemed struggling to command his feelings sufficiently to enable him to speak, and then, nodding his head toward his manuscript, ejaculated in a broken voice, " Friend of mine—oh ! how sad !" and burst into tears. We were so moved at his distress that we did not think to call him back and endeavour to comfort him until he was gone and it was too late. The paper had already gone to press, but knowing that our friend would consider the publication of this item important, and cherishing the hope that to print it would afford a melancholy satisfaction to his sorrowing heart, we stopped the press at once and inserted it in our columns:—

DISTRESSING ACCIDENT.—Last evening, about six o'clock, as Mr. William Schuyler, an old and respectable citizen of South Park, was leaving his residence to go down town, as has been his usual custom for many years with the exception only of a short interval in the spring of 1850, during which he was confined to his bed by injuries received in attempting to stop a run-away horse by thoughtlessly placing himself directly in its wake and throwing up his hands and shouting, which if he had done so even a single moment sooner, must inevitably have frightened the animal still more instead of checking its speed, although disastrous enough to himself as it was, and rendered more melancholy and distressing by reason of the presence of his wife's mother, who was there and saw the sad occurrence, notwithstanding it is at least likely, though not necessarily so, that she should be reconnoitering in another direction when incidents occur, not being vivacious and on the look out, as a general thing, but even the reverse, as her own mother is said to have stated, who is no more, but died in the full hope of a glorious resurrection, upwards of three years ago, aged eighty-six, being a Christian woman and without guile, as it were, or property, in consequence of the fire of 1819, which destroyed every single thing she had in the world. But such is life. Let us all take warning by this solemn occurrence, and let us endeavour so to conduct ourselves that when we come to die we can do it. Let us place our hands upon our heart, and say with earnestness and sincerity that from this day forth we will beware of the intoxicating bowl. —*First Edition of the Californian.*

The head editor has been in here raising the mischief, and tearing his hair and kicking the furniture about, and abusing me like a pick-pocket. He says that every time he leaves me in charge of the paper for half an hour, I get imposed upon by the first infant or the first idiot that comes along And he says that that distressing item of Mr. Bloke's is nothing but a lot of distressing bosh, and has no point to it, and no sense in it, and no information in it, and that there was no sort of necessity for stopping the press to publish it.

Now all this comes of being good-hearted. If I had been as unaccommodating and unsympathetic as some people, I would have told Mr. Bloke that I wouldn't receive his communication at such a late hour ; but no, his snuffling distress touched my heart, and I jumped at the

chance of doing something to modify his misery. I
never read his item to see whether there was anything
wrong about it, but hastily wrote the few lines which
preceded it, and sent it to the printers.   And what has
my kindness done for me?   It has done nothing but
bring down upon me a storm of abuse and ornamental
blasphemy.

Now I will read that item myself, and see if there is any
foundation for all this fuss.   And if there is, the author
of it shall hear from me.

    *   *   *   *   *   *   *   *   *

I have read it, and I am bound to admit that it seems
a little mixed at a first glance.   However, I will peruse
it once more.

    *   *   *   *   *   *   *   *   *

I have read it again, and it does really seem a good deal
more mixed than ever.

    *   *   *   *   *   *   *   *   *

I have read it over five times, but if I can get at the
meaning of it, I wish I may get my just deserts.   It
won't bear analysis.   There are things about it which I
cannot understand at all.   It don't say whatever became
of William Schuyler.   It just says enough about him to
get one interested in his career, and then drops him.   Who
is William Schuyler, anyhow, and what part of South
Park did he live in, and if he started down town at six
o'clock, did he ever get there, and if he did, did anything
happen to him?   Is *he* the individual that met with the
‘ distressing accident?”   Considering the elaborate cir-

cumstantiality of detail observable in the item, it seems
to me that it ought to contain more information than it
does.   On the contrary, it is obscure—and not only obscure, but utterly incomprehensible.   Was the breaking
of Mr. Schuyler's leg, fifteen years ago, the "distressing
accident" that plunged Mr. Bloke into unspeakable grief,
and caused him to come up here at dead of night and stop
our press to acquaint the world with the circumstance ?
Or did the "distressing accident" consist in the destruction of Schuyler's mother-in-law's property in early times ?
Or did it consist in the death of that person herself
three years ago ? (albeit it does not appear that she died
by accident.)   In a word, what *did* that "distressing accident" consist in ?   What did that drivelling ass of a
Schuyler stand *in the wake* of a runaway horse for, with
his shouting and gesticulating, as if he wanted to stop
him ?   And how the mischief could he get run over by
a horse that had already passed beyond him ?   And what
are we to take "warning" by ? and how is this extraordinary chapter of incomprehensibilities going to be a "lesson"
to us ?   And, above all, what has the intoxicating "bowl"
got to do with it, anyhow ?   It is not stated that Schuyler
drank, or that his wife drank, or that his mother-in-law
drank, or that the horse drank—wherefore, then, the refer-
ence to the intoxicating bowl ?   It does seem to me that
if Mr. Bloke had let the intoxicating bowl alone himself,
he never would have got into so much trouble about this
exasperating imaginary accident.   I have read this absurd
item over and over again, with all its insinuating plausi-

bility, until my head swims; but I can make neither head nor tail of it. There certainly seems to have been an accident of some kind or other, but it is impossible to determine what the nature of it was, or who was the sufferer by it. I do not like to do it, but I feel compelled to request that the next time anything happens to one of Mr. Bloke's friends, he will append such explanatory notes to his account of it as will enable me to find out what sort of an accident it was and whom it happened to. I had rather all his friends should die than that I should be driven to the verge of lunacy again in trying to cipher out the meaning of another such production as the above.

A MEDIÆVAL ROMANCE.

CHAPTER I.—THE SECRET REVEALED.

IT was night. Stillness reigned in the grand old feudal Castle of Klugenstein. The year 1222 was drawing to a close. Far away up in the tallest of the castle's towers a single light glimmered. A secret council was being held there. The stern old lord of Klugenstein sat in a chair of state meditating. Presently he said, with a tender accent—"My daughter?"

A young man of noble presence, clad from head to heel in knightly mail, answered—"Speak, father!"

"My daughter, the time has come for the revealing of the mystery that hath puzzled all your young life. Know, then, that it had its birth in the matters which I shall now unfold. My brother Ulrich is the great Duke of Brandenburgh. Our father, on his deathbed, decreed that if no son were born to Ulrich the succession should pass to my house, provided a *son* were born to me. And further, in case no son were born to either, but only daughters, then the succession should pass to Ulrich's daughter if she proved stainless; if she did not, my daughter should succeed if she retained a blameless name

And so I and my old wife here prayed fervently for the good boon of a son, but the prayer was vain. You were born to us. I was in despair. I saw the mighty prize slipping from my grasp—the splendid dream vanishing away! And I had been so hopeful! Five years had Ulrich lived in wedlock, and yet his wife had borne no heir of either sex.

"'But hold,' I said, 'all is not lost.' A saving scheme had shot athwart my brain. You were born at midnight. Only the leech, the nurse, and six waiting-women knew your sex. I hanged them every one before an hour sped. Next morning all the barony went mad with rejoicing over the proclamation that a *son* was born to Klugenstein —an heir to mighty Bradenburgh! And well the secret has been kept. Your mother's own sister nursed your infancy, and from that time forward we feared nothing.

"When you were ten years old a daughter was born to Ulrich. We grieved, but hoped for good results from measles, or physicians, or other natural enemies of infancy, but were always disappointed. She lived, she throve—Heaven's malison upon her! But it is nothing. We are safe. For, ha! ha! have we not a son? And is not our son the future Duke? Our well-beloved Conrad, is it not so?—for woman of eight-and-twenty years as you are, my child, none other name than that hath ever fallen to *you!*

"Now it hath come to pass that age hath laid its hand upon my brother, and he waxes feeble. The cares of state do tax him sore, therefore he wills that you shall come to him and be already Duke in act, though not yet in name. Your servitors are ready — you journey forth to-night.

"Now listen well. Remember every word I say. There is a law as old as Germany, that if any woman sit for a single instant in the great ducal chair before she hath been absolutely crowned in presence of the people—SHE SHALL DIE! So heed my words. Pretend humility. Pronounce your judgments from the Premier's chair, which stands at the *foot* of the throne. Do this until you are crowned and safe. It is not likely that your sex will ever be discovered, but still it is the part of wisdom to make all things as safe as may be in this treacherous earthly life."

"O my father! is it for this my life hath been a lie: Was it that I might cheat my unoffending cousin of her rights? Spare me, father, spare your child?"

"What, hussy! Is this my reward for the august fortune my brain has wrought for thee? By the bones of my father, this puling sentiment of thine but ill accords with my humour. Betake thee to the Duke instantly, and beware how thou meddlest with my purpose!"

Let this suffice of the conversation. It is enough for us to know that the prayers, the entreaties, and the tears of the gentle-natured girl availed nothing. Neither they nor anything could move the stout old lord of Klugenstein. And so, at last, with a heavy heart, the daughter saw the castle gates close behind her, and found herself riding away in the darkness surrounded by a knightly array of armed vassals and a brave following of servants.

The old baron sat silent for many minutes after his daughter's departure, and then he turned to his sad wife, and said—

"Dame, our matters seem speeding fairly. It is ful three months since I sent the shrewd and handsome Count Detzin on his devilish mission to my brother's daughter Constance. If he fail we are not wholly safe, but if he do succeed no power can bar our girl from being Duchess, e'en though ill fortune should decree she never should be Duke!"

"My heart is full of bodings; yet all may still be well."

"Tush, woman! Leave the owls to croak. To bed with ye, and dream of Brandenburgh and grandeur!"

CHAPTER II.—FESTIVITY AND TEARS.

Six days after the occurrences related in the above chapter, the brilliant capitol of the Duchy of Brandenburgh was resplendent with military pageantry, and noisy with the rejoicings of loyal multitudes, for Conrad, the young heir to the crown, was come. The old Duke's heart was full of happiness, for Conrad's handsome person and graceful bearing had won his love at once. The great halls of the palace were thronged with nobles, who welcomed Conrad bravely; and so bright and happy did all things seem, that he felt his fears and sorrows passing away, and giving place to a comforting contentment.

But in a remote apartment of the palace a scene of a different nature was transpiring. By a window stood the

Duke's only child, the Lady Constance. Her eyes were red and swollen, and full of tears. She was alone. Presently she fell to weeping anew, and said aloud—

"The villain Detzin is gone—has fled the dukedom! I could not believe it at first, but, alas! it is too true. And I loved him so. I dared to love him though I knew the Duke my father would never let me wed him. I loved him—but now I hate him! With all my soul I hate him! Oh, what is to become of me? I am lost, lost, lost! I shall go mad!"

CHAPTER III.—THE PLOT THICKENS.

A few months drifted by. All men published the praises of the young Conrad's government, and extolled the wisdom of his judgments, the mercifulness of his sentences, and the modesty with which he bore himself in his great office. The old Duke soon gave everything into his hands, and sat apart and listened with proud satisfaction while his heir delivered the decrees of the crown from the seat of the Premier. It seemed plain that one so loved and praised and honoured of all men as Conrad was could not be otherwise than happy. But, strangely enough, he was not. For he saw with dismay that the Princess Constance had begun to love him! The love of the rest of the world was happy fortune for him, but this was freighted with danger! And he saw, moreover, that the delighted Duke had discovered his daughter's passion likewise, and was already dreaming of a marriage. Every day somewhat of the deep sadness that had been in the princess's face faded away; every day hope and animation beamed brighter from her eye; and by and by even vagrant smiles visited the face that had been so troubled.

Conrad was appalled. He bitterly cursed himself for having yielded to the instinct that had made him seek the companionship of one of his own sex when he was new and a stranger in the palace—when he was sorrowful and yearned for a sympathy such as only women can give or feel. He now began to avoid his cousin. But this only made matters worse, for naturally enough, the more he avoided her the more she cast herself in his way. He marvelled at this at first, and next it startled him. The girl haunted him; she hunted him; she happened upon him at all times and in all places, in the night as well as in the day. She seemed singularly anxious. There was surely a mystery somewhere.

This could not go on forever. All the world was talking about it. The Duke was beginning to look perplexed. Poor Conrad was becoming a very ghost through dread and dire distress. One day as he was emerging from a private ante room attached to the picture gallery Constance confronted him, and seizing both his hands in hers, exclaimed—

"Oh, why do you avoid me? What have I done— what have I said, to lose your kind opinion of me—for surely I had it once? Conrad, do not despise me, but pity a tortured heart? I cannot, cannot hold the words unspoken longer, lest they kill me—I LOVE YOU, CONRAD!

There despise me if you must, but they *would* be uttered!"

Conrad was speechless. Constance hesitated a moment, and then, misinterpreting his silence, a wild gladness flamed in her eyes, and she flung her arms about his neck and said—

"You relent! you relent! You *can* love me—you *will* love me! Oh, say you will, my own, my worshipped Conrad!"

Conrad groaned aloud. A sickly pallor overspread his countenance, and he trembled like an aspen. Presently, in desperation, he thrust the poor girl from him, and cried—

"You know not what you ask! It is forever and ever impossible!" And then he fled like a criminal, and left the Princess stupified with amazement. A minute afterward she was crying and sobbing there, and Conrad was crying and sobbing in his chamber. Both were in despair. Both saw ruin staring them in the face.

By and by Constance rose slowly to her feet and moved away, saying—

"To think that he was despising my love at the very moment that I thought it was melting his cruel heart! I hate him! He spurned me—did this man—he spurned me from him like a dog!"

CHAPTER IV.—THE AWFUL REVELATION.

Time passed on. A settled sadness rested once more upon the countenance of the good Duke's daughter. She and Conrad were seen together no more now. The Duke grieved at this. But as the weeks wore away Conrad's colour came back to his cheeks, and his old-time vivacity to his eye, and he administered the government with a clear and steadily ripening wisdom.

Presently a strange whisper began to be heard about the palace. It grew louder; it spread farther. The gossips of the city got hold of it. It swept the dukedom. And this is what the whisper said—

"The Lady Constance hath given birth to a child!"

When the lord of Klugenstein heard it he swung his plumed helmet thrice around his head and shouted—

" Long live Duke Conrad!—for, lo, his crown is sure from this day forward! Detzin has done his errand well, and the good scoundrel shall be rewarded!"

And he spread the tidings far and wide, and for eight-and-forty hours no soul in all the barony but did dance and sing, carouse and illuminate, to celebrate the great event, and all at proud and happy old Klugenstein's expense.

CHAPTER V.—THE FRIGHTFUL CATASTROPHE.

The trial was at hand. All the great lords and barons of Brandenburg were assembled in the Hall of Justice in the ducal palace. No space was left unoccupied where there was room for a spectator to stand or sit. Conrad, clad in purple and ermine, sat in the Premier's chair, and on either side sat the great judges of the realm. The old Duke had sternly commanded that the trial of his daughter should proceed without favour, and then had taken to his bed broken-hearted. His days were numbered. Poor Conrad had begged, as for his very life, that he might be spared the misery of sitting in judgement upon his cousin's crime, but it did not avail.

The saddest heart in all that great assemblage was in Conrad's breast.

The gladdest was in his father's, for, unknown to his daughter "Conrad," the old Baron Klugenstein was come, and was among the crowd of nobles triumphant in the swelling fortunes of his house.

After the heralds had made due proclamation and the other preliminaries had followed, the venerable Lord Chief-Justice said—"Prisoner, stand forth !"

The unhappy princess rose, and stood unveiled before the vast multitude. The Lord Chief-Justice continued—

"Most noble lady, before the great judges of this realm it hath been charged and proven that out of holy wedlock your Grace hath given birth unto a child, and by our ancient law the penalty is death excepting in one sole contingency, whereof his Grace the acting Duke, our good Lord Conrad, will advertise you in his solemn sentence now ; wherefore give heed."

Conrad stretched forth his reluctant sceptre, and in the self-same moment the womanly heart beneath his robe yearned pityingly toward the doomed prisoner, and the tears came into his eyes. He opened his lips to speak but the Lord Chief-Justice said quickly—

" Not there, your Grace, not there ! It is not lawful to pronounce judgment upon any of the ducal line SAVE FROM THE DUCAL THRONE !"

A shudder went to the heart of poor Conrad, and a tremor shook the iron frame of his old father likewise. CONRAD HAD NOT BEEN CROWNED—dared he profane the throne ? He hesitated and turned pale with fear. But it must be done. Wondering eyes were already upon him. They would be suspicious eyes if he hesitated longer. He ascended the throne. Presently he stretched forth the sceptre again, and said—

" Prisoner, in the name of our sovereign Lord Ulrich, Duke of Brandenburgh, I proceed to the solemn duty that hath devolved upon me. Give heed to my words. By the ancient law of the land, except you produce the partner of your guilt and deliver him up to the executioner you must surely die. Embrace this opportunity— save yourself while yet you may. Name the father of your child !"

A solemn hush fell upon the great court—a silence so profound that men could hear their own hearts beat. Then the princess slowly turned, with eyes gleaming with hate, and pointing her finger straight at Conrad said—

" Thou art the man !"

An appalling conviction of his helpless, hopeless peril struck a chill to Conrad's heart like the chill of death it-self. What power on earth could save him ? To disprove the charge he must reveal that he was a woman, and for an uncrowned woman to sit in the ducal chair was death! At one and the same moment he and his grim old father swooned and fell to the ground.

*　*　*　*　*　*　*　*　*

The remainder of this thrilling and eventful story will NOT be found in this or any other publication, either now or at any future time.

The truth is, I have got my hero (or heroine) into such a particularly close place that I do not see how I am ever going to get him (or her) out of it again, and therefore I will wash my hands of the whole business, and leave that person to get out the best way that offers—or else stay there. I thought it was going to be easy enough to straighten out that little difficulty, but it looks different now.

AFTER-DINNER SPEECH.

[AT A FOURTH-OF-JULY GATHERING, IN LONDON, OF
AMERICANS.]

———

M R. CHAIRMAN AND LADIES AND GENTLEMEN: I
thank you for the compliment which has just been
tendered me, and to show my appreciation of it I will not
afflict you with many words. It is pleasant to celebrate
in this peaceful way, upon this old mother soil, the anniversary of an experiment which was born of war with
this same land so long ago, and wrought out to a successful issue by the devotion of our ancestors. It has taken
nearly a hundred years to bring the English and Americans into kindly and mutually appreciative relations, but
I believe it has been accomplished at last. It was a great
step when the two last misunderstandings were settled
by arbitration instead of cannon. It is another great
step when England adopts our sewing machines without
claiming the invention—as usual. It was another when
they imported one of our sleeping cars the other day.
And it warmed my heart more than I can tell, yesterday,
when I witnessed the spectacle of an Englishman ordering
an American sherry cobbler of his own free will and ac-

cord—and not only that but with a great brain and a level head reminding the bar-keeper not to forget the strawberries.   With a common origin, a common language, a common literature, a common religion and—common drinks, what is longer needful to the cementing of the two nations together in a permanent bond of brotherhood ?

This is an age of progress, and ours is a progressive land.   A great and glorious land, too—a land which has developed a Washington, a Franklin, a Wm. M. Tweed, a Longfellow, a Motley, a Jay Gould, a Samuel C. Pomeroy, a recent Congress which has never had its equal (in some respects) and a United States Army which conquered sixty Indians in eight months by tiring them out—which is much better than uncivilized slaughter, God knows. We have a criminal jury system which is superior to any in the world ; and its efficiency is only marred by the difficulty of finding twelve men every day who don't know anything and can't read.   And I may observe that we have an insanity plea that would have saved Cain.   I think I can say, and say with pride, that we have some legislatures that bring higher prices than any in the world.

I refer with effusion to our railway system, which consents to let us live, though it might do the opposite, being our owners.   It only destroyed three thousand and seventy lives last year by collisions, and twenty-seven thousand two hundred and sixty by running over heedless and unnecessary people at crossings.   The companies seriously regretted the killing of these thirty thousand people, and went so far as to pay for some of them—voluntarily, of course, for the meanest of us would not claim that we possess a court treacherous enough to enforce a law against a railway company.   But thank Heaven the railway companies are generally disposed to do the right and kindly thing without compulsion.   I know of an instance which greatly touched me at the time.   After an accident the company sent home the remains of a dear distant old relative of mine in a basket, with the remark, " Please state what figure you hold him at—and return the basket."   Now there couldn't be anything friendlier than that.

But I must not stand here and brag all night.   However, you won't mind a body bragging a little about his country on the fourth of July.   It is a fair and legitimate time to fly the eagle.   I will say only one more word of brag—and a hopeful one.   It is this.   We have a form of government which gives each man a fair chance and no favour.   With us no individual is born with a right to look down upon his neighbour and hold him in contempt. Let such of us as are not dukes find our consolation in that.   And we may find hope for the future in the fact that as unhappy as is the condition of our political morality to-day, England has risen up out of a far fouler since the days when Charles I. ennobled courtezans and all political place was a matter of bargain and sale.   There is hope for us yet. *

* At least the above is the speech which I was *going* to make, but our minister, Gen. Schenck, presided, and after the blessing, got up and made a great long, inconceivably dull harangue, and wound up by saying that inas-

LIONISING MURDERERS.

I HAD heard so much about the celebrated fortune-teller Madame ——, that I went to see her yesterday. She has a dark complexion naturally, and this effect is heightened by artificial aids which cost her nothing. She wears curls—very black ones, and I had an impression that she gave their native attractiveness a lift with rancid butter. She wears a reddish check handkerchief, cast loosely around her neck, and it was plain that her other one is slow in getting back from the wash. I presume she takes snuff. At any rate, something resembling it had lodged among the hairs sprouting from her upper lip. I know she likes garlic—I knew that as soon as she sighed. She looked at me searchingly for nearly a minute, with her black eyes, and then said—

---

much as speech-making did not seem to exhilarate the guests much, all further oratory would be dispensed with, during the evening, and we could just sit and talk privately to our elbow-neighbours and have a good sociable time. It is known that in consequence of that remark forty-four perfected speeches died in the womb. The depression, the gloom, the solemnity that reigned over the banquet from that time forth will be a lasting memory with many that were there. By that one thoughtless remark Gen. Schenck lost forty-four of the best friends he had in England. More than one said that night, "And this is the sort of person that is sent to represent us in a great sister-empire!"

"It is enough.   Come!"

She started down a very dark and dismal corridor—I stepping close after her.   Presently she stopped, and said that, as the way was so crooked and dark, perhaps she had better get a light.   But it seemed ungallant to allow a woman to put herself to so much trouble for me, and so I said—

"It is not worth while, madam.   If you will heave another sigh, I think I can follow it."

So we got along all right.   Arrived at her official and mysterious den, she asked me to tell her the date of my birth, the exact hour of that occurrence, and the colour of my grandmother's hair.   I answered as accurately as I could.   Then she said—

"Young man, summon your fortitude—do not tremble. I am about to reveal the past."

"Information concerning the *future* would be, in a general way, more"——

"Silence!   You have had much trouble, some joy, some good fortune, some bad.   Your great-grandfather was hanged."

"That is a l—."

"Silence!   Hanged, sir.   But it was not his fault.   He could not help it."

"I am glad you do him justice."

"Ah—grieve, rather, that the jury did.   He was hanged.   His star crosses yours in the fourth division, fifth sphere.   Consequently you will be hanged also."

"In view of this cheerful"——

"I *must* have silence. Yours was not, in the beginning, a criminal nature, but circumstances changed it. At the age of nine you stole sugar. At the age of fifteen you stole money. At twenty you stole horses. At twenty-five you committed arson. At thirty, hardened in crime, you became an editor. You are now a public lecturer. Worse things are in store for you. You will be sent to Congress. Next, to the penitentiary. Finally, happiness will come again—all will be well—you will be hanged."

I was now in tears. It seemed hard enough to go to Congress; but to be hanged—this was too sad, too dreadful. The woman seemed surprised at my grief. I told her the thoughts that were in my mind. Then she comforted me.

"Why, man," * she said, "hold up your head—*you*

---

* In this paragraph the fortune-teller details the exact history of the Pike-Brown assassination case in New Hampshire, from the succouring and saving of the stranger Pike by the Browns, to the subsequent hanging and coffining of that treacherous miscreant. She adds nothing, invents nothing, exaggerates nothing (see any New England paper for November 1869). This Pike-Brown case is selected merely as a type, to illustrate a custom that prevails, not in New Hampshire alone, but in every State in the union—I mean the sentimental custom of visiting, petting, glorifying, and snuffling over murderers like this Pike, from the day they enter the jail under sentence of death until they swing from the gallows. The following extract from the *Temple Bar* (1866) reveals the fact that this custom is not confined to the United States:—"On December 31st, 1841, a man named John Johnes, a shoemaker, murdered his sweetheart, Mary Hallam, the daughter of a respectable labourer, at Mansfield, in the county of Nottingham. He was executed on March 23, 1842. He was a man of unsteady habits, and gave way to violent fits of passion. The girl declined his addresses, and he said if he did not have her no one else should. After he had inflicted the first wound, which was not immediately fatal, she begged for her life, but seeing him

have nothing to grieve about.   Listen.   You will live in
New Hampshire.   In your sharp need and distress the
Brown family will succour you—such of them as Pike the
assassin left alive.   They will be benefactors to you.
When you shall have grown fat upon their bounty, and
are grateful and happy, you will desire to make some
modest return for these things, and so you will go
to the house some night and brain the whole family with
an axe.   You will rob the dead bodies of your benefactors, and disburse your gains in riotous living among the
rowdies and courtesans of Boston.   Then you will be arrested, tried, condemned to be hanged, thrown into pri-
son.   Now is your happy day.   You will be converted—
you will be converted just as soon as every effort to com-
pass pardon, commutation, or reprieve has failed—and
then!   Why then, every morning and every afternoon,
the best and purest young ladies of the village
will assemble in your cell and sing hymns.   This will
show that assassination is respectable.   Then you will
write a touching letter, in which you will forgive all those

resolved, asked for time to pray   He said that he would pray for both, and
completed the crime   The wounds were inflicted by a shoemaker's knife,
and her throat was cut barbarously   After this he dropped on his knees some
time, and prayed God to have mercy on two unfortunate lovers.   He made
no attempt to escape, and confessed the crime.   After his imprisonment he
behaved in the most decorous manner ; he won upon the good opinion of the
jail chaplain, and he was visited by the Bishop of Lincoln.   It does not appear that he expressed any contrition for the crime, but seemed to pass
away with triumphant certainty that he was going to rejoin his victim in
heaven.   *He was visited by some pious and benevolent ladies of Nottingham,
some of whom declared he was a child of God, if ever there was one.   One of the
ladies sent him a white camelia to wear at his execution.*"

recent Browns. This will excite the public admiration. No public can withstand magnanimity. Next, they will take you to the scaffold, with great *eclat*, at the head of an imposing procession composed of clergymen, officials, citizens generally, and young ladies walking pensively two and two, and bearing bouquets and immortelles. You will mount the scaffold, and while the great concourse stand uncovered in your presence, you will read your sappy little speech which the minister has written for you. And then, in the midst of a grand and impressive silence, they will swing you into per—— Paradise, my son. There will not be a dry eye on the ground. You will be a hero! Not a rough there but will envy you. Not a rough there but will resolve to emulate you. And next, a great procession will follow you to the tomb—will weep over your remains—the young ladies will sing again the hymns made dear by sweet associations connected with the jail, and, as a last tribute of affection, respect, and appreciation of your many sterling qualities, they will walk two and two around your bier, and strew wreaths of flowers on it. And lo! you are canonized. Think of it, son—ingrate, assassin, robber of the dead, drunken brawler among thieves and harlots in the slums of Boston one month, and the pet of the pure and innocent daughters of the land the next! A bloody and hateful devil—a bewept, bewailed, and sainted martyr—all in a month! Fool!—so noble a fortune, and yet you sit here grieving."

"No madame," I said, "you do me wrong, you do indeed. I am perfectly satisfied. I did not know before that my great-grandfather was hanged, but it is of no consequence. He has probably ceased to bother about it by this time—and I have not commenced yet. I confess, madame, that I do something in the way of editing and lecturing, but the other crimes you mentioned have escaped my memory. Yet I must have committed them, —you would not deceive a stranger. But let the past be as it was, and let the future be as it may—these are nothing. I have only cared for one thing. I have always felt that I should be hanged some day, and somehow the thought has annoyed me considerably; but if you can only assure me that I shall be hanged in New Hampshire "——

" Not a shadow of doubt !"

" Bless you, my benefactress !—excuse this embrace— you have removed a great load from my breast. To be hanged in New Hampshire is happiness—it leaves an honoured name behind a man, and introduces him at once into the best New Hampshire society in the other world."

I then took leave of the fortune-teller. But, seriously, is it well to glorify a murderous villain on the scaffold, as Pike was glorified in New Hampshire ? Is it well to turn the penalty for a bloody crime into a reward ? Is it just to do it ? Is it sate ?

A NEW CRIME.

LEGISLATION NEEDED.

THIS country, during the last thirty or forty years, has produced some of the most remarkable cases of insanity of which there is any mention in history. For instance, there was the Baldwin case, in Ohio, twenty-two years ago. Baldwin, from his boyhood up, had been of a vindictive, malignant, quarrelsome nature. He put a boy's eye out once, and never was heard upon any occasion to utter a regret for it. He did many such things. But at last he did something that was serious. He called at a house just after dark, one evening, knocked, and when the occupant came to the door, shot him dead, and then tried to escape, but was captured. Two days before, he had wantonly insulted a helpless cripple, and the man he afterward took swift vengeance upon with an assassin bullet had knocked him down. Such was the Baldwin case. The trial was long and exciting: the community was fearfully wrought up. Men said this spiteful, bad-hearted villain had caused grief enough in his time, and now he should satisfy the law. But they were mistaken; Baldwin was *insane* when he did the deed — they had not thought of that. By the arguments of counsel it was shown that at half-past ten in the morning on the day of the murder, Baldwin became insane, and remained so for eleven hours and a half exactly. This just covered the case comfortably, and he was acquitted. Thus, if an unthinking and excited community had been listened to instead of the arguments of counsel, a poor crazy creature would have been held to a fearful responsibility for a mere freak of madness. Baldwin went clear, and although his relatives and friends were naturally incensed against the community for their injurious suspicions and remarks, they said let it go for this time and did not prosecute. The Baldwins were very wealthy. This same Baldwin had momentary fits of insanity twice afterward, and on both occasions killed people he had grudges against. And on both these occasions the circumstances of the killing were so aggravated, and the murders so seemingly heartless and treacherous, that if Baldwin had not been insane he would have been hanged without the shadow of a doubt. As it was, it required all his political and family influence to get him clear in one of the cases, and cost him no less than $10,000 to get clear in the other. One of these men he had notoriously been threatening to kill for twelve years. The poor creature happened, by the merest piece of ill fortune, to come along a dark alley at the very moment that Baldwin's insanity came upon him, and so he was shot in the back with a gun loaded with slugs.

Take the case of Lynch Hackett, of Pennsylvania.

Twice, in public, he attacked a German butcher by the name of Beinis Feldner, with a cane, and both times Feldner whipped him with his fists. Hackett was a vain, wealthy, violent gentleman, who held his blood and family in high esteem, and believed that a reverent respect was due to his great riches. He brooded over the shame of his chastisement for two weeks, and then, in a momentary fit of insanity, armed himself to the teeth, rode into town, waited a couple of hours until he saw Feldner coming down the street with his wife on his arm, and then, as the couple passed the doorway in which he had partially concealed himself, he drove a knife into Feldner's neck, killing him instantly. The widow caught the limp form and eased it to the earth. Both were drenched with blood. Hackett jocosely remarked to her that as a professional butcher's recent wife she could appreciate the artistic neatness of the job that left her in a condition to marry again, in case she wanted to. This remark, and another which he made to a friend, that his position in society made the killing of an obscure citizen simply an "eccentricity" instead of a crime, were shown to be evidences of insanity, and so Hackett escaped punishment. The jury were hardly inclined to accept these as proofs, at first, inasmuch as the prisoner had never been insane before the murder, and under the tranquilizing effect of the butchering had immediately regained his right mind ; but when the defence came to show that a third cousin of Hackett's wife's stepfather was insane, and not only insane, but had a nose the very counterpart of Hackett's, it was plain that insanity was hereditary in the family, and Hackett had come by it by legitimate inheritance. Of course the jury then acquitted him. But it was a merciful providence that Mrs. H.'s people had been afflicted as shown, else Hackett would certainly have been hanged.

However, it is not possible to recount all the marvellous cases of insanity that have come under the public notice in the last thirty or forty years. There was the Durgin case in New Jersey, three years ago. The servant girl, Bridget Durgin, at dead of night, invaded her mistress' bedroom and carved the lady literally to pieces with a knife. Then she dragged the body to the middle of the floor, and beat and banged it with chairs and such things. Next she opened the feather beds, and strewed the contents around, saturated everything with kerosene, and set fire to the general wreck. She now took up the child of the murdered woman in her blood-smeared hands, and walked off, through the snow, with no shoes on, to a neighbour's house a quarter of a mile off, and told a string of wild, incoherent stories about some men coming and setting fire to the house ; and then she cried piteously, and, without seeming to think there was anything suggestive about the blood upon her hands, her clothing, and the baby, volunteered the remark that she was afraid those men had murdered her mistress ! Afterward, by her own confession and other testimony, it was proved that the mistress had always been kind to the girl, consequently there was no revenge in the murder ; and it was also shown that the girl took nothing away from the burning house, not even her own shoes, and consequently robbery was not the motive. Now, the reader says, "Here comes that same old plea of insanity again." But the reader has deceived himself this time. No such plea was offered in her defence. The judge sentenced her, nobody persecuted the Governor with petitions for her pardon and she was promptly hanged.

There was that youth in Pennsylvania, whose curious confession was published some years ago. It was simply a conglomeration of incoherent drivel from beginning to end, and so with his lengthy speech on the scaffold afterward. For a whole year he was haunted with a desire to disfigure a certain young woman, so that no one would marry her. He did not love her himself, and did not want to marry her, but he did not want anybody else to do it. He would not go anywhere with her, and yet was opposed to anybody else's escorting her. Upon one occasion he declined to go to a wedding with her, and when she got other company, lay in wait for the couple by the road, intending to make them go back or kill the escort. After spending sleepless nights over his ruling desire for a full year, he at last attempted its execution—that is, attempted to disfigure the young woman. It was a success. It was permanent. In trying to shoot her cheek (as she sat at the supper table with her parents and brothers and sisters) in such a manner as to mar its comeliness, one of his bullets wandered a little out of its course, and she dropped dead. To the very last moment

of his life he bewailed the ill luck that made her move
her face just at the critical moment. And so he died,
apparently about half persuaded that somehow it was
chiefly her own fault that she got killed. This idiot was
hanged. The plea of insanity was not offered.

Insanity certainly is on the increase in the world, and
crime is dying out. There are no longer any murders—
none worth mentioning, at any rate. Formerly, if you
killed a man, it was possible that you were insane—but
now, if you, having friends and money, kill a man, it is
evidence that you are a lunatic. In these days, too, if a
person of good family and high social standing steals
anything, they call it *kleptomania*, and send him to the
lunatic asylum. If a person of high standing squanders
his fortune in dissipation, and closes his career with
strychnine or a bullet, "Temporary Aberration" is what
was the trouble with *him*.

Is not this insanity plea becoming rather common? Is
it not so common that the reader confidently expects to
see it offered in every criminal case that comes before the
courts? And is it not so cheap, and so common, and
often so trivial, that the reader smiles in derision when
the newspaper mentions it? And is it not curious to
note how very often it wins acquittal for the prisoner?
Of late years it does not seem possible for a man to so
conduct himself, before killing another man, as not to be
manifestly insane. If he talks about the stars, he is
insane. If he appears nervous and uneasy an hour before the killing, he is insane. If he weeps over a great

grief, his friends shake their heads, and fear that he is " not right." If, an hour after the murder, he seems ill at ease, pre-occupied and excited, he is unquestionably insane.

Really, what we want now, is not laws against crime, but a law against *insanity* There is where the true evil lies

A CURIOUS DREAM.

CONTAINING A MORAL.

.

———

NIGHT before last I had a singular dream. I seemed
to be sitting on a door-step (in no particular city
perhaps), ruminating, and the time of night appeared to
be about twelve or one o'clock. The weather was balmy
and delicious. There was no human sound in the air,
not even a footstep. There was no sound of any kind to
emphasize the dead stillness, except the occasional hollow
barking of a dog in the distance and the fainter answer
of a further dog. Presently up the street I heard a
bony clack-clacking, and guessed it was the castanets of
a serenading party. In a minute more a tall skeleton,
hooded, and half clad in a tattered and mouldy shroud,
whose shreds were flapping about the ribby lattice-work
of its person, swung by me with a stately stride, and disappeared in the grey gloom of the starlight. It had a
broken and worm-eaten coffin on its shoulder and a bun-
dle of something in its hand. I knew what the clack-
clacking was then; it was this party's joints working together, and his elbows knocking against his sides as he
walked. I may say I was surprised. Before I could
collect my thoughts and enter upon any speculations as

to what this apparition might portend, I heard another one coming—for I recognized his clack-clack. He had two-thirds of a coffin on his shoulder, and some foot and head-boards under his arm. I mightily wanted to peer under his hood and speak to him, but when he turned and smiled upon me with his cavernous sockets and his projecting grin as he went by, I thought I would not detain him. He was hardly gone when I heard the clacking again, and another one issued from the shadowy half-light. This one was bending under a heavy gravestone, and dragging a shabby coffin after him by a string. When he got to me he gave me a steady look for a moment or two, and then rounded to and backed up to me, saying:

"Ease this down for a fellow, will you?"

I eased the gravestone down till it rested on the ground, and in doing so noticed that it bore the name of "John Baxter Copmanhurst," with "May 1839," as the date of his death. Deceased sat wearily down by me, and wiped his os frontis with his major maxillary—chiefly from former habit I judged, for I could not see that he brought away any perspiration.

"It is too bad, too bad," said he, drawing the remnant of the shroud about him and leaning his jaw pensively on his hand. Then he put his left foot upon his knee and fell to scratching his ankle bone absently with a rusty nail which he got out of his coffin.

"What is too bad, friend?"

"Oh, everything, everything. I almost wish I never had died."

" You surprise me. Why do you say this? Has anything gone wrong? What is the matter?"

"Matter! Look at this shroud—rags. Look at this gravestone, all battered up. Look at that disgraceful old coffin. All a man's property going to ruin and destruction before his eyes, and ask him if anything is wrong! Fire and brimstone!"

" Calm yourself, calm yourself," I said. " It is too bad—it is certainly too bad, but then I had not supposed that you would much mind such matters, situated as you are "

" Well, my dear sir, I *do* mind them. My pride is hurt, and my comfort is impaired—destroyed, I might say. I will state my case—I will put it to you in such a way that you can comprehend it, if you will let me," said the poor skeleton, tilting the hood of his shroud back, as if he were clearing for action, and thus unconsciously giving himself a jaunty and festive air very much at variance with the grave character of his position in life—so to speak—and in prominent contrast with his distressful mood.

"Proceed," said I.

" I reside in the shameful old graveyard a block or two above you here, in this street—there, now, I just expected that cartilage would let go!—third rib from the bottom, friend, hitch the end of it to my spine with a string, if you have got such a thing about you, though a bit of silver wire is a deal pleasanter, and more durable and becoming, if one keeps it polished—to think of shredding out and going to pieces in this way, just on account of the indifference and neglect of one's posterity?"—and the poor ghost grated his teeth in a way that give me a wrench and a shiver—for the effect is mightily increased by the absence of muffling flesh and cuticle. "I reside in that old graveyard, and have for these thirty years; and I tell you things are changed since I laid this old tired frame there, and turned over, and stretched out for a long sleep, with a delicious sense upon me of being *done* with bother, and grief, and anxiety, and doubt, and fear, for ever and ever, and listening with comfortable and increasing satisfaction to the sexton's work, from the startling clatter of his first spadeful on my coffin till it dulled away to the faint patting that shaped the roof of my new home—delicious! My! I wish you could try it to night!" and out of my reverie deceased fetched me with a rattling slap with a bony hand.

"Yes, sir, thirty years ago I laid me down there, and was happy. For it was out in the country, then—out in the breezy, flowery, grand old woods, and the lazy winds gossiped with the leaves, and the squirrels capered over us and around us, and the creeping things visited us, and the birds filled the tranquil solitude with music. Ah, it was worth ten years of a man's life to be dead then! Everything was pleasant. I was in a good neighbourhood, for all the dead people that lived near me belonged to the best families in the city. Our posterity appeared to think the world of us. They kept our graves in the very best condition; the fences were always in faultless repair, head-boards were kept painted or whitewashed, and were replaced with new ones as soon as they began to look rusty or decayed ; monuments were kept upright, railings intact and bright, the rosebushes and shrubbery trimmed, trained, and free from blemish, the walks clean and smooth and gravelled. But that day is gone by. Our descendants have forgotten us. My grandson lives in a stately house built with money made by these old hands of mine, and I sleep in a neglected grave with invading vermin that gnaw my shroud to build them nests withal ! I and friends that lie with me founded and secured the prosperity of this fine city, and the stately bantling of our loves leaves us to rot in a dilapidated cemetery which neighbours curse and strangers scoff at. See the difference between the old time and this—for instance : our graves are all caved in, now ; our head-boards have rotted away and tumbled down , our railings reel this way and that, with one foot in the air, after a fashion of unseemly levity ; our monuments lean wearily, and our gravestones bow their heads discouraged, there be no adornments any more—no roses, nor shrubs, nor gravelled walks, nor anything that is a comfort to the eye ; and even the paintless old board fence that did make a show of holding us sacred from the companionship with beasts and the defilement of heedless feet, has tottered till it overhangs the street, and only advertises the presence of our dismal resting-place and invites yet more derision to it. And now we cannot hide our poverty and tatters in the friendly woods, for the city has stretched its withering arms abroad and taken us in, and all that remains of the cheer of our old home is the cluster of lugubrious forest trees that stand, bored and weary of a city life, with their feet in our coffins, looking into the hazy distance and wishing they were there. I tell you it is disgraceful!

"You begin to comprehend—you begin to see—how it is. While our descendants are living sumptuously on our money, right around us in the city, we have to fight hard to keep skull and bones together. Bless you, there isn't a grave in our cemetery that doesn't leak—not one. Every time it rains in the night we have to climb out and roost in the trees—and sometimes we are wakened suddenly by the chilling water trickling down the back of our necks. Then I tell you there is a general heaving up of old graves and kicking over of old monuments, and scampering of old skeletons for the trees! Bless me, if you had gone along there some such nights after twelve you might have seen as many as fifteen of us roosting on one limb, with our joints rattling drearily and the wind wheezing through our ribs! Many a time we have perched there for three or four dreary hours, and then come down, stiff and chilled through and drowsy, and borrowed each other's skulls to bale out our graves with —if you will glance up in my mouth, now as I tilt my head back, you can see that my head-piece is half full of old dry sediment—how top-heavy and stupid it makes me sometimes! Yes, sir, many a time if you had happened to come along just before the dawn you'd have caught us baling out our graves and hanging our shrouds on the fence to dry. Why, I had an elegant shroud stolen from there one morning—think a party by the name of Smith took it, that resides in a plebeian graveyard over yonder—I think so, because the first time I ever saw him he hadn't anything on but a check shirt, and the last time I saw him, which was at a social gathering in the new cemetery, he was the best dressed corpse in the company—and it is a significant fact that he left when he saw me; and presently an old woman from here missed her coffin — she generally took it with her when she went anywhere, because she was liable to take cold and bring on the spasmodic rheumatism that originally killed her if she exposed herself to the night air too much. She was named Hotchkiss—Anna Matilda Hotchkiss — you might know her? She has two upper front teeth, is tall, but a good deal inclined to stoop, one rib on the left side gone, has one shred of rusty hair hanging from the left side of her head, and one little tuft just above and a little forward of her right ear, has her under jaw wired on one side where it had worked loose, small bone of left forearm gone — lost in a fight—has a kind of swagger in her gait and a 'gallus' way of going with her arms akimbo and her nostrils in the air—has been pretty free and easy, and is all damaged and battered up till she looks like a queens-ware crate in ruins—maybe you have met her?"

"God forbid!" I involuntarily ejaculated, for somehow I was not looking for that form of question, and it caught me a little off my guard. But I hastened to make amends for my rudeness, and say, "I simply meant I had not had the honour—for I would not deliberately speak discourteously of a friend of yours. You were saying that you were robbed—and it was a shame, too—but it appears by what is left of the shroud you have on that it was a costly one in its day. How did——"

A most ghastly expression began to develop among the decayed features and shrivelled integuments of my guest's face, and I was begining to grow uneasy and distressed, when he told me he was only working up a deep, sly smile, with a wink in it, to suggest that about the time he acquired his present garment a ghost in a neighbouring cemetery missed one. This reassured me, but I begged him to confine himself to speech thenceforth, because his facial expression was uncertain. Even with the most elaborate care it was liable to miss fire. Smiling should especially be avoided. What *he* might honestly consider a shining success was likely to strike me in a very different light. I said I liked to see a skeleton cheerful, even decorously playful, but I did not think smiling was a skeleton's best hold.

"Yes, friend," said the poor skeleton, "the facts are just as I have given them to you. Two of these old graveyards—the one that I reside in and one further along—have been deliberately neglected by our descendants of to-day until there is no occupying them any longer. Aside from the osteological discomfort of it—and that is no light matter this rainy weather—the present state of things is ruinous to property. We have got to move or be content to see our effects wasted away and utterly destroyed.

Now, you will hardly believe it, but it is true, nevertheless, that there isn't a single coffin in good repair among all my acquaintance—now that is an absolute fact. I do not refer to low people who come in a pine box mounted on an express waggon, but I am talking about your high toned, silver mounted burial-case, your monumental sort, that travel under black plumes at the head of a procession and have choice of cemetery lots—I mean folk like the Jarvises, and the Bledsoes and Burlings, and such. They are all about ruined. The most substantial people in our set, they were. And now look at them—utterly used up and poverty-stricken. One of the Bledsoes actually traded his monument to a late bar-keeper for some fresh shavings to put under his head. I tell you it speaks volumes, for there is nothing a corpse takes so much pride in as his monument. He loves to read the inscription. He comes after awhile to believe what it says himself, and then you may see him sitting on a fence night after night enjoying it. Epitaphs are cheap, and they do a poor chap a world of good after he is dead, especially if he had hard luck while he was alive. I wish they were used more. Now, I don't complain, but confidentially I *do* think it was a little shabby in my descendants to give me nothing but this old slab of a gravestone—and all the more that there isn't a compliment on it. It used to have

'GONE TO HIS JUST REWARD'

on it, and I was proud when I first saw it, but by-and-by I noticed that whenever an old friend of mine came along he would hook his chin on the railing and pull a long face and read along down till he came to that, and then he would chuckle to himself and walk off, looking satisfied and comfortable. So I scratched it off to get rid of those fools. But a dead man always takes a deal of pride in his monument. Yonder goes half-a-dozen of the Jarvises, now, with the family monument along. And Smithers and some hired spectres went by with his a while ago. Hello, Higgins, good-bye, old friend! That's Meredith Higgins—died in '44—belongs to our set in the cemetery—fine old family—great-grandmother was an Injun—I am on the most familiar terms with him— he didn't hear me was the reason he didn't answer me And I am sorry, too, because I would have liked to introduce you. You would admire him. He is the most disjointed, sway-backed, and generally distorted old skeleton you ever saw, but he is full of fun. When he laughs it sounds like rasping two stones together, and he always starts it off with a cheery screech like raking a nail across a window-pane. Hey, Jones! That is old Columbus Jones—shroud cost four hundred dollars— entire trousseau, including monument, twenty-seven hundred. That was in the Spring of '26. It was enormous style for those days. Dead people came all the way from the Alleghanies to see his things—the party that occupied the grave next to mine remembers it well. Now do you see that individual going along with a piece of a head-board under his arm, one leg-bone below his knee gone, and not a thing in the world on? That is

Barstow Dalhousie, and next to Columbus Jones he was the most sumptuously outfitted person that ever entered our cemetery. We are all leaving. We cannot tolerate the treatment we are receiving at the hands of our descendants. They open new cemeteries, but they leave us to our ignominy. They mend the streets, but they never mend anything that is about us or belongs to us. Look at that coffin of mine—yet I tell you in its day it was a piece of furniture that would have attracted attention in any drawing-room in this city. You may have it if you want it—I can't afford to repair it. Put a new bottom in her, and part of a new top, and a bit of fresh lining along the left side, and you'll find her about as comfortable as any receptacle of her species you ever tried. No thanks —no, don't mention it—you have been civil to me, and I would give you all the property I have got before I would seem ungrateful. Now this winding-sheet is a kind of a sweet thing in its way, if you would like to——. No? Well, just as you say, but I wished to be fair and liberal— there's nothing mean about *me*. Good-by, friend, I must be going. I may have a good way to go to-night—don't know. I only know one thing for certain, and that is, that I am on the emigrant trail, now, and I'll never sleep in that crazy old cemetery again. I will travel till I find respectable quarters, if I have to hoof it to New Jersey. All the boys are going. It was decided in public conclave, last night, to emigrate, and by the time the sun rises there won't be a bone left in our old habitations. Such cemeteries may suit my surviving friends, but they do not suit the remains that have the honour to make these remarks. My opinion is the general opinion. If you doubt it, go and see how the departing ghosts upset things before they started. They were almost riotous in their demonstration of distaste. Hello, here are some of the Bledsoes, and if you will give me a lift with this tombstone I guess I will join company and jog along with them—mighty respectable old family, the Bledsoes, and used to always come out in six-horse hearses, and all that sort of thing fifty years ago when I walked these streets in daylight. Good-by, friend."

And with his gravestone on his shoulder he joined the grisly procession, dragging his damaged coffin after him, for notwithstanding he pressed it upon me so earnestly, I utterly refused his hospitality. I suppose that for as much as two hours these sad outcasts went clacking by, laden with their dismal effects, and all that time I sat pitying them. One or two of the youngest and least dilapidated among them inquired about midnight trains on the railways, but the rest seemed unacquainted with that mode of travel, and merely asked about common public roads to various towns and cities, some of which are not on the map now, and vanished from it and from the earth as much as thirty years ago, and some few of them never *had* existed anywhere but on maps, and private ones in real estate agencies at that. And they asked about the condition of the cemeteries in these towns and cities, and about the reputation the citizens bore as to reverence for the dead.

This·whole matter interested me deeply, and likewise compelled my sympathy for these homeless ones. And it all seeming real, and I not knowing it was a dream, I mentioned to one shrouded wanderer an idea that had entered my head to publish an account of this curious and very sorrowful exodus, but said also that I could not describe it truthfully, and just as it occurred, without seeming to trifle with a grave subject and exhibit an irreverence for the dead that would shock and distress their surviving friends. But this bland and stately remnant of a former citizen leaned him far over my gate and whispered in my ear, and said :—

"Do not let that disturb you. The community that can stand such graveyards as those we are emigrating from can stand anything a body can say about the neglected and forsaken dead that lie in them."

At that very moment a cock crowed, and the weird procession vanished and left not a shred or a bone behind. I awoke, and found myself lying with my head out of the bed "sagging" downwards considerably—a position favourable to dreaming dreams with morals in them, maybe, but not poetry.

NOTE.—The reader is assured that if the cemeteries in his town are kept in good order, this Dream is not levelled at his town at all, but is levelled particularly and venomously at the *next* town.

THE SIAMESE TWINS.

I DO not wish to write of the personal *habits* of these strange creatures solely, but also of certain curious details of various kinds concerning them, which belonging only to their private life, have never crept into print. Knowing the Twins intimately, I feel that I am peculiarly well qualified for the task I have taken upon myself.

The Siamese Twins are naturally tender and affectionate in disposition, and have clung to each other with singular fidelity throughout a long and eventful life. Even as children they were inseparable companions ; and it was noticed that they always seemed to prefer each other's society to that of any other persons. They nearly always played together ; and, so accustomed was their mother to this peculiarity, that, whenever both of them chanced to be lost, she usually only hunted for one of them—satisfied that when she found that one she would find his brother somewhere in the immediate neighbourhood. And yet these creatures were ignorant and unlettered—barbarians themselves and the offspring of barbarians, who knew not the light of philosophy and science. What a withering rebuke is this to our boasted civilization, with its quarrellings, its wranglings, and its separations of brothers !)

As men, the Twins have not always lived in perfect accord ; but still there has always been a bond between them which made them unwilling to go away from each other and dwell apart. They have even occupied the same house, as a general thing, and it is believed that they have never failed to even sleep together on any night since they were born. How surely do the habits of a lifetime become second nature to us ! The Twins always go to bed at the same time ; but Chang usually gets up about an hour before his brother. By an understanding between themselves, Chang does all the in-door work, and Eng runs all the errands. This is because Eng likes to go out ; Chang's habits are sedentary. However, Chang always goes along. Eng is a Baptist, but Chang is a Roman Catholic ; still, to please his brother, Chang consented to be baptized at the same time that Eng was, on condition that it should not " count." During the War they were strong partizans, and both fought gallantly all through the great struggle—Eng on the Union side and Chang on the Confederate. They took each other prisoners at Seven Oaks, but the proofs of capture were so evenly balanced in favour of each, that a general army court had to be assembled to determine which one was properly the captor, and which the captive. The jury was unable to agree for a long time ; but the vexed question was finally decided by agreeing to consider them both prisoners, and then exchanging them. At one time

Chang was convicted of disobedience of orders, and sentenced to ten days in the guard-house, but Eng, in spite of all arguments, felt obliged to share his imprisonment, notwithstanding he himself was entirely innocent ; and so, to save the blameless brother from suffering, they had to discharge both from custody—the just reward of faithfulness.

Upon one occasion the brothers fell out about something, and Chang knocked Eng down, and then tripped and fell on him, whereupon both clinched and began to beat and gouge each other without mercy. The bystanders interferred, and tried to separate them, but they could not do it, and so allowed them to fight it out. In the end both were disabled, and were carried to the hospital on one and the same shutter.

Their ancient habit of going always together had its drawbacks when they reached man's estate, and entered upon the luxury of courting. Both fell in love with the same girl. Each tried to steal clandestine interviews with her, but at the critical moment the other would always turn up. By and by Eng saw, with distraction, that Chang had won the girl's affections ; and, from that day forth, he had to bear with the agony of being a witness to all their dainty billing and cooing. But with a magnanimity that did him infinite credit, he succumbed to his fate, and gave countenance and encouragement to a state of things that bade fair to sunder his generous heartstrings. He sat from seven every evening until two in the morning, listening to the fond foolishness of the two lovers, and to the concussion of hundreds of squandered kisses—for the privilege of sharing only one of which he would have given his right hand. (But he sat patiently and waited, and gaped, and yawned, and stretched, and longed for two o'clock to come.   And he took long walks with the lovers on moonlight evenings—sometimes tra, versing ten miles, notwithstanding he was usually suffer-ing from rheumatism.   He is an inveterate smoker ; but he could not smoke on these occasions, because the young lady was painfully sensitive to the smell of tobacco.   Eng cordially wanted them married, and done with it ; but although Chang often asked the momentous question, the young lady could not gather sufficient courage to answer it while Eng was by.   However, on one occasion, after having walked some sixteen miles, and sat up till nearly daylight, Eng dropped asleep, from sheer exhaus-t:,n, and then the question was asked and answered. The lovers were married. All acquainted with the circum-stances applauded the noble brother-in-law.   His unwav-ering faithfulness was the theme of every tongue. He had stayed by them all through their long and arduous court-ship ; and when at last they were married, he lifted his hands above their heads, and said with impressive unc-tion, " Bless ye, my children, I will never desert ye !" and he kept his word.   Fidelity like this is all too rare in this cold world.

By and by Eng fell in love with his sister-in law's sister, and married her, and since that day they have all lived together, night and day, in an exceeding sociability which is touching and beautiful to behold, and is a scathing rebuke to our boasted civilization.

The sympathy existing between these two brothers is so close and so refined that the feelings, the impulses, the emotions of the one are instantly experienced by the other. When one is sick, the other is sick, when one feels pain, the other feels it; when one is angered, the other's temper takes fire. We have already seen with what happy facility they both fell in love with the same girl. Now, Chang is bitterly opposed to all forms of intemperance, on principal; but Eng is the reverse—for, while these men's feelings and emotions are so closely wedded, their reasoning faculties are unfettered; their *thoughts* are free. .Chang belongs to the Good Templars, and is a hard working, enthusiastic supporter of all temperance reforms. But, to his bitter distress, every now and then Eng gets drunk, and, of course, that makes Chang drunk too This unfortunate thing has been a great sorrow to Chang(for it almost destroys his usefulness in his favourite field of effort) As sure as he is to head a great temperance procession Eng ranges up alongside of him, prompt to the minute, and drunk as a lord; but yet no more dismally and hopelessly drunk than his brother, who has not tasted a drop. (And so the two begin to hoot and yell, and throw mud and bricks at the Good Templars, and of course they break up the procession) It would be manifestly wrong to punish Chang for what Eng does, and, therefore, the Good Templars accept the untoward situation, and suffer in silence and sorrow. They have officially and deliberately examined into the matter, and find Chang blameless. They have taken the two brothers and filled Chang full of warm water and sugar and Eng full of whiskey, and in twenty-five minutes it was not possible to tell which was the drunkest. Both were as drunk as loons—and on hot whiskey punches, by the smell of their breath. Yet all the while Chang's moral principles were unsullied, his conscience clear; and so all just men were forced to confess that he was not morally, but only physically drunk. By every right and by every moral evidence the man was strictly sober; and, therefore, it caused his friends all the more anguish to see him shake hands with the pump, and try to wind his watch with his night-key.

There is a moral in these solemn warnings—or, at least, a warning in these solemn morals; one or the other. No matter, it is somehow. Let us heed it; let us profit by it.

I could say more of an instructive nature about these interesting beings, but let what I have written suffice.

Having forgotten to mention it sooner, I will remark in conclusion, that the ages of the Siamese Twins are respectively fifty-one and fifty-three years.

SPEECH AT THE SCOTTISH BANQUET IN LONDON.

A T the anniversary festival of the Scottish Corporation of London on Monday evening, in response to the toast of " The Ladies," MARK TWAIN replied. The following is the speech as reported in the London Observer :

"I am proud, indeed, of the distinction of being chosen to respond to this especial toast, to ' The Ladies,' or to women if you please, for that is the preferable term, perhaps ; it is certainly the older, and therefore the more entitled to reverence. (Laughter.) I have noticed that the Bible, with that plain, blunt honesty which is such a conspicuous characteristic of the Scriptures, is always particular to never refer to even the illustrious mother of all mankind herself as a 'lady,' but speaks of her as a woman. (Laughter.) It is odd, but you will find it is so. I am peculiarly proud of this honour, because I think that the toast to women is one which, by right and by every rule of gallantry, should take precedence of all others — of the army. of the navy, of even royalty itself—perhaps, though the latter is not necessary in this day and in this land, for the reason that, tacitly, you do drink a broad general health to all good women when you drink the health of the Queen of England and the Princess of Wales. (Loud cheers.) I have in mind a poem just now which is familiar to you all, familiar to everybody. And what an inspiration that was (and how instantly the present toast recalls the verses to all our minds) when the most noble, the most gracious, the purest, and sweetest of all poets says :—

> " ' Woman ! O woman !—er—
> Wom——'

(Laughter) However, you remember the lines ; and you remember how feelingly, how daintily, how almost imperceptibly, the verses raise up before you, feature by feature, the ideal of a true and perfect woman ; and how, as you contemplate the finished marvel, your homage grows into worship of the intellect that could create so fair a thing out of mere breath, mere words. And you call to mind now, as I speak, how the poet, with stern fidelity to the history of all humanity, delivers this beautiful child of his heart and his brain over to the trials and the sorrows that must come to all, sooner or later, that abide in the earth, and how the pathetic story culminates in that apostrophe—so wild, so regretful, so full of mournful retrospection. The lines run thus :—

> " ' Alas !—alas !—a—alas !
> — —Alas !— —- — —alas !'

—and so on. (Laughter.) I do not remember the rest; but, taken altogether, it seems to me that poem is the noblest tribute to woman that human genius has ever brought forth — (laughter) — and I feel that if I were to talk hours I could not do my great theme completer or more graceful justice than I have now done in simply quoting that poet's matchless words. (Renewed laughter.) The phases of the womanly nature are infinite in their variety   Take any type of woman, and you shall find in it something to respect, something to admire, something to love.   And you shall find the whole joining you heart and hand.   Who was more patriotic than Joan of Arc? Who was braver? Who has given us a grander instance of self sacrificing devotion? Ah! you remember, you remember well, what a throb of pain, what a great tidal wave of grief swept over us all when Joan of Arc fell at Waterloo (Much laughter.)   Who does not sorrow for the loss of Sappho, the sweet singer of Israel? (Laughter.) Who among us does not miss the gentle ministrations, the softening influences, the humble piety, of Lucretia Borgia? (Laughter.) Who can join in the heartless libel that says woman is extravagant in dress when he can look back and call to mind our simple and lowly mother Eve arrayed in her modification of the Highland costume. (Roars of laughter.) Sir, women have been soldiers, women have been painters, women have been poets. As long as language lives the name of Cleopatra will live. And not because she conquered George III. —(laughter)—but because she wrote those divine lines—

> " ' Let dogs delight to bark and bite,
>   For God hath made them so.'

(More laughter.) The story of the world is adorned with the names of illustrious ones of our own sex—some of them sons of St. Andrew, too—Scott, Bruce, Burns, the warrior Wallace, Ben Nevis—(laughter)—the gifted Ben Lomond, and the great new Scotchman, Ben Disraeli.* (Great laughter.)

---

* Mr. Benjamin Disraeli, at that time Prime Minister of England, had just been elected Lord Rector of Glasgow University, and had made a speech which gave rise to a world of discussion.

Out of the great plains of history tower whole mountain ranges of sublime women — the Queen of Sheba, Josephine, Semiramis, Sairey Gamp; the list is endless -- (laughter) — but I will not call the mighty roll, the names rise up in your own memories at the mere suggestion, luminous with the glory of deeds that cannot die, hallowed by the loving worship of the good and the true of all epochs and all climes. (Cheers.) Suffice it for our pride and our honour that we in our day have added to it such names as those of Grace Darling and Florence Nightingale. (Cheers.) Woman is all that she should be—gentle, patient, long suffering, trustful, unselfish, full of generous impulses. It is her blessed mission to comfort the sorrowing, plead for the erring, encourage the faint of purpose, succour the distressed, uplift the fallen, befriend the friendless—in a word, afford the healing of her sympathies and a home in her heart for all the bruised and persecuted children of misfortune that knock at its hospitable door. (Cheers.) And when I say, God bless her, there is none among us who has known the ennobling affection of a wife, or the steadfast devotion of a mother but in his heart will say, Amen! (Loud and prolonged cheering.)

A GHOST STORY.

I TOOK a large room, far up Broadway, in a huge old building whose upper stories had been wholly unoccupied for years, until I came. The place had long been given up to dust and cobwebs, to solitude and silence. I seemed groping among the tombs and invading the privacy of the dead, that first night I climbed up to my quarters. For the first time in my life a superstitious dread came over me; and as I turned a dark angle of the stairway and an invisible cobweb swung its slazy woof in my face and clung there, I shuddered as one who had encountered a phantom. I was glad enough when I reached my room and locked out the mould and the darkness. A cheery fire was burning in the grate, and I sat down before it with a comforting sense of relief. For two hours I sat there, thinking of bygone times; recalling old scenes, and summoning half forgotten faces out o. the mist of the past; listening in fancy to voices that long ago grew silent for all time, and to once familiar songs that nobody sings now. And as my reverie softened down to a sadder and sadder pathos, the shrieking of the winds outside softened to a wail, the angry beating of the rain against the panes diminished to a tranquil patter, and one by one the noises in the street subsided, until the hurrying footsteps of the last belated straggler died away in the distance and left no sound behind.

The fire had burned low. A sense of loneliness crept over me. I arose and undressed, moving on tip-toe about the room, doing stealthily what I had to do, as if I were environed by sleeping enemies whose slumbers it would be fatal to break. I covered up in bed, and lay listening to the rain and wind and the faint creaking of distant shutters, till they lulled me to sleep.

I slept profoundly, but how long I do not know. All at once I found myself awake, and filled with a shuddering expectancy. All was still. All but my own heart— I could hear it beat. Presently the bed clothes began to slip away slowly toward the foot of the bed, as if some one were pulling them! I could not stir; I could not speak. Still the blankets slipped deliberately away, till my breast was uncovered. Then with a great effort I seized them and drew them over my head. I waited, listened, waited. Once more that steady pull began, and once more I lay torpid a century of dragging seconds till my breast was naked again. At last I roused my energies and snatched the covers back to their place and held them with a strong grip. I waited. By and bye I felt a faint tug, and took a fresh grip. The tug strengthened to a steady strain—it grew stronger and stronger. My hold parted, and for the third time the blankets slid away. I groaned. An answering groan came from the foot of

the bed! Beaded drops of sweat stood upon my forehead.
I was more dead than alive. Presently I heard a heavy
footstep in my room—the step of an elephant, it seemed
to me—it was not like anything human. But it was
moving *from* me—there was relief in that. I heard
it· approach the door—pass out without moving bolt
or lock—and wander away among the dismal corridors, straining the floors and joists till they creaked
again as it passed—and then silence reigned once
more.

When my excitement had calmed, I said to myself,
"This is a dream—simply a hideous dream." And so I
lay thinking it over until I convinced myself that it *was*
a dream, and then a comforting laugh relaxed my lips
and I was happy again. I got up and struck a light; and
when I found that the locks and bolts were just as I had
left them, another soothing laugh welled in my heart and
rippled from my lips. I took my pipe and lit it, and was
just sittting down before the fire, when—down went the
pipe out of my nerveless fingers, the blood forsook my
cheeks, and placid breathing was cut short with a gasp!
In the ashes on the hearth, side by side with my own
bare footprint, was another, so vast that in comparison
mine was but an infant's! Then I had *had* a visitor, and
the elephantine tread was explained.

I put out the light and returned to bed, palsied with
fear. I lay a long time, peering into the darkness, and
listening. Then I heard a grating noise overhead, like
the dragging of a heavy body across the floor; then the

throwing down of the body, and the shaking of my windows in response to the concussion. In distant parts of the building I heard the muffled slamming of doors. I heard, at intervals, stealthy footsteps creeping in and out among the corridors, and up and down the stairs. Sometimes these noises approached my door, hesitated, and went away again. I heard the clanking of chains faintly in remote passages, and listened while the clanking grew nearer—while it wearily climbed the stairways, marking each move by the loose surplus of chain that fell with an accented rattle upon each succeeding step as the goblin that bore it advanced. I heard muttered sentences; half-uttered screams that seemed smothered violently; and the swish of invisible garments, the rush of invisible wings. Then I became conscious that my chamber was invaded—that I was not alone. I heard sighs and breathings about my bed, and mysterious whisperings. Three little spheres of soft phosphorescent light appeared on the ceiling directly over my head, clung and glowed there a moment, and then dropped—two of them upon my face and one upon the pillow They spattered, liquidly, and felt warm. Intuition told me they had turned to gouts of blood as they fell—I needed no light to satisfy myself of that. Then I saw pallid faces, dimly luminous, and white uplifted hands, floating bodiless in the air,—floating a moment and then disappearing. The whispering ceased, and the voices and the sounds, and a solemn stillness followed. I waited, and listened. I felt that I must have light, or die. I was weak with fear.

I slowly raised myself toward a sitting posture, and my face came in contact with a clammy hand! All strength went from me, apparently, and I fell back like a stricken invalid. Then I heard the rustle of a garmênt—it seemed to pass to the door and go out.

When everything was still once more, I crept out of bed, sick and feeble, and lit the gas with a hand that trembled as if it were aged with a hundred years. The light brought some little cheer to my spirits. I sat down and fell into a dreamy contemplation of that great footprint in the ashes. By and bye its outlines began to waver and grow dim. I glanced up and the broad gas flame was slowly wilting away. In the same moment I heard that elephantine tread again. I noted its approach, nearer and nearer, along the musty halls, and dimmer and dimmer the light waned. The tread reached my very door and paused—the light had dwindled to a sickly blue, and all things about me lay in a spectral twilight. The door did not open, and yet I felt a faint gust of air fan my cheek, and presently was conscious of a huge, cloudy presence before me. I watched it with fascinated eyes. A pale glow stole over the Thing; gradually its cloudy folds took shape — an arm appeared, then legs, then a body, and last a great sad face looked out of the vapour. Stripped of its filmy housings, naked, muscular and comely, the majestic Cardiff Giant loomed above me!

All my misery vanished—for a child might know that no harm could come with that benignant countenance. My cheerful spirits returned at once, and in sympathy with them the gas flamed up brightly again. Never a lonely outcast was so glad to welcome company as I was to greet the friendly giant. I said:

"Why, is it nobody but you? Do you know, I have been scared to death for the last two or three hours? I am most honestly glad to see you. I wish I had a chair———. Here, here, don't try to sit down in that thing!"

But it was too late. He was in it before I could stop him, and down he went—I never saw a chair shivered so in my life.

"Stop, stop, you'll ruin ev——"

Too late again. There was another crash, and another chair was resolved into its original elements.

"Confound it, haven't you got any judgment at all? Do you want to ruin all the furniture on the place? Here, here, you petrified fool——"

But it was no use. Before I could arrest him he had sat down on the bed and it was a melancholy ruin.

"Now what sort of a way is that to do? First you come lumbering about the place bringing a legion of vagabond goblins along with you to worry me to death, and then when I overlook an indelicacy of costume which would not be tolerated anywhere by cultivated people except in a respectable theatre, and not even there if the nudity were of *your* sex, you repay me by wrecking all the furniture you can find to sit down on. And why will you? You damage yourself as much as you do me. You have broken off the end of your spinal column, and littered up the floor with chips off your hams till the place looks like a marble yard. You ought to be ashamed of yourself—you are big enough to know better."

"Well, I will not break any more furniture. But what am I to do? I have not had a chance to sit down for a century." And the tears came into his eyes.

"Poor devil," I said, "I should not have been so harsh with you. And you are an orphan, too, no doubt. But sit down on the floor here—nothing else can stand your weight—and besides, we cannot be sociable with you away up there above me, I want you down where I can perch on this high counting-house stool and gossip with you face to face."

So he sat down on the floor, and lit a pipe which I gave him, threw one of my red blankets over his shoulders, inverted my sitz-bath on his head, helmet fashion, and made himself picturesque and comfortable. Then he crossed his ankles, while I renewed the fire, and exposed the flat, honey-combed bottoms of his prodigious feet to the grateful warmth.

"What is the matter with the bottom of your feet and the back of your legs, that they are gouged up so?"

"Infernal chilblains—I caught them clear up to the back of my head, roosting out there under Newell's farm. But I love the place; I love it as one loves his old home. There is no peace for me like the peace I feel when I am there."

We talked along for half an hour, and then I noticed that he looked tired, and spoke of it.

"Tired ?" he said. "Well I should think so. And now I will tell you all about it, since you have treated me so well. I am the spirit of the Petrified Man that lies across the street there in the Museum. I am the ghost of the Cardiff Giant. I can have no rest, no peace, till they have given that poor body burial again. Now what was the most natural thing for me to do, to make men satisfy this wish? Terrify them into it!—haunt the place where the body lay! So I haunted the museum night after night. I even got other spirits to help me. But it did no good, for nobody ever came to the museum at midnight. Then it occured to me to come over the way and haunt this place a little. I felt that if I ever got a hearing I must succeed, for I had the most efficient company that perdition could furnish. Night after night we have shivered around through these mildewed halls, dragging chains, groaning, whispering, tramping up and down stairs, till to tell you the truth I am almost worn out But when I saw a light in your room to-night I roused my energies again and went at it with a deal of the old freshness. But I am tired out—entirely fagged out. Give me, I beseech you, give me some hope!"

I lit off my perch in a burst of excitement, and exclaimed :

" This transcends everything! everything that ever did occur! Why you poor blundering old fossil, you have had all your trouble for nothing—you have been haunting a *plaster cast* of yourself—the real Cardiff Giant is in Albany !* Confound it, don't you know your own remains ?"

I never saw such an eloquent look of shame, of pitiable humiliation, overspread a countenance before.

The Petrified Man rose slowly to his feet, and said:

"Honestly, *is* that true ?"

"As true as I am sitting here."

He took the pipe from his mouth and laid it on the mantel, then stood irresolute a moment (unconsciously, from old habit, thrusting his hands where his pantaloons pockets should have been, and meditatively dropping his chin on his breast), and finally said:

"Well—I *never* felt so absurd before. The Petrified Man has sold everybody else, and now the mean fraud has ended by selling its own ghost! My son, if there is any charity left in your heart for a poor friendless phantom like me, don't let this get out. Think how *you* would feel if you had made such an ass of yourself."

I heard his stately tramp die away, step by step down the stairs and out into the deserted street, and felt sorry that he was gone, poor fellow—and sorrier still that he had carried off my red blanket and my bath-tub.

* A fact. The original fraud was ingeniously and fraudfully duplicated, and exhibited in New York as the "only genuine" Cardiff Giant, (to the unspeakable disgust of the owners of the real colossus,) at the very same time that the latter was drawing crowds at a museum in Albany.

THE CAPITOLINE VENUS.

CHAPTER I.

[Scene—An Artist's Studio in Rome.]

"OH, George, I *do* love you!"

"Bless your dear heart, Mary, I know that—*why* is your father so obdurate?"

"Georgy, he means well, but art is folly to him—he only understands groceries. He thinks you would starve me."

"Confound his wisdom—it savours of inspiration. Why am I not a money-making, bowelless grocer, instead of a divinely-gifted sculptor with nothing to eat?"

"Do not despond, George, dear—all his prejudices will fade away as soon as you shall have acquired fifty thousand dol—"

"Fifty thousand demons! Child, I am in arrears for my board!"

CHAPTER II.

[Scene—A Dwelling in Rome.]

"My dear sir, it is useless to talk. I haven't anything against you, but I can't let my daughter marry a hash of love, art, and starvation—I believe you have nothing else to offer."

"Sir, I am poor, I grant you.   But is fame nothing?
The Hon. Bellamy Foodle, of Arkansas, says that my
new statue of America is a clever piece of sculpture, and
he is satisfied that my name will one day be famous."

"Bosh !   What does that Arkansas ass know about it ?
Fame's nothing—the market price of your marble scare-
crow is the thing to look at.   It took you six months to
chisel it, and you can't sell it for a hundred dollars.   No,
sir !   Show me fifty thousand dollars and you can have
my daughter—otherwise she marries young Simper.   You
have just six months to raise the money in.   Good morning, sir."

"Alas !   Woe is me !"

CHAPTER III.

[Scene—The Studio.]

"Oh, John, friend of my boyhood, I am the unhappiest
of men."

"You're a simpleton !"

"I have nothing left to love but my poor statue of
America—and see, even she has no sympathy for me in her
cold marble countenance—so beautiful and so heartless !"

"You're a dummy !"

"Oh, John !"

"Oh, fudge !   Didn't you say you had six months to
raise the money in ?"

"Don't deride my agony, John.   If I had six centuries
what good would it do ?   How could it help a poor
wretch without name, capital or friends ?"

"Idiot! Coward! Baby! Six months to raise the money in—and five will do!"

" Are you insane ?"

"Six months—an abundance. Leave it to me. I'll raise it."

" What do you mean, John ? How on earth can you raise such a monstrous sum for *me* ?"

" *Will* you let that be *my* business, and not meddle ? Will you leave the thing in my hands ? Will you swear to submit to whatever I do ? Will you pledge me to find no fault with my actions ?"

"I am dizzy—bewildered—but I swear."

John took up a hammer and deliberately smashed the nose of America ! He made another pass and two of her fingers fell to the floor—another, and part of an ear came away—another, and a row of toes was mangled and dismembered—another, and the left leg, from the knee down, lay a fragmentary ruin !

John put on his hat and departed.

George gazed speechless upon the battered and grotesque nightmare before him for the space of thirty seconds, and then wilted to the floor and went into convulsions.

John returned presently with a carriage, got the broken-hearted artist and the broken-legged statue aboard, and drove off, whistling low and tranquilly. He left the artist at his lodgings, and drove off and disappeared down the *Via Quirinalis* with the statue.

CHAPTER IV.

[Scene—The Studio.]

"**The six** months will be up at two o'clock to-day! Oh, agony! My life is blighted. I would that I were dead. I had no supper yesterday. I have had no breakfast to-day. I dare not enter an eating-house. And hungry?— don't mention it! My bootmaker duns me to death—my tailor duns me—my landlord haunts me. I am miserable. I haven't seen John since that awful day. *She* smiles on me tenderly when we meet in the great thoroughfares, but her old flint of a father makes her look in another direction in short order. Now who is knocking at that door? Who is come to persecute me? That malignant villain, the bootmaker, I'll warrant. *Come in!*"

"Ah, happiness attend your highness—Heaven be propitious to your grace! I have brought my lord's new boots—ah, say nothing about the pay, there is no hurry, none in the world. Shall be proud if my noble lord will continue to honour me with his custom—ah, adieu!"

"Brought the boots himself! Don't want his pay! Takes his leave with a bow and a scrape fit to honour majesty withal! Desires a continuance of my custom! Is the world coming to an end? Of all the—*come in!*"

"Pardon, signor, but I have brought your new suit of clothes for——"

"*Come in!!*"

"A thousand pardons for this intrusion, your worship! But I have prepared the beautiful suite of rooms below for you—this wretched den is but ill suited to——"

"*Come in ! ! !*"

" I have called to say that your credit in our bank, some time since unfortunately interrupted, is entirely and most satisfactorily restored, and we shall be most happy if you will draw upon us for any——"

" COME IN !!!!"

" My noble boy, she is yours! She'll be here in a moment! Take her—marry her—love her--be happy! God bless you both! Hip, hip, hur——"

" COME IN !!!!!"

" Oh, George, my own darling, we are saved!"

" Oh, Mary, my own darling, we *are* saved—but I'll swear I don't know why nor how!"

CHAPTER V.

[Scene—A Roman Cafe.]

One of a group of American gentlemen reads and translates from the weekly edition of *Il Slangwhanger di Roma* as follows :

"WONDERFUL DISCOVERY!—Some six months ago Signor John Smitthe, an American gentleman now some years a resident of Rome, purchased for a trifle a small piece of ground in the Campagna, just beyond the tomb of the Scipio family, from the owner, a bankrupt relative of the Princess Borghese. Mr Smitthe afterwards went to the minister of the Public Records and had the piece of ground transferred to a poor American artist named George Arnold, explaining that he did it as payment and satisfaction for pecuniary damage accidentally done by him long since upon property belonging to Signor Arnold, and further observed that he would make additional satisfaction by improving the ground for Signor A., at his own charge and cost Four weeks ago, while making some necessary excavations upon the property, Signor Smitthe unearthed the most remarkable ancient statue that has ever been added to the opulent art treasures of Rome. It was an exquisite figure of a woman, and though sadly stained by the soil and the mould of ages, no eye can look unmoved upon its ravishing beauty. The nose, the left leg from the knee down, an ear, and also the toes of the right foot and two fingers of one of the hands, were gone, but otherwise the noble figure was in a remarkable state of preservation. The government at once took military possession of the statue, and appointed a commission of art critics, antiquaries and cardinal princes of the church to assess its value and determine the remuneration that must go to the owner of the ground in which it was found. The whole affair was kept a profound secret until last night. In the meantime the commission sat with closed doors, and deliberated. Last night they decided unanimously that the statue is a Venus, and the work of some unknown but sublimely gifted artist of the third century before Christ. They consider it the most faultless work of art the world has any knowledge of.

"At midnight they held a final conference and decided that the Venus was worth the enormous sum of *ten million francs!* In accordance with Roman law and Roman usage, the government being half owner in all works of art found in the Campagna, the State has naught to do but pay five million francs to Mr. Arnold and take permanent possession of the beautiful statue. This morning the Venus will be removed to the Capitol, there to remain, and at noon the commission will wait upon Signor Arnold with His Holiness the Pope's order upon the Treasury for the princely sum of five million francs in gold."

Chorus of Voices.—"Luck! It's no name for it!"

Another Voice.—"Gentlemen, I propose that we immediately form an American joint-stock company for the purchase of lands and excavations of statues, here, with proper connections in Wall Street to bull and bear the stock."

All.—"Agreed!"

CHAPTER VI.

[Scene—The Roman Capitol Ten Years Later.]

"Dearest Mary, this is the most celebrated statue in the world. This is the renowned 'Capitoline Venus'

you have heard so much about.   Here she is with her
little blemishes ' restored' (that is, patched) by the most
noted Roman artists—and the mere fact that they did
the humble patching of so noble a creation will make
their names illustrious while the world stands.   How
strange it seems—this place !   The day before I last stood
here, ten happy years ago, I wasn't a rich man—bless
your soul, I hadn't a cent.   And yet I had a good deal to
do with making Rome mistress of this grandest work of
ancient art the world contains."

"The worshipped, the illustrious Capitoline Venus—and
what a sum she is valued at !   Ten millions of francs ?"

"Yes—*now* she is."

"And oh, Georgy, how divinely beautiful she is !"

"Ah, yes—but nothing to what she was before that
blessed John Smith broke her leg and battered her nose.
Ingenious Smith !—gifted Smith—noble Smith !   Author
of all our bliss !   Hark !   Do you know what that wheeze
means ?   Mary, that cub has got the whooping cough.
Will you *never* learn to take care of the children !"

THE END.

The Capitoline Venus is still in the Capitol at Rome,
and is still the most charming and most illustrious work
of ancient art the world can boast of.   But if ever it shall
be your fortune to stand before it and go into the customary ecstacies over it, don't permit this true and secret
history of its origin to mar your bliss—and when you

read about a gigantic Petrified Man being dug up near Syracuse, in the State of New York, or near any other place, keep your own counsel,—and if the Barnum that buried him there offers to sell to you at an enormous sum, don't you buy. Send him to the Pope !

Note.—The above sketch was written at the time the famous swindle of the " Petrified Giant " was the sensation of the day in the United States.

SPEECH ON ACCIDENT INSURANCE.

DELIVERED IN HARTFORD, AT A DINNER TO CORNELIUS
WALFORD, OF LONDON.

———

GENTLEMEN: I am glad indeed to assist in welcoming the distinguished guest of this occasion to a city whose fame as an insurance centre has extended to all lands, and given us the name of being a quadruple band of brothers working sweetly hand in hand, — the Colt's arms company making the destruction of our race easy and convenient, our life insurance citizens paying for the victims when they pass away, Mr. Batterson perpetuating their memory with his stately monuments, and our fire insurance comrades taking care of their hereafter. I am glad to assist in welcoming our guest—first, because he is an Englishman, and I owe a heavy debt of hospitality to certain of his fellow-countrymen ; and secondly, because he is in sympathy with insurance and has been the means of making other men cast their sympathies in the same direction.

Certainly there is no nobler field for human effort than the insurance line of business—especially accident insurance. Ever since I have been director in an accident in-

surance company I have felt that I am a better man.
Life has seemed more precious. Accidents have assumed
a kindlier aspect. Distressing special providences have
lost half their horror. I look upon a cripple, now, with
affectionate interest—as an advertisement. I do not seem
to care for poetry any more. I do not care for politics
—even agriculture does not excite me. But to me, now,
there is a charm about a railway collision that is unspeakable.

There is nothing more beneficent than accident insurance. I have seen an entire family lifted out of poverty
and into affluence by the simple boon of a broken leg.
I have had people come to me on crutches, with tears in
their eyes, to bless this beneficent institution. In all my
experience of life, I have seen nothing so seraphic as the
look that comes into a freshly mutilated man's face when
he feels in his vest pocket with his remaining hand and
finds his accident ticket all right. And I have seen
nothing so sad as the look that came into another splint-
ered customer's face, when he found he couldn't collect
on a wooden leg.

I will remark here, by way of advertisement, that the
noble charity which we have named the HARTFORD AC-
CIDENT INSURANCE COMPANY,* is an institution which is
peculiarly to be depended upon. A man is bound to
prosper who gives it his custom. No man can take out
a policy in it and not get crippled before the year is out.
Now there was one indigent man who had been disap-

---

* The speaker is a director of the company named.

pointed so often with other companies that he had grown disheartened, his appetite left him, he ceased to smile— said life was but a weariness. Three weeks ago I got him to insure with us, and now he is the brightest, happiest spirit in this land — has a good steady income and a stylish suit of new bandages every day, and travels around on a shutter.

I will say, in conclusion, that my share of the welcome to our guest is none the less hearty because I talk so much nonsense, and I know that I can say the same for the rest of the speakers.

JOHN CHINAMAN IN NEW YORK.

AS I passed along by one of those monster American tea-stores in New York, I found a Chinaman sitting before it acting in the capacity of a sign. Everybody that went by gave him a steady stare as long as their heads would twist over their shoulders without danger of dislocating their necks, and a group had stopped to stare deliberately.

Is it not a shame that we, who prate so much about civilization and humanity are content to degrade a fellow-being to such an office as this? Is it not time for reflection when we find ourselves willing to see in such a being, matter for frivolous curiosity instead of regret and grave reflection? Here was a poor creature whom hard fortune had exiled from his natural home beyond the seas, and whose troubles ought to have touched these idle strangers that thronged about him; but did it? Apparently not. Men calling themselves the superior race, the race of culture and of gentle blood, scanned his quaint Chinese hat, with peaked roof and ball on top, and his long queue dangling down his back; his short silken blouse, curiously frogged and figured (and like the rest of his raiment, rusty, dilapidated, and awkwardly put on); his blue cotton, tight-legged pants, tied close around the ankles; and his clumsy blunt-toed shoes with thick cork soles; and having so scanned him from head to foot, cracked some unseemly joke about his outlandish attire or his melancholy face and passed on. In my heart I pitied the friendless Mongol. I wondered what was passing behind his sad face, and what distant scene his vacant eye was dreaming of. Were his thoughts with his heart, ten thousand miles away, beyond the bil-lowy wastes of the Pacific? among the rice-fields and plumy palms of China? under the shadows of remembered mountain-peaks, or in groves of bloomy shrubs and strange forest trees unknown to climes like ours? And now and then, rippling among his visions and his dreams, did he hear familiar laughter and half-forgotten voices, and did he catch fitful glimpses of the friendly faces of a bygone time? A cruel fate it is, I said, that is befallen this bronzed wanderer. In order that the group of idlers might be touched at least by the words of the poor fellow, since the appeal of his pauper dress and dreary exile was lost upon them, I touched him on the shoulder and said—

" Cheer up—don't be down-hearted. It is not America that treats you in this way, it is merely one citizen, whose greed of gain has eaten the humanity out of his heart. America has a broader hospitality for the exiled and op-pressed. America and Americans are always ready to help the unfortunate. Money shall be raised—you shall go back to China—you shall see your friends again. What wages do they pay you here?"

"Divil a cint but four dollars a week and find meself; but it's aisy, barrin the troublesome furrin clothes that's so expinsive."

The exile remains at his post. The New York tea-merchants who need picturesque signs are not likely to run out of Chinamen.

HOW I EDITED AN AGRICULTURAL PAPER.

I DID not take temporary editorship of an agricultural paper without misgivings. Neither would a landsman take command of a ship without misgivings. But I was in circumstances that made the salary an object. The regular editor of the paper was going off for a holiday, and I accepted the terms he offered, and took his place.

The sensation of being at work again was luxurious, and I wrought all the week with unflagging pleasure. We went to press, and I waited a day with some solicitude to see whether my effort was going to attract any notice. As I left the office, toward sundown, a group of men and boys at the foot of the stairs dispersed with one impulse, and gave me passage-way, and I heard one or two of them say: "That's him!" I was naturally pleased with this incident. The next morning I found a similar group at the foot of the stairs, and scattering couples and individuals standing here and there in the street, and over the way, watching me with interest. The group separated and fell back as I approached, and I heard a man say, "Look at his eye!" I pretended not to observe the notice I was attracting, but secretly I was pleased with it, and was purposing to write an account of it to my aunt. ' I went up the short flight of stairs, and heard cheery voices and a ringing laugh as I drew near the door, which I opened, and caught a glimpse of two young rural-looking men, whose faces blanched and lengthened when they saw me, and then they both plunged through the window with a great crash. I was surprised.

In about half an hour an old gentleman, with a flowing beard and a fine but rather austere face, entered and sat down at my invitation. He seemed to have something on his mind. He took off his hat and set it on the floor, and got out of it a red silk handkerchief and a copy of our paper.

He put the paper on his lap, and while he polished his spectacles with his handkerchief, he said, " Are you the new editor ? "

I said I was.

" Have you ever edited an agricultural paper before ? "

" No," I said ; " this is my first attempt."

" Very likely. Have you had any experience in agriculture practically ? "

" No ; I believe I have not."

" Some instinct told me so," said the old gentleman, putting on his spectacles, and looking over them at me with asperity, while he folded his paper into a convenient shape. " I wish to read you what must have made me have that instinct. It was this editorial. Listen, and see if it was you that wrote it :—

"Turnips should never be pulled, it injures them. It is much better to send a boy up and let him shake the tree."

" Now, what do you think of that ?—for I really suppose you wrote it ? "

"Think of it ?   Why, I think it is good.   I think it is
sense.   I have no doubt that every year millions and
millions of bushels of turnips are spoiled in this township
alone by being pulled in a half-ripe condition, when, if
they had sent a boy up to shake the tree"—

"Shake your grandmother!   Turnips don't grow on
trees !"

" Oh, they don't, don't they ? Well, who said they did ?
The language was intended to be figurative, wholly figurative.   Anybody that knows anything will know that I
meant that the boy should shake the vine."

Then this old person got up and tore his paper all into
small shreds, and stamped on them, and broke several
things with his cane, and said I did not know as much
as a cow ; and then went out and banged the door after
him, and, in short, acted in such a way that I fancied he
was displeased about something.   But not knowing what
the trouble was, I could not be any help to him.

Pretty soon after this a long cadaverous creature, with
lanky locks hanging down to his shoulders, and a week's
stubble bristling from the hills and valleys of his face,
darted within the door, and halted, motionless, with finger
on lip, and head and body bent in listening attitude.   No
sound was heard.   Still he listened.   No sound.   Then
he turned the key in the door, and came elaborately tip-
toeing toward me till he was within long reaching distance of me, when he stopped, and after scanning my face

with intense interest for a while, drew a folded copy of our paper from his bosom, and said—

"There, you wrote that. Read it to me—quick! Relieve me. I suffer."

I read as follows; and as the sentences fell from my lips I could see the relief come, I could see the drawn muscles relax, and the anxiety go out of the face, and rest and peace steal over the features like the merciful moonlight over a desolate landscape:

"The guano is a fine bird, but great care is necessary in rearing it. It should not be imported earlier than June or later than September. In the winter it should be kept in a warm place, where it can hatch out its young.

"It is evident that we are to have a backward season for grain. Therefore it will be well for the farmer to begin setting out his cornstalks and planting his buckwheat cakes in July instead of August.

"Concerning the pumpkin.—This berry is a favourite with the natives of the interior of New England, who prefer it to the gooseberry for the making of fruit-cake, and who likewise give it the preference over the raspberry for feeding cows, as being more filling and fully as satisfying. The pumpkin is the only esculent of the orange family that will thrive in the North, except the gourd and one or two varieties of the squash. But the custom of planting it in the front yard with the shrubbery is fast going out of vogue, for it is now generally conceded that the pumpkin as a shade tree is a failure.

"Now, as the warm weather approaches, and the ganders begin to spawn——"

The excited listener sprang toward me to shake hands, and said—

"There, there—I know I am all right now, because you have read it just as I did, word for word. But, stranger, when I read it this morning, I said to myself, I never, never believed it before, notwithstanding my friends kept

me under watch so strict, but now I believe I *am* crazy ;
and with that I fetched a how! that you might have
heard two miles,and started out to kill somebody—because,
you know, I knew it would come to that sooner or later,
and so I might as well begin. I read one of them paragraphs again, so as to be certain, and then I burned my
house down and started. I have crippled several people,
and have got one fellow up a tree, where I can get him
if I want him. But I thought I would call in here as I
passed along and make the thing perfectly certain ; and
now it *is* certain, and I tell you it is lucky for the chap
that is in the tree. I should have killed him, sure, as I
went back. Good-bye, sir, good-bye ; you have taken a
great load off my mind. My reason has stood the strain
of one of your agricultural articles, and I know that nothing can ever unseat it now. *Good*-bye, sir."

I felt a little uncomfortable about the cripplings and
arsons this person had been entertaining himself with,
for I could not help feeling remotely accessory to them.
But these thoughts were quickly banished, for the regular
editor walked in ! [I thought to myself, Now if you had
gone to Egypt as I recommended you to, I might have
had a chance to get my hand in ; but you wouldn't do it,
and here you are. I sort of expected you.]

The editor was looking sad and perplexed and de-
ected.

He surveyed the wreck which the old rioter and those
two young farmers had made, and then said, "This is a sad
business—a very sad business. There is the mucilage

bottle broken, and six panes of glass, and a spittoon and
two candlesticks.   But that is not the worst.   The reputation of the paper is injured—and permanently, I fear.
True, there never was such a call for the paper before,
and it never sold such a large edition or soared to such
celebrity;—but does one want to be famous for lunacy,
and prosper upon the infirmities of his mind ? My friend,
as I am an honest man, the street out here is full of people, and others are roosting on the fences, waiting to get
a glimpse of you, because they think you are crazy.   And
well they might after reading your editorials.   They are
a disgrace to journalism.   Why, what put it into your
head that you could edit a paper of this nature ?   You
do not seem to know the first rudiments of agriculture.
You speak of a furrow and a harrow as being the same
thing ; you talk of the moulting season for cows ; and
you recommend the domestication of the pole-cat on account of its playfulness and its excellence as a ratter!
Your remark that clams will lie quiet if music be played
to them was superfluous—entirely superfluous.   Nothing
disturbs clams.   Clams *always* lie quiet.   Clams care
nothing whatever about music.   Ah, heavens and earth,
friend ! if you had made the acquiring of ignorance the
study of your life, you could not have graduated with
higher honour than you could to-day.   I never saw anything like it.   Your observation that the horse-chestnut
as an article of commerce is steadily gaining in favour, is
simply calculated to destroy this journal.   I want you
to throw up your situation and go.   I want no more

holiday—I could not enjoy it if I had it.   Certainly not
with you in my chair.   I would always stand in dread
of what you might be going to recommend next.   It
makes me lose all patience every time I think of your
discussing oyster-beds under the head of 'Landscape
Gardening.'   I want you to go.   Nothing on earth could
persuade me to take another holiday.   Oh ! why didn't
you *tell* me you didn't know anything about agriculture ? "

" *Tell* you, you cornstalk, you cabbage, you son of a
cauliflower ?   It's the first time I ever heard such an un-
feeling remark.   I tell you I have been in the editorial
business going on fourteen years, and it is the first time
I ever heard of a man's having to know anything in
order to edit a newspaper.   You turnip !   Who write
the dramatic critiques for second-rate papers ?   Why, a
parcel of promoted shoemakers and apprentice apothe-
caries, who know just as much about good acting as I do
about good farming and no more.   Who review the books?
People who never wrote one.   Who do up the heavy
leaders on finance ?   Parties who have had the largest
opportunities for knowing nothing about it.   Who criti-
cise the Indian campaigns ?   Gentlemen who do not
know a war-whoop from a wigwam, and who never have
had to run a foot-race with a tomahawk, or pluck arrows
out of the several members of the family to build the
evening camp-fire with.   Who write the temperance ap-
peals and clamour about the flowing bowl ?   Folk who
will never draw another sober breath till they do it in

the grave.   Who edit the agricultural papers, you—yam ?
Men, as a general thing, who fail in the poetry line, yellow
coloured novel line, sensation-drama line, city-editor line,
and finally fall back on agriculture as a temporary reprieve from the poorhouse.   *You* try to tell *me* anything
about the newspaper business!   Sir, I have been through
it from Alpha to Omaha, and I tell you that the less a
man knows the bigger the noise he makes and the higher
the salary he commands.   Heaven knows if I had been
ignorant instead of cultivated, and impudent instead of
diffident, I could have made a name for myself in this
cold selfish world.   I take my leave, sir.   Since I have
been treated as you have treated me, I am perfectly willing to go.   But I have done my duty.   I have fulfilled
my contract as far as I was permitted to do it.   I said I
could make your paper of interest to all classes — and I
have.   I said I could run your circulation up to twenty
thousand copies, and if I had had two more weeks I'd
have done it.   And I'd have given you the best class of
readers that ever an agricultural paper had—not a farmer
in it, nor a solitary individual who could tell a water-
melon tree from a peach-vine to save his life.   *You* are
the loser by this rupture, not me, Pie-plant.   Adios."

   I then left.

THE PETRIFIED MAN.

NOW, to show how really hard it is to foist a moral or a truth upon an unsuspecting public through a burlesque without entirely and absurdly missing one's mark, I will here set down two experiences of my own in this thing. In the fall of 1862, in Nevada and California, the people got to running wild about extraordinary petrifications and other natural marvels. One could scarcely pick up a paper without finding in it one or two glorified discoveries of this kind. The mania was becoming a little ridiculous. I was a bran-new local editor in Virginia City, and I felt called upon to destroy this growing evil; we all have our benignant fatherly moods at one time or another, I suppose. I chose to kill the petrifaction mania with a delicate, a very delicate satire. But maybe it was altogether too delicate, for nobody ever perceived the satire part of it at all. I put my scheme in the shape of the discovery of a remarkably petrified man.

I had had a temporary falling out with Mr. ———, the new coroner and justice of the peace of Humboldt, and thought I might touch him up a little at the same time and make him ridiculous, and thus combine pleasure with

business. So I told, in patient, belief-compelling detail, all
about the finding of a petrified man at Gravelly Ford
(exactly a hundred and twenty miles, over a breakneck
mountain trail, from where —— lived) ; how all the savants of the immediate neighbourhood had been to examine it (it was notorious that there was not a living
creature within fifty miles of there, except a few starving
Indians, some crippled grasshoppers, and four or five buz-
zards out of meat and too feeble to get away) ; how those
savants all pronounced the petrified man to have been in
a state of complete petrification for over ten generations ;
and then, with a seriousness that I ought to have been
ashamed to assume, I stated that as soon as Mr. —— heard
the news he summoned a jury, mounted his mule, and
posted off, with noble reverence for official duty, on that
awful five days' journey, through alkali, sage-brush, peril
of body, and imminent starvation, to *hold an inquest* on
this man that had been dead and turned to everlasting
stone for more than three hundred years ! And then my
hand being "in," so to speak, I went on with the same
unflinching gravity, to state that the jury returned a verdict that deceased came to his death from *protracted ex-
posure.* This only moved me to higher flights of imagination, and I said that the jury, with that charity so
characteristic of pioneers, then dug a grave and were about
to give the petrified man Christian burial, when they
found that for ages a limestone sediment had been trickling down the face of the stone against which he was sitting, and this stuff had run under him and cemented him

fast to the " bed-rock ;" that the jury (they were all silver miners) canvassed the difficulty a moment and then got out their powder and fuse, and proceeded to drill a hole under him, in order to *blast him from his position,* when Mr. ——, "with that delicacy so characteristic of him, forbade them, observing that it would be little less than sacrilege to do such a thing."

From beginning to end the "petrified man" was a string of roaring absurdities, albeit they were told with an unfair pretence of truth that even imposed upon me to some extent, and I was in some danger of believing in my own fraud. But I really had no desire to deceive anybody, and no expectation of doing it. I depended on the way the petrified man was *sitting* to explain to the public that he was a swindle. Yet I purposely mixed that up with other things, hoping to make it obscure— and I did. I would describe the position of one foot, and then say his right thumb was against the side of his nose ; then talk about his other foot, and presently come back and say the fingers of his right hand were spread apart ; then talk about the back his head a little, then return and say the left thumb was hooked into the right little finger ; then ramble off about something else, and by and by drift back again and remark that the fingers of the left hand were spread like those of the right. But it was too ingenious. I mixed it up rather too much ; and so all that description of the attitude, as a key to the humbuggery of the article, was entirely lost, for nobody but me ever discovered and comprehended the peculiar and suggestive position of the petrified man's hands.

As a *satire* on the petrifaction mania, or anything else, my Petrified Man was a disheartening failure ; for everybody received him in innocent good faith, and I was stunned to see the creature I had begotten to pull down the wonder-business with, and bring derision upon it, calmly exalted to the grand chief place in the list of the genuine marvels our Nevada had produced.   I was so disappointed at the curious miscarriage of my scheme, that at first I was angry, and did not like to think about it ; but by and by, when the exchanges began to come in with the Petrified Man copied and guilelessly glorified, I began to feel a soothing secret satisfaction ; and as my gentleman's field of travels broadened, and by the exchanges I saw that he steadily and implacably penetrated territory after territory, State after State, and land after land, till he swept the great globe and culminated in sublime and unimpeached legitimacy in the august London *Lancet*, my cup was full, and I said I was glad I had done it.   I think that for about eleven months, as nearly as I can remember, Mr. ——'s daily mail-bag continued to be swollen by the addition of half a bushel of newspapers hailing from many climes with the Petrified Man in them, marked around with a prominent belt of ink.   I sent them to him.   I did it for spite, not for fun.   He used to shovel them into his back yard and curse.   And every day during all those months the miners, his constituents (for miners never quit joking a person when they get started), would call on him and ask if he could tell them where they could get hold of a paper with the Petrified Man in it. He could have accomodated a continent with them. I hated —— in those days, and these things pacified me and pleased me. I could not have gotten more real comfort out of him without killing him.

MY BLOODY MASSACRE.

THE other burlesque I have referred to was my fine
satire upon the financial expedient of "cooking
dividends," a thing which became shamefully frequent on
the Pacific coast for a while.   Once more, in my
self-complacent simplicity, I felt that the time had arrived for me to rise up and be a reformer.   I put this re-
formatory satire in the shape of a fearful " Massacre at
Empire City."   The San Francisco papers were making a
great outcry about the iniquity of the Daney Silver-Mining Company, whose directors had declared a " cooked "
or false dividend, for the purpose of increasing the value
of their stock, so that they could sell out at a comfortable
figure, and then scramble from under the tumbling concern.   And while abusing the Daney, those papers did
not forget to urge the public to get rid of all their silver
stocks and invest in sound and safe San Francisco stocks,
such as the Spring Valley Water Company, etc.   But
right at this unfortunate juncture, behold the Spring
Valley cooked a dividend too ! And so, under the insidi-
ous mask of an invented " bloody massacre," I stole upon
the public unawares with my scathing satire upon the
dividend-cooking system.   In about half a column of im-

aginary human carnage I told how a citizen had murdered
his wife and nine children, and then committed suicide.
And I said slyly, at the bottom, that the sudden madness
of which this melancholy massacre was the result, had
been brought about by his having allowed himself to be
persuaded by the California papers to sell his sound and
lucrative Nevada silver stocks, and buy into Spring Valley
just in time to get cooked along with that company's
fancy dividend, and sink every cent he had in the
world.

Ah, it was a deep, deep satire, and most ingeniously
contrived.   But I made the horrible details so carefully
and conscientiously interesting that the public devoured
them greedily, and wholly overlooked the following dis-
tinctly-stated facts, to wit :—The murderer was perfectly
well known to every creature in the land as a *bachelor*,
and consequently he could not murder his wife and nine
children ; he murdered them "in his splendid dressed-
stone mansion just in the edge of the great pine forest
between Empire City and Dutch Nick's," when even the
very pickled oysters that came on our tables knew that
there was not a "dressed-stone mansion " in all Nevada
Territory ; also that, so far from there being a "great
pine forest between Empire City and Dutch Nick's," there
wasn't a solitary tree within fifteen miles of either place;
and, finally, it was patent and notorious that Empire
City and Dutch Nick's were one and the same place, and
contained only six houses anyhow, and consequently
there could be no forest *between* them ; and on top of all

these absurdities I stated that this diabolical murderer, after inflicting a wound upon himself that the reader ought to have seen would kill an elephant in the twinkling of an eye, jumped on his horse and rode *four miles*, waving his wife's reeking scalp in the air, and thus performing entered Carson City with tremendous *eclat*, and dropped dead in front of the chief saloon, the envy and admiration of all beholders.

Well, in all my life I never saw anything like the sensation that little satire created. It was the talk of the town, it was the talk of the Territory. Most of the citizens dropped gently into it at breakfast, and they never finished their meal. There was something about those minutely faithful details that was a sufficing substitute for food. Few people that were able to read took food that morning. Dan and I (Dan was my reportorial associate) took our seats on either side of our customary table in the "Eagle Restaurant," and, as I unfolded the shred they used to call a napkin in that establishment, I saw at the next table two stalwart innocents with that sort of vegetable dandruff sprinkled about their clothing which was the sign and evidence that they were in from the Truckee with a load of hay. The one facing me had the morning paper folded to a long narrow strip, and I knew, without any telling, that that strip represented the column that contained my pleasant financial satire From the way he was excitedly mumbling, I saw that the heedless son of a hay-mow was skipping with all his might, in order to get to the bloody details as quickly as possible ; and so he was missing the guideboards I had set up to warn him that the whole thing was a fraud. Presently his eyes spread wide open, just as his jaws swung asunder to take in a potato approaching it on a fork ; the potato halted, the face lit up redly, and the whole man was on fire with excitement. Then he broke into a disᐧointed checking off of the particulars—his potato cooling in mid-air meantime, and his mouth‚ making a reach for it occasionally, but always bringing up suddenly against a new and still more direful performance of my hero. At last he looked his stunned and rigid comrade impressively in the face, and said, with an expression of concentrated awe—

"Jim, he b'iled his baby, and he took the old 'oman's skelp. Cuss'd if *I* want any breakfast !"

And he laid his lingering potato reverently down, and he and his friend departed from the restaurant empty but satisfied.

He *never got down* to where the satire part of it began. Nobody ever did. They found the thrilling particulars sufficient. To drop in with a poor little moral at the fag-end of such a gorgeous massacre, was to follow the expiring sun with a candle, and hope to attract the world's attention to it.

The idea that anybody could ever take my massacre for a genuine occurrence never once suggested itself to me, hedged about as it was by all those tell-tale absurdities and impossibilities concerning the "great pine forest," the "dressed-stone mansion," etc. But I found out then, and never have forgotten since, that we never *read* the dull explanatory surroundings of marvellously exciting things when we have no occasion to suppose some irresponsible scribbler is trying to defraud us; we skip all that, and hasten to revel in the blood-curdling particulars and be happy.

CONCERNING CHAMBERMAIDS.

AGAINST all chambermaids, of whatsoever age or nationality, I launch the curse of bachelordom ! Because:

They always put the pillows at the opposite end of the bed from the gas-burner, so that while you read and smoke before sleeping (as is the ancient and honoured custom of bachelors), you have to hold your book aloft in an uncomfortable position, to keep the light from dazzling your eyes.

When they find the pillows removed to the other end of the bed in the morning, they receive not the suggestion in a friendly spirit ; but, glorying in their absolute sovereignty, and unpitying your helplessness, they make the bed just as it was originally, and gloat in secret over the pang their tyranny will cause you.

Always after that, when they find you have transposed the pillows, they undo your work, and thus defy and seek to embitter the life that God has given you.

If they cannot get the light in an inconvenient position any other way, they move the bed.

If you pull your trunk out six inches from the wall, so that the lid will stay up when you open it, they always shove that trunk back again. They do it on purpose.

If you want the spittoon in a certain spot, where it will be handy, they don't, and so they move it.

They always put your other boots into inaccessible places. They chiefly enjoy depositing them as far under the bed as the wall will permit. It is because this compels you to get down in an undignified attitude and make wild sweeps for them in the dark with the boot jack, and swear.

They always put the match-box in some other place. They hunt up a new place for it every day, and put up a bottle, or other perishable glass thing, where the box stood before. This is to cause you to break that glass thing, groping in the dark, and get yourself into trouble.

They are forever moving the furniture. When you come in, in the night, you can calculate on finding the bureau where the wardrobe was in the morning. And when you go out in the morning, if you leave the slop-bucket by the door and the rocking-chair by the window, when you come in at midnight, or thereabouts, you will fall over that rocking-chair, and you will proceed toward the window and sit down in that slop-tub. This will disgust you. They like that.

No matter where you put anything, they are not going to let it stay there. They will take it and move it the first chance they get. It is their nature. And, besides, it give them pleasure to be mean and contrary this way. They would die if they couldn't be villains.

They always save up all the old scraps of printed rubbish you throw on the floor, and stack them up carefully on the table, and start the fire with your valuable manuscripts. If there is any one particular old scrap that you are more down on than any other, and which you are gradually wearing your life out trying to get rid of, you may take all the pains you possibly can in that direction, but it won't be of any use, because they will always fetch that old scrap back and put it in the same old place again every time. It does them good.

And they use up more hair-oil than any six men. If charged with purloining the same, they lie about it. What do they care about a hereafter? Absolutely nothing.

If you leave the key in the door for convenience sake, they will carry it down to the office and give it to the clerk. They do this under the vile pretence of trying to protect your property from thieves; but actually they do it because they want to make you tramp back downstairs after it, when you come home tired, or put you to the trouble of sending a waiter for it, which waiter will expect you to pay him something. In which case I suppose the degraded creatures divide.

They keep always trying to make your bed before you get up, thus destroying your rest and inflicting agony upon you; but after you get up, they don't come any more till the next day.

They do all the mean things they can think of, and they do them just out of pure cussedness, and nothing else.

Chambermaids are dead to every human instinct.

If I can get a bill through the legislature abolishing chambermaids, I mean to do it.

ABOUT BARBERS.

ALL things change except barbers, the ways of barbers, and the surroundings of barbers. These never change. What one experiences in a barber's shop the first time he enters one is what he always experiences in barber's shops afterwards till the end of his days. I got shaved this morning as usual. A man approached the door from Jones Street as I approached it from Main— a thing that always happens. I hurried up, but it was of no use; he entered the door one little step ahead of me, and I followed in on his heels and saw him take the only vacant chair, the one presided over by the best barber. It always happens so. I sat down, that I might fall heir to the chair belonging to the better of the remaining two barbers, for he had already begun combing his man's hair, while his comrade was not yet quite done rubbing up and oiling his customer's locks. I watched the probabilities with strong interest. When I saw that No. 2 was gaining on No. 1 my interest grew to solicitude. When No. 1 stopped a moment to make change on a bath ticket for a new comer, and lost ground in the race, my solicitude rose to anxiety. When No. 1 caught up again, and both he and his comrade were pulling the towels away and

brushing the powder from their customers' cheeks, and it
was about an even thing which one would say "Next!"
first, my very breath stood still with the suspense. But
when at the culminating moment No. 1 stopped to pass a
comb a couple of times through his customer's eyebrows, I
saw that he had lost the race by a single instant, and I rose
indignant and quitted the shop, to keep from falling into
the hands of No. 2; for I have none of that enviable
firmness that enables a man to look calmly into the eyes
of a waiting barber and tell him he will wait for his fel-
low-barber's chair.

I stayed out fifteen minutes, and then went back, hoping for better luck. Of course all the chairs were occupied now, and four men sat waiting, silent, unsociable,
distraught, and looking bored, as men always do who are
awaiting their turn in a barber's shop. I sat down in
one of the iron-armed compartments of an old sofa, and
put in the time for a while reading the framed advertise-
ments of all sorts of quack nostrums for dyeing and
colouring the hair. Then I read the greasy names on the
private bay rum bottles; read the names and noted the
numbers on the private shaving cups in the pigeon-holes;
studied the stained and damaged cheap prints on the
walls, of battles, early Presidents, and voluptuous recum-
bent sultanas, and the tiresome and everlasting young
girl putting her grandfather's spectacles on; execrated in
my heart the cheerful canary and the distracting parrot
that few barbers' shops are without. Finally, I searched
out the least dilapidated of last year's illustrated papers

that littered the foul centre-table, and conned their un-
justifiable misrepresentation of old forgotten events.

At last my turn came.   A voice said "Next!" and I
surrendered to—No. 2, of course.   It always happens so
I said meekly that I was in a hurry, and it affected him
as strongly as if he had never heard it.   He shoved up
my head, and put a napkin under it.   He ploughed his
fingers into my collar and fixed a towel there.   He explored my hair with his claws and suggested that it
needed trimming.   I said I did not want it trimmed   He
explored again and said it was pretty long for the present
style—better have a little taken off; it needed it behind
especially.   I said I had had it cut only a week before.
He yearned over it reflectively a moment, and then asked
with a disparaging manner, who cut it?   I came back at
him promptly with a "You did!"   I had him there.
Then he fell to stirring up his lather and regarding himself in the glass, stopping now and then to get close and
examine his chin critically or inspect a pimple.   Then he
lathered one side of my face thoroughly, and was about
to lather the other when a dog fight attracted his attention, and he ran to the window and stayed and saw it
out, losing two shillings on the result in bets with the
other barbers, a thing which gave me great satisfaction.
He finished lathering and then began to rub in the suds
with his hand.

He now began to sharpen his razor on an old sus-
pender, and was delayed a good deal on account of a
controversy about a cheap masquerade ball he had figured

at the night before, in red cambric and bogus ermine, as some kind of a king. He was so gratified with being chaffed about by some damsel whom he had smitten with his charms that he used every means to continue the controversy by pretending to be annoyed at the chaffings of his fellows. This matter begot more surveying of himself in the glass, and he put down his razor and brushed his hair with elaborate care, plastering an inverted arch of it down on his forehead, accomplishing an accurate "part" behind, and brushing the two wings forward over his ears with nice exactness. In the meantime the lather was drying on my face, and apparently eating into my vitals.

Now he began to shave, digging his fingers into my countenance to stretch the skin and bundling and tumbling my head this way and that as convenience in shaving demanded. As long as he was on the tough sides of my face I did not suffer; but when he began to rake and rip, and tug at my chin, the tears came. He now made a handle of my nose, to assist him in shaving the corners of my upper lip, and it was by this bit of circumstantial evidence that I discovered that a part of his duties in the shop was to clean the kerosene lamps. I had often wondered in an indolent way whether the barbers did that, or whether it was the boss.

About this time I was amusing myself trying to guess where he would be most likely to cut me this time, but he got ahead of me and sliced me on the end of the chin before I had got my mind made up. He immediate'

sharpened his razor—he might have done it before. I
do not like a close shave and would not let him go over
me a second time. I tried to get him to put up his razor,
dreading that he would make for the side of my chin,
my pet tender spot, a place where a razor cannot touch
twice without making trouble; but he said he only
wanted to just smooth off one little roughness, and in the
same moment he slipped his razor along the forbidden
ground, and the dreaded pimple-signs of a close shave
rose up smarting and answered to the call. Now he
soaked his towel in bay rum, and slapped it all over my
face nastily; slapped it over as if a human being ever
yet washed his face in that way. Then he dried it by
slapping with the dry part of the towel, as if a human
being ever dried his face in such a fashion; but a barber
seldom rubs you like a Christian. Next he poked bay
rum into the cut places with his towel, then choked the
wound with powdered starch, then soaked it with bay
rum again, and would have gone on soaking and powder-
ing it for evermore, no doubt, if I had not rebelled and
begged off. He powdered my whole face now, straight-
ened me up, and began to plough my hair thoughtfully
with his hands. Then he suggested a shampoo, and said
my hair needed it badly, very badly. I observed that I
shampooed it myself very thoroughly in the bath yesterday. I " had him " again. He next recommended some of
" Smith's Hair Glorifier," and offered to sell me a bottle.
I declined. He praised the new perfume, " Jones' Delight of the Toilet," and proposed to sell me some of that.

I declined again. He tendered me a tooth-wash atrocity of his own invention, and when I declined offered to trade knives with me.

He returned to business after the miscarriage of this last enterprise, sprinkled me all over, legs and all, greased my hair in defiance of my protest against it, rubbed and scrubbed a good deal of it out by the roots, and combed and brushed the rest, parting it behind, and plastering the eternal and inverted arch of hair down on my forehead, and then, while combing my scant eyebrows and defiling them with pomade, strung out an account of the achievements of a six-ounce black and tan terrier of his till I heard the whistles blow for noon, and knew I was five minutes too late for the train. Then he snatched away the towel, brushed it lightly over my face, passed his comb through my eyebrows once more, and gaily sang out " Next !"

This barber fell down and died of apoplexy two hours later. I am waiting over a day for my revenge — I am going to attend his funeral.

HISTORY REPEATS ITSELF.

———

THE following I find in a Sandwich Island paper which some friend has sent me from that tranquil far-off retreat. The coincidence between my own experience and that here set down by the late Mr. Benton is so remarkable that I cannot forbear publishing and commenting upon the paragraph. The Sandwich Island paper says :—

"How touching is this tribute of the late Hon. T. H. Benton to his mother's influence :—' My mother asked me never to use tobacco ; I have never touched it from that time to the present day. She asked me not to gamble, and I have never gambled. I cannot tell who is losing in games that are being played. She admonished me, too, against liquor-drinking, and whatever capacity for endurance I have at present, and whatever usefulness I may have attained through life I attribute to having complied with her pious and correct wishes. When I was seven years of age, she asked me not to drink, and then I made a resolution of total abstinence ; and that I have adhered to it through all time I owe to my mother.'"

I never saw anything so curious. It is almost an exact epitome of my own moral career—after simply substituting a grandmother for a mother. How well I remember my grandmother's asking me not to use tobacco, good old soul ! She said, "You're at it again, are you, you whelp ? Now, don't let me ever catch you chewing tobacco before breakfast again, or I'll black-snake you within an inch of your life !" I have never touched it at that hour of the morning from that time to the present day.

She asked me not to gamble. She whispered and said, " Put up those wicked cards this minute !—two pair and a jack, you numskull, and the other fellow's got a flush ! "

I never have gambled from that day to this—never once—without a " cold deck " in my pocket. I cannot even tell who is going to lose in games that are being played unless I dealt myself.

When I was two years of age she asked me not to drink, and then I made a resolution of total abstinence. That I have adhered to it and enjoyed the beneficent effects of it through all time, I owe to my grandmother. I have never drunk a drop from that day to this of any kind of water.

FIRST INTERVIEW WITH ARTEMUS WARD.

I HAD never seen him before. He brought letters of introduction from mutual friends in San Francisco, and by invitation I breakfasted with him. It was almost religion, there in the silver mines, to precede such a meal with whiskey cocktails. Artemus, with the true cosmopolitan instinct, always deferred to the customs of the country he was in, and so he ordered three of those abominations. Hingston was present. I said I would rather not drink a whiskey cocktail. I said it would go right to my head, and confuse me so that I would be in a helpless tangle in ten minutes. I did not want to act like a lunatic before strangers. But Artemus gently insisted, and I drank the treasonable mixture under protest, and felt all the time that I was doing a thing I might be sorry for. In a minute or two I began to imagine that my ideas were clouded. I waited in great anxiety for the conversation to open, with a sort of vague hope that my understanding would prove clear, after all, and my misgivings groundless.

Artemus dropped an unimportant remark or two, and then assumed a look of superhuman earnestness, and made the following astounding speech. He said :—

'" Now there is one thing I ought to ask you about before I forget it. You have been here in Silverland—here in Nevada,—two or three years, and, of course, your position on the daily press has made it necessary for you to go down in the mines· and examine them carefully in detail, and therefore you know all about the silver-mining business. Now, what I want to get at is—is, well, the way the deposits of ore are made, you know. For instance. Now, as I understand it, the vein which contains the silver is sandwiched in between casings of granite, and runs along the ground, and sticks up like a curb-stone. Well, take a vein forty feet thick, for example, or eighty, for that matter, or even a hundred—say you go down on it with a shaft, straight down, you know, or with what you call 'incline,' maybe you go down five hundred feet, or maybe you don't go down but two hundred—any way you go down, and all the time this vein grows narrower, when the casings come nearer or approach each other, you may say—that is, when they do approach, which of course they do not always do, particularly in cases where the nature of the formation is such that they stand apart wider than they otherwise would, and which geology has failed to account for, although everything in that science goes to prove that, all things being equal, it would if it did not, or would not certainly if it did, and then of course they are. Do not you think it is ?"

I said to myself:—

" Now I just knew how it would be—that whiskey

cocktail has done the business for me; I don't understand any more than a clam."

And then I said aloud:—

" I—I—that is—if you don't mind, would you—would
you say that over again ? I ought "——

" Oh, certainly, certainly! You see I am very un-
familiar with the subject, and perhaps I don't present my
case clearly, but I "——

"No, no—no, no—you state it plain enough, but that
cocktail has muddled me a little. But I will—no, I do understand for that matter; but I would get the hang of it
all the better if you went over it again—and I'll pay better attention this time."

He said, " Why, what I was after was this."

[Here he became even more fearfully impressive than
ever, and emphasized each particular point by checking it
off on his finger ends.]

"This vein, or lode, or ledge, or whatever you call it,
runs along between two layers of granite, just the same
as if it were a sandwich. Very well. Now, suppose you
go down on that, say a thousand feet, or maybe twelve
hundred (it don't really matter), before you drift,
and then you start your drifts, some of them across
the ledge, and others along the length of it, where
the sulpherets,—I believe they call them sulpherets,
though why they should, considering that, so far
as I can see, the main dependence of a miner does not so
lie, as some suppose, but in which it cannot be successful-
ly maintained, wherein the same should not continue,

while part and parcel of the same ore not committed to
either in the sense referred to, whereas, under different
circumstances, the most inexperienced among us could
not detect it if it were, or might overlook it if it did, or
scorn the very idea of such a thing, even though it were
palpably demonstrated as such.   Am I not right?"

I said, sorrowfully—"I feel ashamed of myself, Mr.
Ward.   I know I ought to understand you perfectly well,
but you see that treacherous whiskey cocktail has got into my head, and now I cannot understand even the simplest proposition.   I told you how it would be."

"Oh, don't mind it, don't mind it; the fault was my
own, no doubt—though I did think it clear enough
for"——

"Don't say a word.   Clear!   Why, you stated it as
clear as the sun to anybody but an abject idiot; but its
that confounded cocktail that has played the mischief."

"No; now don't say that.   I'll begin it all over again,
and"——

"Don't now—for goodness sake don't do anything of
the kind, because I tell you my head is in such a condition that I don't believe I could understand the most
trifling question a man could ask me."

"Now, don't you be afraid.   I'll put it so plain this
time that you can't help but get the hang of it.   We will
begin at the very beginning."   [Leaning far across the
table, with determined impressiveness wrought upon his
every feature, and fingers prepared to keep tally of each
point as enumerated; and I, leaning forward with painful

interest, resolved to comprehend or perish.] "You know the vein, the ledge, the thing that contains the metal, whereby it constitutes the medium between all other forces, whether of present or remote agencies, so brought to bear in favour of the former against the latter, or the latter against the former or all, or both, or compromising the relative differences existing within the radius whence culminate the several degrees of similarity to which"——

I said—"Oh, hang my wooden head, it ain't any use! —it ain't any use to try—I can't understand anything. The plainer you get it the more I can't get the hang of it."

I heard a suspicious noise behind me, and turned in time to see Hingston dodging behind a newspaper, and quaking with a gentle ecstasy of laughter. I looked at Ward again, and he had thrown off his dread solemnity and was laughing also. Then I saw that I had been sold —that I had been made the victim of a swindle in the way of a string of plausibly worded sentences that didn't mean anything under the sun. Artemus Ward was one of the best fellows in the world, and one of the most companionable. It has been said that he was not fluent in conversation, but with the above experience in my mind, I differ.

NIAGARA.

NIAGARA FALLS is a most enjoyable place of resort. The hotels are excellent, and the prices not at all exorbitant. The opportunities for fishing are not surpassed in the country; in fact, they are not even equalled elsewhere. Because, in other localities, certain places in the streams are much better than others; but at Niagara one place is just as good as another, for the reason that the fish do not bite anywhere, and so there is no use in your walking five miles to fish, when you can depend on being just as unsuccessful nearer home. The advantages of this state of things have never heretofore been properly placed before the public.

The weather is cool in summer, and the walks and drives are all pleasant and none of them fatiguing. When you start out to " do " the Falls you first drive down about a mile, and pay a small sum for the privilege of looking down from a precipice into the narrowest part of the Niagara river. A railway "cut" through a hill would be as comely if it had the angry river tumbling and foaming through its bottom. You can descend a staircase here a hundred and fifty feet down, and stand at the edge of the water.   After you have done it, you will wonder why you did it; but you will then be too late.

The guide will explain to you, in his blood-curdling way, how he saw the little steamer, *Maid of the Mist*, descend the fearful rapids—how first one paddle-box was out of sight behind the raging billows, and then the other, and at what point it was that her smokestack toppled overboard, and where her planking began to break and part asunder—and how she did finally live through the trip, after accomplishing the incredible feat of travelling seventeen miles in six minutes, or six miles in seventeen minutes, I have really forgotten which.   But it was very extraordinary, anyhow.   It is worth the price of admission to hear the guide tell the story nine times in succession to different parties, and never miss a word or alter a sentence or a gesture.

Then you drive over the Suspension Bridge, and divide your misery between the chances of smashing down two hundred feet into the river below, and the chances of having the railway train over head smashing down on to you.   Either possibility is discomforting taken by itself, but mixed together, they amount in the aggregate to positive unhappiness.

On the Canada side you drive along the chasm between long ranks of photographers standing behind their cameras, ready to make an ostentatious frontispiece of you and your decaying ambulance, and your solemn crate with a hide on it, which you are expected to regard in the light of a horse, and a diminished and unimportant background of sublime Niagara ; and a great many people *have* the incredible effrontery or the native depravity to aid and abet this sort of crime.

Any day, in the hands of these photographers, you may see stately pictures of papa and mamma, Johnny and Bub and Sis, or a couple of country cousins, all smiling vacantly, and all disposed in studied and uncomfortable attitudes in their carriage, and all looming up in their awe-inspiring imbecility before the snubbed and diminished presentment of that majestic presence whose ministering spirits are the rainbows, whose voice is the thunder, whose awful front is veiled in clouds, who was monarch here dead and forgotten ages before this hackful of small reptiles was deemed temporarily necessary to fill a crack in the world's unnoted myriads, and will still be monarch here ages and decades of ages after they shall have gathered themselves to their blood relations, the other worms, and been mingled with the unremembering dust.

There is no actual harm in making Niagara a background whereon to display one's marvellous insignificance in a good strong light, but it requires a sort of superhuman self-complacency to enable one to do it.

When you have examined the stupendous Horseshoe Fall till you are satisfied you cannot improve on it, you return to America by the new suspension bridge, and follow up the bank to where they exhibit the Cave of the Winds.

Here I followed instructions, and divested myself of all

my clothing, and put on a waterproof jacket and over-
alls. This costume is picturesque, but not beautiful. A
guide, similarly dressed, led the way down a flight of
winding stairs, which wound and wound, and still kept
on winding long after the thing ceased to be a novelty,
and then terminated long before it had begun to be a
pleasure. We were then well down under the precipice,
but still considerably above the level of the river.

We now began to creep along flimsy bridges of a
single plank, our persons shielded from destruction by a
crazy wooden railing, to which I clung with both hands
—not because I was afraid, but because I wanted to.
Presently the descent became steeper, and the bridge
flimsier, and sprays from the American Fall began
to rain down on us in fast-increasing sheets that
soon became blinding, and after that our progress was
mostly in the nature of groping. Now a furious wind
began to rush out from behind the waterfall, which
seemed determined to sweep us from the bridge, and
scatter us on the rocks and among the torrents below.
I remarked that I wanted to go home; but it was too
late. We were almost under the monstrous wall of water
thundering down from above, and speech was in vain in
the midst of such a pitiless crash of sound.

In another moment the guide disappeared behind the
deluge, and bewildered by the thunder, driven helplessly
by the wind, and smitten by the arrowy tempest of rain,
I followed. All was darkness. Such a mad storming,
roaring, and bellowing of warring wind and water never

crazed my ears before. I bent my head and seemed to
receive the Atlantic on my back. The world seemed
going to destruction. I could not see anything, the
flood poured down so savagely. I raised my head, with
open mouth, and the most of the American cataract went
down my throat. If I had sprung a leak now, I had
been lost. And at this moment I discovered that the
bridge had ceased, and we must trust for a foothold to
the slippery and precipitous rocks. I never was so scared
before and survived it. But we got through at last, and
emerged into the open day, where we could stand in front
of the laced and frothy and seething world of descending
water, and look at it. When I saw how much of it there
was, and how fearfully in earnest it was, I was sorry I
had gone behind it.

The noble Red Man has always been a friend and darling of mine. I love to read about him in tales and
legends and romances. I love to read of his inspired
sagacity, and his love of the wild free life of mountain
and forest, and his general nobility of character, and his
stately metaphorical manner of speech, and his chivalrous
love for the dusky maiden, and the picturesque pomp of
his dress and accoutrements. Especially the picturesque
pomp of his dress and accoutrements. When I found the
shops at Niagara Falls full of dainty Indian bead-work,
and stunning moccasins, and equally stunning toy figures
representing human beings who carried their weapons in
holes bored through their arms and bodies, and had feet
shaped like a pie, I was filled with emotion. I knew that

now, at last, I was going to come face to face with the noble Red Man.

A lady clerk in a shop told me, indeed, that all her grand array of curiosities were made by the Indians, and that they were plenty about the Falls, and that they were friendly, and it would not be dangerous to speak to them. And sure enough, as I approached the bridge leading over to Luna Island, I came upon a noble Son of the Forest sitting under a tree, diligently at work on a bead reticule. He wore a slouch hat and brogans, and had a short black pipe in his mouth. Thus does the baneful contact with our effeminate civilization dilute the picturesque pomp which is so natural to the Indian when far removed from us in his native haunts. I addressed the relic as follows:—

" Is the Wawhoo-Wang-Wang of the Whack-a-Whack happy ? Does the great Speckled Thunder sigh for the war path, or is his heart contented with dreaming of the dusky maiden, the Pride of the Forest ? Does the mighty Sachem yearn to drink the blood of his enemies, or is he satisfied to make bead reticules for the papooses of the paleface ? Speak, sublime relic of bygone grandeur— venerable ruin, speak ! "

The relic said—

" An' is it mesilf, Dennis Hooligan, that ye'd be takin for a dirty Injin, ye drawlin', lantern-jawed, spider-legged divil ! By the piper that played before Moses, I'll ate ye! "

I went away from there.

By and by, in the neighbourhood of the Terrapin Tower, I came upon a gentle daughter of the aborigines in fringed and beaded buckskin moccasins and leggins, seated on a bench, with her pretty wares about her. She had just carved out a wooden chief that had a strong family resemblance to a clothes-pin, and was now boring a hole through his abdomen to put his bow through. I hesitated a moment, and then addressed her:

"Is the heart of the forest maiden heavy? Is the Laughing Tadpole lonely? Does she mourn over the extinguished council-fires of her race, and the vanished glory of her ancestors? Or does her sad spirit wander afar towards the hunting-grounds whither her brave Gobler-of-the-Lightnings is gone? Why is my daughter silent? Has she aught against the paleface stranger?"

The maiden said—

"Faix, an' is it Biddy Malone ye dare to be callin' names? Lave this, or I'll shy your lean carcass over the cataract, ye snivelling blaggard!"

I adjourned from there also.

"Confound these Indians!" I said. "They told me they were tame; but, if appearances go for anything, I should say they were all on the war path."

I made one more attempt to fraternize with them, and only one. I came upon a camp of them gathered in the shade of a great tree, making wampum and moccasins, and addressed them in the language of friendship :—

"Noble Red Men, Braves, Grand Sachems, War Chiefs, Squaws, and High Muck a-Mucks, the paleface

from the land of the setting sun greets you ! You, Beneficent Polecat—you, Devourer of Mountains—you, Roaring Thundergust—you, Bully Boy with a Glass eye—
the paleface from beyond the great waters greets you all!
War and pestilence have thinned your ranks, and destroyed your once proud nation. Poker and seven-up, and a
vain modern expense for soap, unknown to your glorious
ancestors, have depleted your purses. Appropriating, in
your simplicity, the property of others, has gotten you
into trouble. Misrepresenting facts, in your simple innocence, has damaged your reputation with the soulless
usurper. Trading for forty-rod whiskey, to enable you
to get drunk and happy and tomahawk your families,
has played the everlasting mischief with the picturesque
pomp of your dress, and here you are, in the broad light
of the nineteenth century, gotten up like the ragtag
and bobtail of the purlieus of New York. For shame !
Remember your ancestors ! Recall their mighty deeds !
Remember Uncas !—and Red Jacket !—and Hole in the
Day !—and Whoopdedoodledo ! Emulate their achievements ! Unfurl yourselves under my banner, noble
savages, illustrious guttersnipes ”——

    “ Down wid him !” “ Scoop the blaggard !” “Burn
him !” “ Hang him !” “Dhround him !”

    It was the quickest operation that ever was. I simply
saw a sudden flash in the air of clubs, brickbats, fists,
bead-baskets, and moccasins—a single flash, and they
all appeared to hit me at once, and no two of them in the
same place. In the next instant the entire tribe was up-

on me. They tore half the clothes off me ; they broke my arms and legs ; they gave me a thump that dented the top of my head till it would hold coffee like a saucer; and, to crown their disgraceful proceedings and add insult to injury, they threw me over the Niagara Falls, and I got wet.

About ninety or a hundred feet from the top, the remains of my vest caught on a projecting rock, and I was almost drowned before I could get loose. I finally fell, and brought up in a world of white foam at the foot of the Fall, whose celled and bubbly masses towered up several inches above my head. Of course I got into the eddy. I sailed round and round in it forty-four times—chasing a chip and gaining on it—each round trip a half mile— reaching for the same bush on the bank forty-four times, and just exactly missing it by a hair's-breadth every time.

At last a man walked down and sat down close to that bush, and put a pipe in his mouth, and lit a match, and followed me with one eye and kept the other on the match, while he sheltered it in his hands from the wind. Presently a puff of wind blew it out. The next time I swept around he said—

"Got a match ?"

"Yes ; in my other vest. Help me out, please."

"Not for Joe."

When I came round again, I said—

"Excuse the seemingly impertinent curiosity of a drowning man, but will you explain this singular conduct of yours ?"

"With pleasure. I am the coroner. Don't hurry on my account. I can wait for you. But I wish I had a match."

I said—"Take my place, and I'll go and get you one."

He declined. This lack of confidence on his part created a coldness between us, and from that time forward I avoided him. It was my idea, in case anything happened to me, to so time the occurrence as to throw my custom into the hands of the opposition coroner over on the American side.

At last a policeman came along, and arrested me for disturbing the peace by yelling at the people on shore for help. The judge fined me, but I had the advantage of him. My money was with my pantaloons and my pantaloons were with the Indians.

Thus I escaped. I am now lying in a very critical condition. At least I am lying anyway—critical or not critical. I am hurt all over, but I cannot tell the full extent yet, because the doctor is not done taking inventory. He will make out my manifest this evening. However, thus far he thinks only sixteen of my wounds are fatal. I don't mind the others.

Upon regaining my right mind, I said—

"It is an awful savage tribe of Indians that do the bead work and moccasins for Niagara Falls, doctor. Where are they from?"

"Limerick, my son."

ANSWERS TO CORRESPONDENTS.

"MORAL STATISTICIAN."—I don't want any of your statistics; I took your whole batch and lit my pipe with it.   I hate your kind of people.   You are always ciphering out how much a man's health is injured, and how much his intellect is impaired, and how many pitiful dollars and cents he wastes in the course of ninety-two years' indulgence in the fatal practice of smoking; and in the equally fatal practice of drinking coffee, and in playing billiards occasionally; and in taking a glass of wine at dinner, etc., etc., etc. And you are always figuring out how many women have been burned to death because of the dangerous fashion of wearing expansive hoops, etc., etc., etc.   You never see more than one side of the question. You are blind to the fact that most old men smoke and drink coffee, although, according to your theory, they ought to have died young; and that hearty old Englishmen drink wine and survive it, and portly old Dutchmen both drink and smoke freely, and yet grow older and fatter all the time.   And you never try to find out how much solid comfort, relaxation, and enjoyment a man derives from smoking in the course of a lifetime (which is worth ten times the money he

would save by letting it alone), nor the appalling aggregate of happiness lost in a lifetime by your kind of people from *not* smoking. Of course you can save money by
denying yourself all those little vicious enjoyments for
fifty years; but then what can you do with it? What
use can you put it to? Money can't save your infinitesi-
mal soul. All the use that money can be put to is to
purchase comfort and enjoyment in this life; therefore,
as you are an enemy to comfort and enjoyment, where is
the use of accumulating cash? It won't do for you to
say that you can use it to better purpose in furnishing a good table, and in charities, and in supporting tract
societies, because you know yourself that you people who
have no petty vices are never known to give away a cent,
and that you stint yourself so in the matter of food that
you are always feeble and hungry. And you never dare
to laugh in the daytime for fear some poor wretch, seeing
you in a good humour, will try to borrow a dollar of you;
and in church you are always down on your knees, with
your eyes buried in the cushion, when the contribution-
box comes around; and you never give the revenue officers a full statement of your income. Now you know
all these things yourself, don't you? Very well, then,
what is the use of your stringing out your miserable lives to
a lean and withered old age? What is the use of your
saving money that is so utterly worthless to you? In a
word, why don't you go off somewhere and die, and not
be always trying to seduce people into becoming as
"ornery" and unlovable as you are yourselves, by your

villainous "moral statistics?" Now, I don't approve of dissipation, and I don't indulge in it either; but I haven't a particle of confidence in a man who has no redeeming petty vices, and so I don't want to hear from you any more. I think you are the very same man who read me a long lecture last week about the degrading vice of smoking cigars, and then came back in my absence, with your reprehensible fire-proof gloves on, and carried off my beautiful parlour stove.

"YOUNG AUTHOR." — Yes, Agassiz *does* recommend authors to eat fish, because the phosphorous in it makes brains. So far you are correct. But I cannot help you to a decision about the amount you need to eat—at least, not with certainty. If the specimen composition you send is about your fair usual average, I should judge that perhaps a couple of whales would be all you would want for the present. Not the largest kind, but simply good, middling-sized whales.

"SIMON WHEELER," *Sonora.* — The following simple and touching remarks and accompanying poem have just come to hand from the rich gold-mining region of Sonora :—

To Mr. Mark Twain: The within parson, which I have set to poetry under the name and style of "He Done His Level Best," was one among the whitest men I ever see, and it an't every man that knowed him that can find it in his heart to say he's glad the poor cuss is busted and gone home to the States. He was here in an early day, and he was the handyest man about takin' holt of anything that come along you most ever see, I judge. He was a cheerful, stirrin' cretur always doin' somethin', and no man can say he ever see him do anything by halvers. Preachin' was his natural gait, but he warn't a man to lay back and twidle his thumbs because there didn't happen to be nothin' doin' in his own especial line—no, sir, he was a man who would meander forth and stir up something for hisself. His last acts was to go his pile on "kings-*and*" (calklatin' to fill, but which he didn't fill), when there was a "flush" out agin him, and naterally, you see, he went under. And so he was cleaned out, as you may say, and he struck the home-trail, cheerful but flat broke. I knowed this talonted man in Arkansaw, and if you would print this humbly tribute to his gorgis abilities, you would greatly obleege his onhappy friend.

HE DONE HIS LEVEL BEST.

Was he a mining on the flat—
  He done it with a zest ;
Was he a leading of the choir—
  He done his level best.

If he'd a reg'lar task to do,
  He never took no rest ;
Or if 'twas off-and-on—the same—
  He done his level best.

If he was preachin' on his beat,
  He'd tramp from east to west,
And north to south—in cold and heat
  He done his level best.

He'd yank a sinner outen (Hades), *
  And land him with the blest ;
Then snatch a prayer'n waltz in again,
  And do his level best.

He'd cuss and sing and howl and pray,
  And dance and drink and jest,
And lie and steal—all one to him—
  He done his level best.

Whate'er this man was sot to do,
  He done it with a zest :
No matter *what* his contract was,
  HE'D DO HIS LEVEL BEST.

---

* Here I have taken a slight liberty with the original MS. "Hades" does not make such good metre as the other word of one syllable, but it sounds better.

Verily, this man *was* gifted with "gorgis abilities," and it is happiness to me to embalm the memory of their lustre in these columns. If it were not that the poet crop is unusually large and rank in California this year I would encourage you to continue writing, Simon Wheeler; but, as it is, perhaps it might be too risky in you to enter against so much opposition.

"PROFESSIONAL BEGGAR."—No; you are not obliged to take greenbacks at par.

"MELTON MOWBRAY," * *Dutch Flat.*—This correspondent sends a lot of doggerel, and says it has been regarded as very good in Dutch Flat. I give a specimen verse:—

> "The Assyrian came down like a wolf on the fold,
>   And his cohorts were gleaming with purple and gold;
>   And the sheen of his spears was like stars on the sea;
>   When the blue wave rolls nightly on deep Galilee."

There, that will do. That may be very good Dutch Flat poetry, but it won't do in the metropolis. It is too smooth and blubbery; it reads like buttermilk gurgling from a jug. What the people ought to have is something spirited—something like "Johnny Comes Marching Home." However, keep on practising, and you may succeed yet. There is genius in you, but too much blubber.

---

* This piece of pleasantry, published in a San Francisco paper, was mistaken by the country journals for seriousness, and many and loud were the denunciations of the ignorance of author and editor, in not knowing that the lines in question were "written by Byron."

"St. Clair Higgins," *Los Angeles.*—"My life is a failure; I have adored, wildly, madly and she whom I love has turned coldly from me and shed her affections upon another. What would you advise me to do?"

You should set your affections on another also—or on several, if there are enough to go round. Also, do everything you can to make your former flame unhappy. There is an absurd idea disseminated in novels, that the happier a girl is with another man, the happier it makes the old lover she has blighted. Don't allow yourself to believe any such nonsense as that. The more cause that girl finds to regret that she did not marry you, the more comfortable you will feel over it. It isn't poetical, but it is mighty sound doctrine.

"Arithmeticus." *Virginia, Nevada.*—"If it would take a cannon ball 3 1-3 seconds to travel four miles, and 33-8 seconds to travel the next four, and 3 5-8 to travel the next four, and if its rate of progress continued to diminish in the same ratio, how long would it take it to go fifteen hundred millions of miles?

I don't know.

"Ambitious Learner," *Oakland.*—Yes; you are right —America was not discovered by Alexander Selkirk.

"Discarded Lover."—"I loved, and still love, the beautiful Edwitha Howard, and intended to marry her. Yet, during my temporary absence at Benicia, last week, alas! she married Jones. Is my happiness to be thus blasted for life? Have I no redress?"

Of course you have. All the law, written and unwritten, is on your side. The *intention* and not the *act* constitutes crime—in other words, constitutes the *deed.* If you call your bosom friend a fool, and *intend* it for an insult, it *is* an insult; but if you do it playfully, and meaning no insult, it is *not* an insult.   If you discharge a pistol *accidentally*, and kill a man, you can go free, for you have done no murder ; but if you try to kill a man, and manifestly *intend* to kill him, but fail utterly to do it, the law still holds that the *intention* constituted the crime, and you are guilty of murder.   Ergo, if you had married Edwitha *accidentally*, and without really *intending* to do it, you would not actually be married to her at all, because the *act* of marriage could not be complete without the *intention*.   And ergo, in the strict spirit of the law, since you deliberately *intended* to marry Edwitha, and dĭdn't do it, you are married to her all the same—because, as I said before, the *intention* constitutes the crime.   It is as clear as day that Edwitha is your wife, and your redress lies in taking a club and mutilating Jones with it as much as you can.   Any man has a right to protect his own wife from the advances of other men.   But you have another alternative—you were married to Edwitha *first*, because of your deliberate intention, and now you can prosecute her for bigamy, in subsequently marrying Jones.   But there is another phase in this complicated case :   You *intended* to marry Edwitha, and consequently, according to law, she is your wife—there is no getting around that ; but she didn't marry you, and if she *never intended* to marry you, *you are not her husband*, of course.   Ergo, in marrying Jones, she was guilty of bigamy, because she was the wife of another man at the time ; which is all very well as far as it goes—but then, don't you see, she had **no**

other *husband* when she married Jones, and, consequently she was *not* guilty of bigamy.   Now, according to this
view of the case, Jones married a *spinster*, who was a
widow at the same time and another man's *wife* at the
same time, and yet who had no *husband* and *never had
one,* and never had any *intention* of getting married, and
therefore, of course, never *had* been married ; and by
the same reasoning you are a *bachelor*, because you have
never been any one's *husband* ; and a *married man*, because you have a wife living ; and to all intents and purposes a *widower*, because you have been deprived of that
wife ; and a consummate *ass* for going off to Benicia in
the first place, while things were so mixed.   And by
this time I have got myself so tangled up in the intrica-
cies of this extraordinary case that I shall have to give
up any further attempt to advise you—I might get confused and fail to make myself understood.   I think I
could take up the argument where I left off, and by following it closely awhile, perhaps I could prove to your
satisfaction, either that you never existed at all, or that
you are dead now, and consequently don't need the faith-
less Edwitha—I think I could do that, if it would afford
you any comfort.

" ARTHUR AUGUSTUS."—No ; you are wrong ; that is
the proper way to throw a brickbat or a tomahawk ; but
it doesn't answer so well for a bouquet ; you will hurt
somebody if you keep it up.   Turn your nosegay upside
down, take it by the stems, and toss it with an upward

sweep. Did you ever pitch quoits? that is the idea. The practice of recklessly heaving immense solid bouquets, of the general size and weight of prize cabbages, from the dizzy altitude of the galleries, is dangerous and very reprehensible. Now, night before last, at the Academy of Music, just after Signorina—— had finished that exquisite melody, "The Last Rose of Summer," one of these floral pile-drivers came cleaving down through the atmosphere of applause, and if she hadn't deployed suddenly to the right, it would have driven her into the floor like a shingle-nail. Of course that bouquet was well meant ; but how would you like to have been the target? A sincere compliment is always grateful to a lady, so long as you don't try to knock her down with it.

"YOUNG MOTHER."—And so you think a baby is a thing of beauty and a joy forever ? Well, the idea is pleasing, but not original ; every cow thinks the same of its own calf. Perhaps the cow may not think it so elegantly, but still she thinks it nevertheless. I honour the cow for it. We all honour this touching maternal instinct wherever we find it, be it in the home of luxury or in the humble cow-shed. But really, madam, when I come to examine the matter in all its bearings, I find that the correctness of your assertion does not assert itself in all cases. A soiled baby, with a neglected nose, cannot be conscientiously regarded as a thing of beauty ; and inasmuch as babyhood spans but three short years, no baby is competent to be a joy "forever." It pains me thus to demolish two-thirds of your pretty sentiments in a single sentence: but the position I hold in this chair requires that I shall not permit you to deceive and mislead the public with your plausible figures of speech. I know a female baby, aged eighteen months, in this city, which cannot hold out as a "joy" twenty-four hours on a stretch, let alone "forever." And it possesses some of the most remarkable eccentricities of character and appetite that have ever fallen under my notice. I will set down here a statement of this infant's operations (conceived, planned, and carried out by itself, and without suggestion or assistance from its mother or any one else), during a single day ; and what I shall say can be substantiated by the sworn testimony of witnesses.

It commenced by eating one dozen large blue-mass pills, box and all ; then it fell down a flight of stairs, and rose with a blue and purple knot on its forehead, after which it proceeded in quest of further refreshment and amusement. It found a glass trinket ornamented with brass-work—smashed up and ate the glass, and then swallowed the brass. Then it drank about twenty drops of laudanum, and more than a dozen tablespoonsful of strong spirits of camphor. The reason why it took no more laudanum was because there was no more to take. After this it lay down on its back, and shoved five or six inches of a silver-headed whale-bone cane down its throat ; got it fast there, and it was all its mother could do to pull the cane out again, without pulling out some of the child with it. Then being hungry for glass again, it broke up several wine-glasses, and fell to eating and swallowing the fragments, not minding a cut or two. Then it ate a quantity of butter, pepper, salt, and California matches, actually taking a spoonful of butter, a spoonful of salt, a spoonful of pepper, and three or four lucifer matches at each mouthful. (I will remark here that this thing of beauty likes painted German lucifers, and eats all she can get of them; but she prefers California matches, which I regard as a compliment to our home manufactures of more than ordinary value, coming, as it does, from one who is too young to flatter.) Then she washed her head with soap and water, and afterwards ate what soap was left, and drank as much of the suds as she had room for; after which she sallied forth and took the cow familiarly by the tail, and got kicked heels over head. At odd times during the day, when this joy for ever happened to have nothing particular on hand, she put in the time by climbing up on places, and falling down off them, uniformly damaging herself in the operation. As young as she is she speaks many words tolerably distinctly; and being plain spoken in other respects, blunt and to the point, she opens conversation with all strangers, male or female, with the same formula, "How do, Jim?" Not being familiar with the ways of children, it is possible that I have been magnifying into matter of surprise things which may not strike any one who is familiar with infancy as being at all astonishing. However, I cannot believe that such is the case, and so I repeat that my report of this baby's performances is strictly true; and if

any one doubts it, I can produce the child. I will further engage that she will devour anything that is given
her (reserving to myself only the right to exclude anvils),
and fall down from any place to which she may be elevat-
ed (merely stipulating that her preference for alighting
on her head shall be respected, and, therefore, that the
elevation chosen shall be high enough to enable her to
accomplish this to her satisfaction.) But I find I have
wandered from my subject; so, without further argument
I will reiterate my conviction that not *all* babies are
things of beauty and joys forever.

"ARITHMETICUS," *Virginia, Nevada.*—"I am an enthusiastic student of
mathematics, and it is so vexatious to me to find my progress constantly im-
peded by these mysterious arithmetical technicalities. Now do tell me
what the difference is between geometry and conchology?"

Here *you* come again with your arithmetical conundrums, when I am suffering death with a cold in the
head. If you could have seen the expression of scorn that
darkened my countenance a moment ago, and was instantly split from the centre in every direction like a fractured
looking-glass by my last sneeze, you never would have
written that disgraceful question. Conchology is a
science which has nothing to do with mathematics: it
relates only to shells. At the same time, however, a man
who opens oysters for a hotel, or shells a fortified town,
or sucks eggs, is not, strictly speaking, a conchologist—a
fine stroke of sarcasm that, but it will be lost on such an
unintellectual clam as you. Now compare conchology
and geometry together, and you will see what the differ-

ence is, and your question will be answered. But don't torture me with any more arithmetical horrors until you know I am rid of my cold. I feel the bitterest animosity towards you at this moment—bothering me in this way, when I can do nothing but sneeze and rage and snort pocket-handkerchiefs to atoms. If I had you in range of my nose, now, I would blow your brains out.

www.ingramcontent.com/pod-product-compliance
Lightning Source LLC
Chambersburg PA
CBHW060536030726
47498CB00004B/1218